CHASING

Grace

BY LILY DURKEE

Ms. Dvorsky,
You're an amazing teacher and I learned so much in your class. Thanks for a great sophomore year!

Lily D
2012

Copyright © 2012 by Lily Durkee
All rights reserved. No part of this book may be reproduced or transmitted in any form or by any means, electronic or mechanical, including photocopying, recording, or by any information storage and retrieval system, without permission in writing from the publisher.

For *Valley Mill,*
for getting me in a boat that first summer,
all those years ago.

Note to non-paddlers:

Paddling terms are used without explanation in much of this novel. Feel free to use the glossary at the end if at any point you do not know what is going on.

Chasing Grace

Part 1
A Runaway

A spark flies out of the fire and lands on my bare leg. I watch it glow and feel a brief, searing pain, before it fades, leaving behind a speck of black dust. I poke at the fire again, sending a flurry of sparks up into the air. A log ignites, and out of the corner of my eye, I notice a pair of eyes hovering only feet to my right.

"Ah!" I shriek, standing abruptly and stumbling backwards in fright. I trip over the log I was sitting on, and as I fall, I see a flash of a striped tail and hear a rustle in the trees. I land in a heap in the bush behind me, and my hair gets tangled in its branches.

My heart is still pounding in my chest. I take a few deep breaths, trying to relax. *It was just a raccoon,* I think. *You're fine.* But maybe camping alone wasn't such a great idea.

I hear another rustle, this one from across the fire ring, and I spring up, ripping half my hair out in the process. I'm about to reach for a piece of firewood to defend myself when a man steps into the glow of the fire. I realize I still have half a bush sticking out of my head and dirt all over my shorts, so I put a grin on my face and hope that he doesn't notice.

"You okay?" the newcomer asks, in a voice that sounds like a young man's. "I heard a scream."

"Yeah," I say rather sheepishly. "A raccoon gave me a bit of a scare." My visitor takes a few steps closer to me, extending his hand.

"Well, I'm Grant, by the way. Sorry for startling you."

"Don't worry about it, I was getting lonely anyway," I answer, meeting his eyes and grasping his hand with my own. He has kind eyes the color of melted chocolate, and they flick upwards briefly and he gives me a small, humored smile as he takes in the leaves in my hair.

"And who are you?" he inquires, that half smile still lingering on his lips.

"I'm Grace," I say. "Well, call me Ginny." I run a hand through my tangled hair, realizing that my old British accent showed as I pronounced "Ginny" as they do in England.

"As in 'Ginny Weasley'?" Grant asks, in a fake British accent mimicking my own. He flashes me a smile. Damn. *He's cute,* I think. *Really, really cute.* Even in the pale glow of the fire, I can tell he has killer looks. I can hear Sara, my best friend back home, whispering in my ear, *"Eye candy, Gins! Go get 'em!"* But of course she's not here, not now, not in the middle of the wilderness with me. She's back home, probably fast asleep in her bed. Or maybe she's worrying about me.

"Yeah," I reply. "As in Ginny Weasley."

"Where are you from?" he asks.

"Bethesda, Maryland," I answer. "And yourself?"

"Fayetteville, West Virginia."

The name rings a bell. "Oh, that's where the New River is, right? And the Gauley?"

Grant nods, looking impressed. "Do you paddle?" he asks. Why would I be at a rural campsite by the Ottawa River, only miles from the put in, and not paddle?

"Yeah, I do," I reply.

"Well, so do I. My buddy Jordi and I are running the Ottawa tomorrow. Garburator's in, and it's supposed to be a beautiful day. I saw the boats on your car—you heading out there as well?"

Well, this guy knows what he's talking about, that's for sure. Maybe, if I play it right, I'll be able to tag along with him and not have to run the river alone. "Yeah, I am. I'm looking for a ride on Garb as well," I reply.

"You do freestyle?"

"Some, but I mostly just run rivers, you know, for fun."

"Nice. Have you been on the Ottawa before?" he asks.

Of course I have. I've run it more times than I can count. But I don't tell him that. "No," I say instead. "Well, I mean, I've never run it at this level. I'm not sure if the lines will be the same." I cross my fingers behind my back and hope that he takes the hint.

"Well, you seem pretty competent," he says. "If you want to come along with us, I'm sure Jordi wouldn't mind at all."

I grin. "Really? That'd actually be amazing. I couldn't convince anyone back home to come with me, and my parents would be extremely grateful if I ran the river with a group." Actually, my parents don't even know I'm here. But that's beside the point.

"I'm camped next to you, a little ways down the road to your right. Bright red truck, hard to miss." Grant gestures to the right, and sure enough, I see another campfire. That's a relief. If I actually get attacked by something vicious tonight, at least there will be someone nearby to help.

"So I guess I'll see you in the morning?" I ask.

"Yup. Rest up, okay? The Ottawa's no cupcake." He meets my eyes, and I nod.

"Sure thing. G'night," I tell him. I raise a hand in farewell as he starts to walk away.

"Sweet dreams," he calls over his shoulder. Then the night swallows him up, and I'm left alone again.

My mind drifts back to the morning I left home. It's only been fourteen hours, and the images of the fight are still flickering through my head.

"Mom, Dad," I said over breakfast. "I've been thinking."

Dad, whose face was in the morning paper, glanced up and straightened his glasses. Mom, who was sitting next to me, looked up from her half finished Sudoku puzzle.

"Yeah, Grace?" Mom said, curiosity in her voice. "Have you made up your mind about the summer internship at Children's Hospital yet?" I resisted the urge to roll my eyes. Mom had her heart set on me volunteering as a children's nurse this summer as part of "career experience." I wouldn't have minded an internship if it had been in something I was interested in. Nursing, though, is not something I want to do with my life.

"Um, no..." I replied. "But I have been thinking about what I want to do this summer."

"Oh?" Dad said, taking a sip of his coffee.

"I'm thinking of training," I said.

"Training for what?" Mom asked.

"Paddling." My answer was met with silence. I swirled the oatmeal around in my bowl, waiting for a reply.

"Why?" Dad finally asked.

"I was thinking..." I took a deep breath, and braced myself for their response. "I was thinking about running Great Falls at the end of the summer." Silence again. Dad was the first to break.

"What?" he shouted, slamming his cup down on the table. I flinched and didn't meet his eyes. "You want to do what?"

"I shouldn't have told you, I guess," I mumbled. I thought it would have been a nice conversation to have over breakfast. My old paddling instructor, Jared, was coming down for the summer, and he was going to help me prepare. We planned to leave Monday for a tour around North Carolina for "college visits".

"Grace, your father asked you a question," Mom said dangerously. "Answer it."

"You heard what I said," I said to Dad. "I want to run Great Falls."

"Well, you're not going to," Dad said. "No daughter of mine is throwing herself off of that. No girl in general should be going off something so dangerous! What is wrong with you, Grace?"

"Um—"

"Your father and I have put up with all this nonsense for years," Mom broke in, her voice rising with every word. "We thought as you grew older, you'd realize how absolutely ridiculous kayaking is. It's quite awful, really. Dreadful. You will not be going off any more waterfalls. Actually, I don't even want you in a boat anymore! Ever! No more kayaking!" This was going too far. I felt anger rising in me dangerously fast, and knew that if they didn't shut up, I was going to explode.

"You can't do that—" I began quietly, only to be interrupted by my dad.

"We can do whatever the hell we want! We are your parents, Grace! We raised you! We fed you! We paid for your schooling, your car, and are now saving everything we can for you to go to college! You cannot tell us what we can and cannot do!" Spit was flying from his mouth, and his face appeared the shade of an overripe tomato. I had never seen him that mad before. I stayed quiet.

"And now we are saying that you can no longer kayak. As a matter of fact, I'm going outside right now and ripping that boat off of your car—" As Dad stood up, I lost it.

"Who the hell do you think you are?" I screamed, standing up and banging my hands on the table. "You obviously don't know me at all! All you think about is yourself and your money. You don't give a flying fuck about me and what I want!"

"Grace," Mom said, her voice low but urgent. "Your father's not serious—"

Dad threw down his mug, spilling coffee all over our table, and stood up. "I was not kidding, Nicole! And I'm not kidding now when I say that you will never be stepping foot into a kayak again!" His eyes were flaming as they glared into mine. He thought, by staring me down, he'd intimidate me. But my mind was already made up.

"Fuck off," I said, my voice surprisingly composed.

Then I turned and walked calmly out of the house.

My father could have gotten up and barred the door, if he had wanted to. But I think he thought I was going to blow off steam for a few hours and then come right back. He didn't think I was strong enough to actually run away. Well, Daddy, you were wrong about me. So very wrong.

So why did I choose the Ottawa? It's not even my favorite river. I guess I needed to be out of the country. And maybe I believed that an epic surf on Garb would clear my head and help me see some sense in my parents' words. Because I want them to love me. But I also know that living without kayaking would be like living without a soul, and there's no way I'd be able to do that.

So I drove off towards the horizon, kayaks on the roof of my car, a bit of money in my pocket, and the waves of the Ottawa River in my mind's eye.

I met Jared, my 23-year-old former paddling instructor and close friend, just outside of Ithaca, New York. When I called and asked if he'd help me over the border, he was hesitant, but he knows how much kayaking means to me. He did it, even if I knew he didn't really want to.

To pass through customs, he pretended he was my cousin, which is believable enough, because we have similar blue eyes and thick hair. We forged a beautiful letter from my mom giving Jared the right to take me up to our uncle's house in Quebec. We separated soon after that, because he had to take care of some business in Ottawa City before heading back into the US. I apologized for not being able to paddle North Carolina with him and he smiled and said that there are better rivers in Canada, anyway. He also gave me a few words of wisdom—be safe, think before I do *anything,* and paddle with a group, or don't paddle at all. I wrapped my arms around him when we parted, not knowing how long it was going to be until I saw him again. Not knowing how long it was going to be before I saw anyone that I knew.

Violent shaking of my tent awakes me from my deep sleep the following morning.

"Um, Ginny? It's 10:30, and we were hoping to get on the water by twelve. You in or out?" It's Grant. I open my eyes, shove myself into a sitting position, and try to smooth down my hair. My fingers come in contact with a stray twig that I missed when combing through my hair last night, and I pull it out quickly and toss it into the corner of my tent.

"I'll be ready," I yawn. "Give me 10 minutes." I immediately change into my bathing suit—it's an old two-piece that I always keep in my gear bag—and put on the shirt and shorts I'd been wearing since I left home. I make a mental note to go shopping later, smooth down my hair some more, and roll out of my tent. I drag out my sleeping gear and begin to roll it up, and while I'm doing this I notice Grant standing off to the side, watching me. I hate to admit it, but he's easily ten times cuter in the daylight. He has a messy, brown mop of hair on his head, smiling brown eyes and strong, paddler's shoulders. He's wearing a shirt, but something tells me that underneath, he has rock hard abs and a life jacket tan. He meets my eyes and grins.

"Morning, Ginny. Sleep well? Any raccoon attacks last night?"

"Thankfully, no. And I slept fine, thanks." I'm too groggy to come up with a clever comeback. "How long have you been up?"

"Oh, since eight or so. J's been patching his skirt and I've been getting some last safety stuff in place. And we cooked an elaborate, but excessive, breakfast. You hungry?"

"Famished, actually. I haven't eaten since lunch yesterday." I flash him a grateful smile. I drove all day yesterday, nonstop, from 10:00 AM to 12:00 AM earlier this morning.

I stuff the last pole into the tent bag and chuck my stuff into the back of my van.

"All ready?" Grant asks, and I nod, and we begin to walk towards his site.

"Who's J?" I ask.

"Jordan. J. Jordi. He has lots of nicknames. He's my best mate." He glances at me. "Why are you travelling alone, anyway?"

I don't feel like lying to him. "It's a long story. But in short, I kind of...ran away from home." Grant's eyebrows shoot up.

"So I'm assisting a runaway?" he says, in mock distress. His voice turns more serious. "Why'd you decide to leave home?"

"Well, I asked my parents if I could run Great Falls. You know, the big V on the Potomac?" Grant nods. "Well, they freaked. Told me I could never paddle again. So...I left." Grant seems to be working through my story in his head.

Finally, he replies, looking down at me. "So you must be really good, huh? Great Falls is no joke." By now we've entered his site, and the smell of bacon is radiating from the picnic table. A guy, maybe 18 or so, is sitting on the bench, head bent over an IR skirt. He looks up as we approach.

"Hey, Jordan, this is the girl who's gonna tag along with us today. Her name's Ginny."

I nod at him and hold out my hand. "Hey," I say, eyeing the bacon hungrily.

"Hey," he says, shaking my hand. He turns back to Grant. "Have you checked the level?" he asks him.

"Yup, same as yesterday. We're good to go." I see Grant place a cell phone into a dry bag and close it up, and toss it into a pile of gear.

Jordan turns back to me. "So have you run the Ottawa before?"

"Yeah," I reply. "But when it was really, really low. I just need pointers on the lines is all." The smell of bacon grease is overwhelming, and I must be beginning to salivate because Jordan laughs. He pushes the plate towards me.

"Here, help yourself," he says, and I immediately begin to stuff my face. "Where are you from?"

"Maryland," I reply, between bites.

"Did you drive all the way here?"

I nod, trying to chew faster. "Yeah. Yesterday."

"Alone?"

"Unfortunately." I swallow loudly, then continue. "I told Grant this earlier, but I actually ran away from home. I don't know what my parents are going to do about it, so if you don't want me paddling with you I understand…"

Jordan just grins. "It takes serious balls to turn on your parents like that. What awful thing did they do to you?"

"They told me I couldn't kayak. And kayaking's basically my life, and I knew if I wanted to ever get in a boat again I'd have to get away from them."

Jordan looks at me, surprised. He glances at Grant and an unsaid message passes between them, and they both smile.

"What boat are you paddling?" Jordan asks me. "We should put it in our truck."

"A blue and yellow Star," I answer, while stuffing a last piece of bacon into my mouth. "What about you guys?"

"I have a red Rockstar, and Grant's in a green All Star," Jordan replies. "Oh, and make sure to grab your gear, too."

I nod. "Sure thing."

I turn around and begin to walk away, and hear Jordan whisper something to Grant. Curious, I slip behind a tree and listen.

"I heard her talking about running Great Falls. So you think she's legit?" Jordan says.

"I mean, she drove all the way from Maryland to Ottawa to be able to paddle...sure sounds legit to me," Grant whispers back. A grin spreads across my face and a warm feeling begins to simmer inside of me. Grant thinks I'm legit! *You have a boyfriend,* I remind myself sternly. *Remember?* Justin. I try to picture his face in my head, his blue eyes and dark hair. But the only face I can picture right now is a tan, floppy haired river rat with a smile that seems to light up the sky.

Justin and I go a long way back. I've known him since Kindergarten, and he was my first friend after I moved to Bethesda from London. My father used to have a job at a branch of his company there, but it fell apart, so we moved back to Bethesda, where he and Mom lived before I was born. I can't say I remember it too well, but the way people pronounced my name there has stuck with me since. I'll always be "Ginn-ey", not the American "Ginny", if you know what I mean.

Anyway, when I first showed up, Justin was really nice to me, and we became pretty close. Then, late in middle school, hormones started kicking in and something about our relationship started to shift, but it seemed natural, so I let it happen. He grew up to be quite the looker, and a fantastic lacrosse player, too. We've been a couple since the fall of 9th grade. He was my first boyfriend—and as Sara jokes, he'll probably be my last. I've never been a flirt, never "expanded my horizons," and have never felt what it's like to actually be crazy about someone. Sara says I could be one of the school hotties, with my thick, wavy brown hair, bright blue eyes, and slim figure, but I've never really made an effort. If only Sara were here, she'd know what to do about the guy sitting in front of me. Even from the back seat of his truck, I get butterflies in my stomach every time I look at the back of his head. Pathetic. It doesn't help that I notice he has a helmet tan along the side of his face.

Sara's always thought my obsession with male paddlers was mental. My room is covered with posters of the big time boaters. There's just something about the build of a kayaker that turns me on. It's weird, I'll admit. But at least I don't fall for Abercrombie models like she does. At least the people I crush on are real.

We're bumping along the dirt road leading up to the

Ottawa parking area when my favorite song comes on. Of course, there are limited wavelengths available in the middle of the wilderness, and the only station we were able to get was country—and I'm a sucker for songs about tractors and cowboys. I can't help but sing along as Lady Antebellum's *Need You Now* begins blaring out of the speakers. I have a pretty good country twang voice, and as I belt out the familiar lyrics, Grant meets my eyes and smirks in the rearview mirror. I feel myself begin to flush, but I keep singing, anyway. We roll into the gravel parking lot, windows down, and every single person turns and stares at us. I just sing louder. By the time the song ends, I'm practically screaming, Grant's cracking up, and Jordan looks like he wants to shoot himself.

At around 12:30, we finally get onto the water. We paddle the first flat section easily, stopping every now and then to throw a couple ends and show off our flatwater playboating skills. Jordan and Grant can both get eight ends, no problem, but I can bow stall better than them both, which surprises us all.

We hop out before the first rapid, McCoy's, to scout, and the moment my eyes find the whitewater, an amazing feelings starts building up in my chest. I can't really describe it. Bubbles seem to be forming, moving upward, and are threatening to make my midsection burst open. A huge grin spreads across my face and stays there, and I know I look like an idiot, but I can't help it.

Grant and Jordan want to run the "man line", the line that takes us through the 4-foot tongue next to the deadly Phil's hole. Though I've done this line before, messing up is really consequential, and I should be nervous. But all I feel right now is the buzz of adrenaline. I peer at the rapid again, note a few landmarks, and am ready to go.

"Are you sure about this line, Ginny?" Jordan asks, concern flickering in his eyes. "I'll take you down the left side of the hole, if you want." I flash him a smile, appreciating him looking out for me but also knowing that I could probably run this line in my sleep.

"Nah, I'll be fine, Jordan, thanks," I reply. He and Grant exchange a glance, and Grant shrugs.

"I'll lead, if that's okay. Jordi can sweep. Let's all catch the eddy below Corner Wave, okay?" Grant gives these instructions with confidence, and he meets my eyes, making sure that I understand. Looking into his brown eyes makes my heart beat a little faster, and this time it has nothing to do with adrenaline.

We hike back to our boats silently, all thinking about the line ahead. We exchange high fives once we're all in our boats again, then Grant exits the eddy, sticks out his tongue at us, and heads down McCoy's. I watch him approach the hole, set his angle, and hit the flush spot perfectly. Jordan nods at me, and I flash him a grin, then aim myself at Phil's hole. I see the green water in the middle of Phil's foam pile, point my bow at it and paddle hard. The water is roaring all around me, and as I nail the line, I laugh spontaneously, loving the river, loving kayaking, and loving life. People search all their lives for happiness, and some die before they even know what they're looking for. But if I'm reading my emotions correctly, I'm pretty sure I've found it. As I paddle down the wave train before Corner, I realize a few things:

1) I know this is what I want to do for the rest of my life

2) Leaving home was the right decision—if my parents don't support my passion then I won't listen to them and

3) Every moment paddling near Grant makes me realize how much I wish he were mine.

I slip to the right of Corner wave and catch the eddy with ease, and paddle over to where Grant's waiting.

"It doesn't seem like you need us, Ginny," he jokes, his eyes laughing. When he meets my eyes, my dumb grin widens. "You know the line for this next part?"

I nod. "Hey diddle diddle, right down the middle," I say, and Grant smiles. Jordan drops into the eddy beside me, and he holds out his fist, and I knock mine against it.

"Sweet line, Ginny," he says, impressed.

"Thanks," I say. "Do you guys mind if I take a surf on Corner?"

"Go for it," Jordan says. "It's kind of hard to catch at this level, so if you wash out, don't screw up Horseshoe, okay?" He winks, and I nod, winking back. Horseshoe is the next hole, and has a nasty part called The Pit on the river right side that I'm not planning on going into.

I focus on the wave and paddle hard, grabbing the pillow with my blade and pulling myself into the trough. I drop in, and I feel my face break into a grin as I feel my boat bounce beneath me. I lean into the pillow and throw in a spin and face forwards again, still on the wave. I hear Grant whoop and I feel my grin widen, and spin again the other way. I front surf a little bit more before flushing out the far side, and point myself down the middle of the next rapid and slip easily down the tongue. I pull up in the large eddy on river left, and watch to make sure Grant and Jordan both get down safely.

First I see Jordan's red boat, but he's way too far right and is heading directly for The Pit. I lift my paddle and point it hard to his left, but he doesn't notice, and falls right into the hole. He flips, the hole rolls him up, and as he begins to get worked I see Grant coming down above him. Grant's boat is sideways and he appears disoriented, and I signal wildly with my paddle, but Grant follows Jordan's line exactly—and falls right into the hole after him. Now both their boats are side by side, getting trashed together.

Adrenaline helps my mind make a plan, and I begin the hardest attainment of my life. I spot the eddy I need to be in—the one behind the submerged rock to the right of the hole—and I start paddling hard. My short boat is not made for moves like this, but I keep pushing, as hard as I can, and I feel myself making progress. I look ahead at the hole—now Grant is upside down and Jordan is being window shaded in rapid succession. If this wasn't real life, I'd probably laugh. What are the odds that two people get stuck in the same hole, one after another? What is this, monkey see, monkey do?

I'm in the eddy now. My muscles seem a lot bigger than they were a few minutes ago—I guess that's the adrenaline kicking in. I actually feel like I could lift a car. I see Jordan roll up and get control of his edges, and I find the safety whistle I always have on my life jacket and blow. He hears the shriek of my whistle and turns his head and glances at me. I've been stuck in this hole before—he needs to side surf his way out. I point my paddle to the left, meaning, "Go left. Hard." I rack my brain for tips on "How to get Group Members Unstuck from Holes" from the whitewater safety books I've been reading, but I come up empty handed. Only one thing comes to mind—"DON'T PANIC." I take a deep breath.

Meanwhile, Jordan grabs the foam pile with his paddle and with great effort, drags himself out of the man-eating hole. Once he's out, he motions to Grant's boat and hits his head lightly with his hand and makes a slicing motion by his throat. I get the message, loud and clear. Grant is unconscious. And unfortunately, I know that the only option I have now is to go in after him.

I begin paddling like crazy and attempt a ferry there's no way I'd be able to make in a normal situation. But there seems to be a strong surge of power behind each of my strokes, and before I know it, I'm right next to the hole.

I see the part Grant's boat is in, and I know he's in trouble. Years of river reading helps me identify the nasty recirculation as something that is extremely deadly—and Grant's boat is in the thick of it. If I go in there, I may not get out, either. I get on the edge of the foam pile and make my way to the right of the hole, but the force of the water is too strong, and I know if I don't act fast, I'll get washed down. So I throw myself into what seems to be a definite trashing.

The hole takes my boat and begins to throw it around. It flips me over, and the roaring of the water sounds like a hundred bears all screaming bloody murder at the same time. I manage to roll up and find myself right next to Grant. I lean into the foam pile and throw myself over his boat. Two boats are much harder to trash than one is. I secure one hand around his hull, wedge my paddle between my body and his boat, and it takes all my strength not go head first into the thick of the hole. But I manage to reach under his boat and curl my hand around the one thing that can save him—his grab loop, the small, life-saving feature on a whitewater skirt that allows you to bail if necessary. I pull it as hard as I can, the skirt pops off, and his boat, the one I'm leaning on, immediately begins to sink. Shit.

Now I know that I have launched myself into a suicide mission because what I do next is crazy enough to make people question my sanity. I take a huge breath, chuck my paddle into what I hope is the main current, and pop my own skirt with my free hand. My other hand is still clutching Grant's grab loop for dear life. I hear a yell from somewhere, probably Jordan, telling me to stop, but I can't, not now. I keep seeing Grant's face in my head—those deep brown eyes emerging from the smoke of the campfire, and I know I can't—I won't—let him die. So with my last ounce of effort, I heave myself out of my boat and dive, head first, into the hole.

My other hand finds his skirt and I work my hands along it until I hit a body. The hole is swirling around me, threatening to tear me to pieces, but I'm not ready to let my guard down quite yet. I wrap my arms around Grant, and I push off against his boat as hard as I can. The last thing I remember is the roar of the hole in my ears and the relief that at least I died trying to save someone's life.

There's a sweet voice singing in my ear. The lyrics don't register, but they seem gentle, sad even. I think that perhaps it's an angel, singing me along on my way to the afterlife, where I'll see my grandfather, and my dog, and maybe even my mom's miscarried baby. Then a voice breaks into my blissful thoughts.

"Ginny. Ginny! Can you hear me? Come on, girl! Up and at 'em! I'm not kidding! You're breathing! I know you are!" The voice is rough, hoarse, and has fear and urgency woven into it. My body jerks. My eyes fly open, and Jordan's face is inches from mine—there's a massive cut along the side of his face, and his eyes are bloodshot and wild. Relief floods them as they meet my own.

"Ginny. Grant is not okay. His pulse is weak and I'm afraid it's going to stop. Are you all right? Can you hear me? Say something, anything." I see Grant to our left, lying on his back, his eyes closed and his chest still. I open my mouth to reply, and immediately start coughing. The coughs become worse, and I vomit up a bunch of water, which is followed my more coughing, then, finally, silence. Jordan leans over and gives Grant a rescue breath, counts to two, and gives him another. I clear my throat.

"I think I'm okay," I rasp, giving Jordan a half smile.
"Are you tired?" I ask Jordan, my brain beginning to work again.

"Yeah, but I'll be okay. One of us needs to get help. We don't get phone service here, but if you run out of the woods far enough, I know there's a road that you'll reach. I have Grant's cell. Go towards the road until you get bars." I nod. I'm an athlete; I have been trained all my life to run.

"And how will I find you again?" I ask. Instead of answering, Jordan begins to take off his gear. He hands me his helmet, life jacket, paddling jacket, booties, skirt, and he's about to take off his swim trunks when I stop him.

"I have my gear too. It's okay. So I'll mark every twenty-five steps or so. I've driven along this river many times and the road isn't too far away. I'll run in a straight line and leave the objects in plain site. You will get all your gear back, I promise." He reaches out a hand and I clasp it, and our eyes meet briefly. He gives me a small nod, hands me Grant's cell phone, and then I'm off. I'm not as strong as I was on the river, and I feel fatigue in my muscles as I begin to run. But I force myself forward. I begin to drop objects and look over my shoulder every few steps to make sure my trail is clear. My mind begins to get tired, too, and soon I focus all my energy on keeping one foot in front of the other. I feel like falling over when I finally hit the road, and leave an obvious red life jacket at the point I exit. The world begins to spin lightly, and I check the phone. My exhausted eyes make out that I have one bar. I plug in 911, hit dial, and mumble my position and Grant's condition to the person on the other end. I sit down to wait and lean against a tree, and before I know it, my eyes are closed, and my world goes black.

My next memories are of people moving me. I feel myself get put onto a stretcher and I hear the faint blare of a siren. I open my eyes part way and see people in masks hustling around. "I left a trail..." I manage to mutter. One of the EMTs looks up and nods at me.

"We found it. We have people on it already." The person appears to be a young woman, maybe 25. "I have them on radio right now. They have a few questions for you, as do I." She presses down a button on a radio, and says, "Team A, come in, this is Base speaking. The patient has woken up."

There's a crackle, then a female voice responds. "This is Team A. Ask the patient how long she thinks her friend was underwater." The EMT turns to me.

"Maybe five minutes? Maybe more. I was unconscious too." The EMT carries on my message. The questions continue, and every time I want to interrupt with my own, another one flies at me. How old is Grant? How long have you been out today? Was he showing any signs of fatigue before the accident? I answer the questions in the same flat voice with none of the panic I'm feeling inside showing. Finally, the woman on Team A says something I'm interested in.

"The patient has been located." I breathe a sigh of relief. I continue to hear the live stream updates on Grant's condition. I hear the muffled sound of an AED giving directions, meaning that his pulse did stop. I hear

Jordan's voice, faintly, every now and then, but mainly just the EMTs yelling at each other. Then I hear a male voice, spoken directly into the radio: "We need an ER. We're not making headway and we may be running out of time. We need to get out quickly and we'll need you to ready the vehicle." The EMT near me frowns in worry, and I realize that a break from life support for the period of time it took me to get to the road could be fatal to his condition. Suddenly I'm on my feet.

"Tell them to wait," I command quietly. The EMT looks at me, surprised. I say it louder. "Tell them to wait or I'll do it myself."

"Sweetie, you're in no condition to—" she begins, but I rip the radio out of her hand.

"Team A," I say with as much authority as I can muster. "Do not try to move the patient. That's an order." I shove the radio back into her hand. "If they protest, tell them to wait, okay? I was the one who saved him. I'm not letting you kill him by trying to bring him here."

Without waiting for a response, I pry open the ambulance door, run down the road, and turn into the woods at the red life jacket.

My mind is a blur as I race through the trees. My thoughts are wild. I get glimpses of being trashed in the hole with him, and the sound of the whitewater as I dove in. I remember the adrenaline rush, the relief at knowing I was ending my life trying to preserve another, and Grant's still body lying on the riverbank. I speed up, leaping logs, dodging trees, and shoving branches out of my path. I don't think about where I'm going, but before I know it, I burst through the woods and into the clearing by the Ottawa. I locate the EMTs immediately, and they all whip their heads around and look at me, surprised. I smile at them briefly before rushing forward towards Grant's body, which has now been moved to a board. I kneel beside him. I see the AED pads hooked up to his bare chest and gently touch his cheek. Then I hear the AED say, "Shock advised", an EMT presses a button, and the AED says, "administering shock. Please stand back." I jerk my hand away and see the shock run through his chest.

"May I do CPR?" I ask. "I'm a lifeguard." A man comes forward and is about to push me aside when a woman grabs his arm.

"Let her try," she says quietly. "You know how dangerous it would be to move him right now." I smile at her gratefully before beginning. I press my mouth against his and give him two breaths, wishing our first kiss could have been a bit more romantic. Then I begin the chest thrusts, making sure to be firm, deliberate, and rhythmic. With every thrust, I chant the words "come back to me" over and over again. I hear the EMTs muttering amongst themselves. I hear the woman's voice, telling the others to calm down, that CPR is CPR and that they can do it no better than I can.

I am aware of the steady rush of the river next to me, the same whitewater that almost ended both of our lives. But the water gives me strength as well—whitewater has been my drug, my life-food and my comfort for as long as I can remember, and having it roaring by me now gives me extra determination. I feel invincible, like I could go on forever. If I'm tiring I'm not aware of it, and my brain remains focused and calm. *Jared would be proud*, I think.

Jared has been my paddling instructor since I started. When I first picked up the sport, I was nine and innocent and he was a mighty fifteen year old. I saw him on the river one day, running the gorge below Great Falls, while on a hike with my parents. His boat was my favorite color (purple), and I thought it was wicked cool that he was floating down giant rapids in it. I ran down the steep bank and said hello, and he gave me his email and told me to contact him if I ever wanted to learn how to kayak. I'm pretty sure he was joking, thinking that I would forget him immediately. But I didn't. I emailed him that night after my parents stopped yelling at me for running down to the river without permission. Jared became my mentor and older brother, of sorts, kind of like the cool older sibling that I never had. He moved to New York to attend Cornell at the end of the summer when I was thirteen. I feel a slight pang as I remember how he was always there when I needed support, and I know if he were here now, Grant wouldn't have gone into that hole. I then feel a rush of regret so strong that my focus wavers—because it's my fault he ran the line wrong in the first place.

"Miss," one of the EMTs says quietly. "Miss, I think—" She never gets a chance to finish her sentence, because just then, in the middle of my second rescue breath after about ten minutes of CPR, I hear Grant begin to cough. His coughs become racking, ripping through his bare torso, and water spills out of his mouth. The EMTs rush forward, excitement in their voices. But just as they begin to push me away, Grant opens his eyes, and meets mine. Between coughs, he manages to speak.

"Ginny...you...incredible..." Then the EMTs block him from my view, and I sink down onto a boulder, finally exhausted.

When I finally wake, I'm moving. I've been strapped to a backboard, and I open one eye and see that there's an IV in my arm that's connected to a fluid bag. I peer around and realize that I'm in an ambulance, probably on the way to the hospital. I see another board to my right and make out Grant's face in the dim lighting. Jordan is sitting on a bench beside me, his eyes closed, his head resting against the wall. Next to him is the EMT who let me give Grant CPR. She smiles when she sees me.

"Hey, I'm Jessie. It's nice to see you awake and functioning." I smile back, not really wanting to speak. Jordan stirs from where he's sitting, and grins at me, too.

"Ginny! My hero!" he greets me.

"Hey, Jordi," I rasp. I realize that I didn't see him when I went back into the woods to help the EMTs. "Where were you during Grant's rescue?"

"Sleeping on the rocks, a little ways away. When the

EMTs showed up I was kind of freaking out. I kept thinking of what it would be like if we lost him, and I got a bit violent and threw a couple of bad punches, which didn't help them work quickly. So they sedated me." He leans in close to me, his face maybe a foot from my own.

"Thanks for going in after him. I…I don't know what I'd do if he never came out of that hole," he murmurs. I see his eyes get moist, and a tear drops down. I reach my arm up, the one not hooked up to the IV, and wipe it away gently.

"I'm glad I could help," I reply. He meets my eyes and smiles.

"You know, I didn't hear the story of how Grant got stuck in the river in the first place," Jessie says, breaking the tender moment.

"Well, I don't know what happened from Ginny's point of view…but I was scared out of my mind," Jordan says. "By the time I realized Grant was unconscious, it was too late for me to do anything about it. So I sent you that message," he says to me. I nod, and he continues. "I expected you to come over to me and help come up with a plan, but you went in after him. I honestly wasn't expecting that. But then I saw you both floating down the river…and I realized that your crazy ass plan must have worked."

I put myself in Jordan's shoes for a moment. Seeing my best friend upside down in a killer hole, then seeing a crazy girl I just met go in after him. Thinking they were both going to die, then seeing them unconscious in the middle of the river, and having to pull them out to save both their lives. I guess between the two of us, we experienced enough fear and adrenaline to last us for a long time.

But then again, I live off adrenaline. I act best when put in tight situations. The higher the stakes, the more effective I am. I shake my head slightly as I think just how high the stakes were this time.

Hospitals always seem the same. Blank walls, rushing

people, antiseptic smell. They wheel me in on a gurney even after I insist that I'm fine, and I'm put in a room with other semi-serious patients in the ER. Grant is whisked off into the Intensive Care Unit. I remember when my grandfather had a heart attack and was sent there. I was little, but one thing stuck out—the feeling of death. I remember it being almost tangible. I'm scared for Grant now. My grandfather never made it out of the ICU.

After getting a check over, the nurse attending me decides that I'm free to roam. I jump out of bed and sprint through the halls, but a door reading "AUTHORIZED PERSONNEL ONLY" stops me in my tracks. I hear Jordan's voice from a corner. He's speaking into a phone, and it sounds like he's talking to Grant's parents.

"Yeah, he's all right now…yes. Yeah, I did give him CPR, but that's not what saved him…yeah. EMTs came. That's right. No need to worry. I'll tell him to call when he's allowed visitors. Thanks, Becca. See you." He shuts his cell, then looks up and sees me.

"Ginny. The nurses say we have to wait," he says. I go over and sit next to him. His eyes are red and his hair is spiked from the river water. I gently touch his arm.

"This must be really hard for you," I murmur. "I'm so sorry." Jordan jerks into a more upright position.

"Ginny! Why the hell are you apologizing? You saved his fucking life! I was the one who sat in the eddy, not knowing what to do. I was the one who went in the hole in the first place. I'm the idiot here, and my best friend is paying for it." He slumps back into the chair and rests his head against the wall, and I see a tear escape out of the corner of his pale blue eye.

"Hey," I say softly. "I was the one who chose to go into the hole after him and almost got myself killed, too. It was all because of you that Grant and I got out alive. If you hadn't been there, we would have both died."

Jordan's eyes meet my own. "I guess."

"We're all alive, Jordan. All of us. We should be thankful for that, and move on." Jordan cracks a smile, but it doesn't reach his eyes. "Forget regret, or life is yours to miss, you know?"

"*Rent*," Jordan says, understanding my reference.

"Exactly," I reply. "Grant's not going to blame you for this, you know. I'm pretty sure he's just going to be glad to be here."

"When did you become so smart?" Jordan jokes, and I see his eyes beginning to light up again.

I shrug. "You've just been unobservant, Jordi," I say with a grin.

"Yeah, right," he says, smiling for real now. He meets my eyes and seems to search them for something, his expression turning more serious. "You know, I think that's what Grant likes about you. You're smart. Independent. You don't really give a shit to what other people think."

At the mention of the words me, Grant, and like in the same sentence, my heart starts pounding a little harder. "Wait, what?"

"Grant hates shallow girls. Hates them. He told me he would get a buzz cut if it would keep the girls off him." He laughs softly. "I convinced him otherwise. I said if he lost his characteristic mop, he wouldn't be my best friend anymore." I laugh too, mostly to keep him talking. "The girl he has now is okay, I guess. What about you? Have a hot boyfriend back home?" He winks at me.

"Yeah. Well, I guess." In an attempt to change the subject, I break into song as *Mine* by Taylor Swift begins to play through the speakers. Before Jordan can punch me for making us the center of attention in the waiting room, a nurse comes out. She glances at her clipboard, then back at us.

"Grant Haney is ready for visitors. Who are you two?" She points her pen at us. I consider lying, but Jordan answers for me.

"I'm Jordan Bolton, and this here is Ginny..." he glances at me, and I finish for him.

"Ginny Kinsey. That's me." The nurse raises her eyebrows.

"Any relation to the patient?"

"We're friends of his. We were also both with him during his accident."

The nurse looks from Jordan, to me, and shrugs and waves us ahead. "Just don't be too loud." She walks away, and Jordan turns to me and grins.

"Let's go make sure the guy we risked our lives for is still living and breathing, shall we?"

Grant's skin is pale, his eyes are closed, and his lips are chapped and peeling. His face looks drained of color and life, and there's a deep bruise forming above his left eyebrow. He looks asleep when we walk in.

"Grant?" Jordan whispers softly. Grant opens his eyes, and he scans both of us. A small smile forms on his lips.

"My heroes. Hey. I hoped you guys would show up." His words are soft, but clear.

"How much do you remember?" Jordan asks softly.

"Being stupid and leading you into that hole, thinking we could get in a quick surf and then get out. I remember you next to me...getting worked for a bit...then flipping. That's it." So he doesn't remember the part where I saved him on the shore. I flash a quick look at Jordan, and another at Grant, and realize that keeping that a secret is probably for the best.

"So how did I get out of the river? No way it was the EMTs, they came too late." Grant looks from Jordan, to me, an expectant look in his eyes and a small smile on his lips. "How'd you guys do it?"

I glance at Jordan, and he nods, telling me to go ahead. "Well," I begin. "Jordan surfed out, and I attained up and went in after you. I popped your skirt and dove in, got you out of your boat and sent us both floating, unconscious, down the river. Jordan then swooped in and saved the day, dragged us out of the river and did CPR on you until the EMTs came."

"Ginny ran to the road and called 911, she's leaving

that part out because she's modest. She marked a trail for them to follow and everything," Jordan adds, flashing me a grin.

Grant's silent for a moment, his eyes wide. He blinks a few times, and then he shakes his head, amazed. "You guys did all of that for me?" Jordan and I exchange a small smile.

"Nah, we didn't do that for you," Jordan says, grinning at him. "I did it for myself, because I knew I would never forgive myself if I let my best friend die in a hole while I watched. Now I have my best friend back and an awesome story to tell my friends." He winks at me as he says this. Meanwhile, I'm watching Grant—memorizing his features, thinking that he may disappear at any moment. I note the way his eyes glow when he smiles, and the way his hair just barely grazes his eyebrows. I notice the perfect curve of his lips, the freckle under his right eye, and the scar running down his left cheekbone. After a bit of silence, he notices me watching him, and his eyes meet mine. A thousand messages seem to flow between us, and I see warmth, compassion, and gratitude in his gaze. Or maybe his eyes always look like that.

"Are you okay?" I find myself asking, just to break the silence. He keeps his eyes on mine as he answers.

"I've honestly never felt better." I give him a quizzical look.

"You what?" I ask.

"I said I've never felt better. I may look like shit but I actually feel more...alive than I have in a long, long time. Near death experiences have a tendency to do that to you." He flashes a grin at Jordan as he says this. I wonder what he could be referencing, and I know by Jordan's return smile that it occurred on one of their past adventures, on some other river, long before they met me. *What am I doing here?* I think. If they hadn't picked me up Grant wouldn't even be here at all. I'm messing with a lifelong friendship. I should be back in Bethesda where I belong.

"Let's not think about the Tellico now," Jordan replies, shaking his head at the memory. "Let's think happy times. Remember our first Ocoee run? Our first surf on Hell Hole?" Grant's face lights up, and they begin to gush about their first runs of rivers, their best wave rides, and their coolest tricks. I look from Grant to Jordan and back again, and feel a surprising flash of envy. What would it feel like to have a paddling buddy? A true best friend? Sara's great, but she's nothing like this. She doesn't even know the difference between an eddy and a hole on a river.

I guess it is sort of my fault that I have no one I'm extremely close to. Anyone who begins to warm up to me I shove violently away. I haven't let someone in my personal bubble in a long time. It all started in 7th grade. My crush had been the hottest guy in the school, Jackson, an 8th grader. We started kissing at a party one night, and I swore to myself that I had fallen in love. My fantasy grew and grew with every day that I saw him, and I probably would have proposed to him if I hadn't caught him making out with another girl in between classes one day. I was sensible enough to be pissed off and talk to him about it, but I didn't expect him to apologize in the way he did. Let's just say things got inappropriate and I ended up running home, curling in a ball, and crying my eyes out. And I told nobody. That was probably the biggest mistake of them all.

Since then, I have shoved away any guy who has acted interested in me. I haven't had a heart-to-heart with a girlfriend, and I haven't used the word "love" to describe anything other than kayaking in five or so years. And I've stayed with Justin since freshman year to prevent myself from ever getting carried away again.

Then why do I seem to have such strong feelings for Grant? I don't know. That's the problem. If he tries to break into my personal bubble, I don't think I'll be able to push him away. I've never had a guy have such a great effect on me before. Which means I have absolutely no idea how to deal with it.

"Are you kids insured?" says a nurse, holding a clipboard under her arm. "We're going to have to bill either you or your parents for ambulance service and medical care. We're planning on releasing Mr. Haney tomorrow if he seems healthy." Jordan and 'Grant exchange a nervous glance, and I speak up.

"I have medical insurance," I say. "It's my parents', and it'll cover for me." The nurse extends a hand, and I hand her the card. She looks at it, scans it briefly, and then hands it back.

"This should be fine. You can talk about payment at the front desk when you check out." She approaches Grant next, checks his IV, fingers his wrist to check his pulse, and marks something on a piece of paper. "I'll bring you food shortly. You two should go eat in the cafeteria and find somewhere to spend the night, because we're keeping him until tomorrow." Jordan and I share a glance then lean over Grant to say goodbye.

"Hey, bro, sleep well, okay? We'll be back in the morning." He reaches out and they clasp hands, and he heads for the door, along with the nurse. I'm left alone at his bedside.

"See you, Grant," I say, and I'm about to follow the others out when he calls me back.

"Ginny."

I stop and turn around, my heart beginning to pound. "Yeah?"

"What you did today was incredible. I have no idea how I could ever repay you. Thanks for saving my butt out there." His eyes are wide and earnest, and gratitude colors his voice. I walk over to his bed and place my hand gently on his cheek.

"I'm glad you're okay," I say quietly. Grant reaches up a hand and wraps it around mine, and his touch sends shivers up my arm.

"I'm glad we found you," he says. He brings my hand

to his mouth and kisses it gently, and meets my eyes once more. "See you tomorrow?" I smile as calmly as I can. My heart seems to be pounding loud enough to rival the sound of a stampede.

"Yeah. I'll be here," I say, and hold his gaze for a moment longer before releasing his hand and walking out the door. Once outside, I lean against the wall for a second and take a few deep breaths. Shit, what's wrong with me? My palms are sweaty, my heart is racing, and my stomach is doing back flips. A hand touches my shoulder and I jump.

"Whoa there, kiddo, it's just me. You okay?" It's Jordan, and a concerned expression is coloring his face. I smile sheepishly.

"I'm fine. Let's roll," I say. Thankfully, he turns his back to lead the way out of the ICU, so he doesn't see my face flush bright red.

Once back in the front of the building, I deal with some financial stuff and Jordan gives the man behind the desk a billing address for both him and Grant. My insurance covers my medical care and I have to pay for the ambulance ride, which I'm able to take out of my wallet.

"I vote we find some nice restaurant and eat there. I'm craving something good," Jordan says once we're outside.

"I'm sure anything is better than the crap they have here," I reply.

"Mexican sound good?"

"Mexican sounds great," I say. "We definitely deserve it."

"Ginny," Jordan says, looking up from his burrito. "You do realize we left the car at the put in, right?" I stop chewing and my fork drops out of my hand and lands with a plop in the middle of my refried beans.

"Oh. Shit," I reply, feeling stupid. "And how are we going to get that? Do cabs go as far as the put in for the Ottawa?" Jordan laughs.

"I'm sure if we pay them enough. I have some money

on me, I carry around a decent amount when we go on river trips, just in case. We'll be okay."

"Are you sure? I have money too."

"Nah, don't worry about it. You saved my best friend, remember?" He winks at me, and he holds up a hand as I open my mouth to protest. "Don't argue with me, if you hadn't gone in after him he'd probably still be in there."

I sigh, but smile. We eat our food without talking for a few minutes. I smother sour cream on my overflowing tortilla and take a gigantic bite, and Jordan laughs as a big chunk of chicken falls out of my fajita and lands on my shirt. I swallow loudly, grab a napkin off my tray, and wipe of my shirt and my face.

"How old are you?" I ask as I finish, realizing that I know next to nothing about him. "Like, are you in school anywhere?"

"Gap year," he replies. "Grant and I just graduated from New River Academy. Have you heard of it?"

My eyes widen in surprise and envy hits me like a bulldozer. "Yes I've heard of it! I've wanted to go there since my paddling friend told me about it years ago, but my parents insisted on me attending a catholic school." I go to St. Anthony's, a private/catholic "College High School" that focuses on education and sports. It's nice because it's pretty close to the river, but everyone there is either preppy, overly sporty, a huge jock, or religious, and I don't fit in anywhere. There's no group for river rats, if you know what I mean. Most kids there don't even know the difference between rowing and whitewater kayaking.

"Yeah, it was great," Jordan continues. "We travelled all over the world, paddling and learning. A lot of kids are taking a gap year with the school, but Grant and I decided to make our own trip. Before the Ottawa we hit the rest of the east coast, starting in North Carolina and moving up through West Virginia and New York. We're planning on driving west from here and hitting Wisconsin and then rolling down to Colorado and going back up through California to Oregon and Washington." He's smiling and has a faraway expression in his eyes, like he's remembering good times. He focuses his eyes back on me. "But to answer your original question, I'm 18, as is Grant. What about you?"

"I'm a rising senior. I'm 17, 18 in October. I go to St. Anthony's High, which is right by the Potomac."

"Nice. And what other rivers have you run?" Jordan asks. "You seem to know a lot about whitewater."

"Well, I've taken a few trips up to Canada with a group from around where I live, and I've been down to North Carolina and Nantahala. I ran the West Virginia rivers, like the Yough and the New, on my own with a bit of help from some raft guides. I've never been to the west coast before, but that's number one on my list after Great Falls."

"That's why you ran away, right? To be able to paddle?" Jordan stops eating to meet my eyes.

"Yeah. Pretty much."

"So do you have a plan?" he asks. I smirk and then begin to laugh.

"Hell no. I never have a plan. I usually go with gut instinct...don't know why exactly, but it usually ends up being right." Jordan gives me a long look, like he can't quite believe what he's hearing. Then he laughs too.

"You're a character, Grace Kinsey, you really are. I've never met anyone quite like you."

I smile at him, wiping my mouth with my napkin before I reply. "I'm glad I met you too, Jordan. Other than the fact that I almost killed you and your best friend, it's been a pretty awesome day."

"It's not one I'd like to relive, but yes, it makes an epic story."

Is that all I'm going to be after this? I think. *A story to tell your friends?* I wonder what I'll do tomorrow once Grant and Jordan are out of my life. I actually think that I'll be lonely. There'll be no one to save me from raccoon attacks, no one to laugh at my sarcastic comments. No one to kill me for singing country music at the top of my lungs. The thought makes me strangely depressed.

"I wish my friends cared about paddling," I say. "If I told them this story, they'd get bored after about three seconds."

"No way! You saved someone's life. That's not boring at all."

"I guess," I answer, unconvinced. "Anyway, what's next on the agenda for you guys?" I try to ask this without hinting anything, but I know I failed.

"I believe we're running the St. Lawrence and surfing up Lachine. Have you been there before?"

I can't suppress the grin that spreads across my face. "Been there. Loved it."

Jordan grins back at me. "Well, I'm sure Grant would love to have you along. In case he gets stuck in any more holes, that is." He winks at me, and I laugh, but it comes out as more of a shout because of the excitement that's building up inside me. Several people turn to look at us, and I cover my mouth with my hand.

"Sorry," I mutter.

"You seem to have a knack for being the center of attention," Jordan comments.

I give him a small smile. "Yeah, I tend to be rather ridiculous when around people I don't know. I mean, I'm never going to see any of these people again, right?"

"Right. Does that apply to us, too?"

"I want to see you guys again tomorrow," I reply quietly.

"That's good," Jordan says, "because I don't think the trip would be the same without you. Welcome aboard the Haney/Bolton express, kiddo." Happiness bubbles in the pit of my stomach, and I realize for the first time in my life, I've found a group of people who accept me for who I am.

"Thank you!" I call to the cab driver, who nods at me and accepts a hefty payment from Jordan. I glance over and see Grant's pickup truck sitting exactly where we parked it this morning, when I was nothing but a tenacious girl and Grant and Jordan were two buddies on a paddling trip. It's crazy how one day can change everything.

"There it is," Jordan says, walking towards the car.

"It feels like a lifetime has passed since we last saw that," I murmur. I realize how lucky I am, all of a sudden. What if Jordan hadn't pulled us out of the river today? I breathe in deeply, taking in my surroundings. I notice the way the sinking sun shines through the deeply leafed trees, casting geometric shapes on the ground. The air smells faintly of river water, but most of all, I smell summer. The air always seems sweeter during the summer months. The smell of the air fills my nose and my body and makes me think of carefree days on the water, warm nights, and skies full of stars.

A car pulling into the parking lot interrupts the silence. It's an old, blue Honda minivan, and there are kayaks on the roof. I see the familiar splotch of red on the passenger door from when I was younger and spilled the red paint from my shed onto the side of his car. What is Jared doing here?

He parks the car and gets out and walks towards us. I'm worried now. When we parted ways at the border, it seemed like we weren't going to be seeing each other again for a while. But now he's here, and it's only been twenty-four hours.

"Uh...Ginny? Who is that?" Jordan asks from beside me. Just as he says this, Jared calls, "Hey, Gins!" I raise a hand in greeting, a confused look still on my face. I turn back to Jordan.

"Jordan, this is Jared, one of my long-time paddling friends. Jared, meet Jordan, my, uh, newer paddling friend." They shake hands.

"Hey," Jordan says. "Nice to meet you."

"What brings you here?" I ask Jared, concern building up in me.

"You, actually," he replies, and I raise my eyebrows.

"What?"

"Your sister contacted me earlier today, said your parents found out where you were, and that they're coming after you."

"Casey? Is she okay?"

"She was left at home, with neighbor supervision."

"How did they find out where I am?" I ask, panic creeping into my voice.

"Casey said they found insurance records online that linked back to a hospital in Ontario. She gave me the name of it, and I drove up there immediately. They said you had checked out, so I checked the next place I thought you'd be. The Ottawa." Jordan and I are both staring at him, wide-eyed and open-mouthed.

"Shit," I mutter.

"I'm supposed to tell you to run," Jared says. "Casey said that your parents are breathing fire and that they'll sear your ass if they catch you. That's a direct quote."

I can't help but smile. "She says I should run, huh?" I say.

"Unless you want to never paddle again, yeah, that's what she said."

"We're headed for Wisconsin. She could come with us. We could skip the Lachine," Jordan says, and both Jared and I turn to look at him.

"I'm not going to make you do that for me," I tell him firmly. "I can take care of this myself."

"I know you're capable," Jordan says. "But we're going there anyway. It's no trouble to take you along for the ride."

"What about my car?" I ask, smacking myself on the forehead as I remember that it's sitting at the campsite we stayed at last night.

"We only need one car. Maybe Jared could do something with yours?" Jordan suggests.

"Sure. I'll take care of it," Jared confirms. "I can get one of my friends to drive it back over the border. It's no problem, really." I smile at him gratefully.

"Just let me know where it ends up. It's a trashy car, anyways. My parents have wanted to get rid of it for a while now."

"Yeah, no problem," he replies. "You wanna give me a phone number I can reach you at, or what?" I look hopefully at Jordan, and he nods, and scribbles his number down on a piece of paper that Jared supplies.

"Here, Jared," I say, tossing him the car keys I had kept in my dry bag during the paddling trip. He grins when he catches them.

"I see you've learned to bring your keys with you, huh," he says, his eyes laughing.

"Shut up!" I say, laughing with him. "I only did that twice!"

Jared raises his eyebrows skeptically. "Yeah, right," he says. I punch him in the shoulder, and my fist is met with solid muscle.

"Someone hasn't gotten any weaker," I comment, rubbing my fist, which I'm sure hurts more than his shoulder does.

"College near whitewater is the way to go," Jared replies, flexing his biceps. "I highly recommend it." Jared goes to Cornell, right by the Cascadilla and Fall Creeks, two epic class V runs that we ran this past spring in prep for Great Falls. "Speaking of schools," he continues. "Where do you go, Jordan?"

"I'm taking a gap year," he answers. "A year full of paddling is ahead for me."

"Ah, the life of a river rat," Jared says, a wistful expression appearing on his face. "Yeah, that'd get you pretty buff, too." Talking about buff paddlers makes me think of the buff paddler who is now sitting in the ICU, who is in no condition to be rushed into a runaway trip across the country.

"Wait, Jordan," I say, "what about Grant?"

"What about him?"

"We can't just yank him out of the ICU. That's not how hospitals work."

"Listen, Ginny," Jordan begins, reaching out a hand and placing it on my shoulder. "I know it seems like we just met you, and that we're strangers or whatever. Well, after all we went through, we're not strangers. We're friends. Okay? And at least in our books, friends don't leave friends behind to get abducted by evil dream-destroyers. Grant will be fine. He may not be a hundred percent but he's as hard core as they come." He drops his hand off my shoulder and turns to Jared. "Has she always been this stubborn?" Jared laughs his light, carefree laugh that has always succeeded in making me smile.

"Hell yes. She's also been good at staying *out* of the hospital. Why exactly did you have to use your parents' insurance yesterday?"

"Well..." I begin, not sure how much to tell him. I don't really want to freak him out. "Grant got stuck in a pretty nasty hole, and then got knocked unconscious. We got him out, but I also, uh, got a little banged up as well. The EMTs who saved Grant also checked over me, so I had to pay for that."

"I see my instructions of 'be safe' may not have been followed..." Jared says, keeping a smile on his face. I feel myself flush slightly despite his joking tone, as guilt begins to rise up in me again. I think back to earlier that day, before the rapid that changed our lives. If we had scouted that rapid the trip would have continued on as planned. No trashings. No suicide missions. And Grant wouldn't be in the ICU.

"We tried," I reply, keeping my voice light. "Unfortunately the river had other ideas." Jared laughs.

"What'd he get stuck in?" he asks.

"The Pit," Jordan answers, grimacing at the memory.

"Oh, that's a nasty one. I guess it is the right level for it, isn't it. How long have you been paddling, kid?" Jared asks, directing the question at Jordan.

"Um, since I was around eleven," he replies.

"And you're now...?"

"Eighteen." Jared nods, and winks at me. I see an unsaid message flickering in his gaze. *Good find, Ginny.* I roll my eyes.

Jordan checks his watch then extends his arm to

Jared. "Hey, I know this has been a brief visit, but we need to get going. I'm not sure how long it takes to bail someone out of the hospital and I think a head start would do us good."

"You do realize that they may not let him out, right?" Jared says. "I mean, I'm not trying to run your trip for you or anything, but sometimes it's better to be safe than sorry in these situations, you know?" As much as I want to get out of here now, I know Jared's right.

"Yeah. You're right," I reply, thinking about Grant and how close we had been to losing him. "We don't want to take any chances."

"I say we hole up by the hospital, maybe chill at an Internet café and try to make some plans," Jordan says, agreeing with me. "I have Grant's laptop in the car, and I'll show you the map we made and where we're planning on going."

I nod. "Good idea."

"Ginny? I think I need to head off. I'm going to give this number to Casey in case she wants to keep you updated," Jared says, holding up the paper with Jordan's number on it. "That's okay with you, Jordan, right?"

"Yeah, no problem. It'll be good to know what's going on with Ginny's parents and all."

"Your sister's at home, Ginny, but knowing her, she's going to come up with some crazy-ass plan to try to help you. I'm going to do my best to make sure she doesn't do anything stupid," Jared informs me. I smile, knowing that that's exactly what Casey's going to do.

"Tell her hey for me, okay? And tell her to be safe, and that I miss her," I say.

"Will do," he answers. "As I understood it, your neighbors are practically living with her, so I don't think she'll be able to do anything too crazy." He opens his arms and I lean into him, smelling his familiar body wash mixed with river water that brings back so many memories of my younger days. I remember my first swim, my first trashing, my first pin—and I remember Jared, always being there when I needed him, always knowing exactly what to say to make me feel better. He was my perfect older brother, the one who never made mistakes, the one who had the answers for all my problems. I was thirteen when he left, and honestly, that was probably the biggest breakthrough of my childhood. I began to think for myself.

"See you, Jared," I say as we pull apart.

"See you out there, girlie," he says, raising a hand in farewell as Jordan and I make our way to the car.

"You seem to know that guy well," Jordan points out.

"I've been paddling with him since the I started, and he's taught me just about everything I know." Jordan gives me a questioning look. "We've never been more than good friends, I promise! He's six years older than me anyway."

Jordan raises his eyebrows skeptically but smiles. "Whatever you say, *girlie*," he mocks, and I take a fake swipe at his head.

"Hey, I was nine when I met him. Be nice," I say. "I was a lot smaller back then. The name was more fitting."

"Whatever you say," he says again as he inserts the key into the car door and unlocks it. I get in the passenger side and he turns the key in the ignition, and we make our way back to the hospital.

"Look under your seat, there should be a laptop case with Grant's name on it. Take it out, and the map should be on the screen." I follow his directions and remove a silver MacBook Pro covered in kayaking stickers from the case. I flip it open and observe the detailed map displayed on the screen. Jordan leans over and confirms that I have the right one, and I begin to decipher the symbols and small text covering the diagram.

I see a circled star with the word "START" in bold letters. It's placed in West Virginia next to a dot that reads "NEW RIVER." There's a line moving southeast with a kayak symbol at each spot they paddled, each with a number in it. The numbers reference a key in the corner. I recognize most of the rivers down south—Russell Fork,

Tellico, Chattooga, Ocoee, Cheoah, Nolichucky, just to name a few. After the North Carolina area, the line moves north again, hitting a few in Virginia and my alma mater, the Potomac. Some other ones I recognize are the Cheat, the Gauley, the Yough, the Big Sandy, and of course, the Ottawa, where I found them. From there the line continues westward, going through Wisconsin, then there's a long haul through the Midwest and more stops in Colorado and Utah. The line snakes through California and up the west coast, with some stops at the ocean with a note in bold and italics stating, "*SUP!!*"

I imagine Grant and Jordan planning this, sitting next to each other by the river, laptop nearby with American Whitewater books surrounding them, picking out rivers and mapping this out. And now they are living it, like really, really living it, like they've been dreaming about for years, and who do they run into? Me. I can't believe I'm about to screw everything up again.

"Jordan, this is incredible," I gush. "Honestly. This is any paddler's dream. This must have taken forever to plan."

"Oh, click on the excel file behind it, we calculated cost, gear, equipment, food, everything." I do so, and my eyes widen at what I find. They must have thought through everything—from nearby hotels to possible souvenir shops, they calculated the cost literally down to the penny. In total it costs about $40,000, with a note stating, "more if fewer nights are spent in tents." In the "total time" column, it says 314 days, starting in June.

"You really thought of everything, didn't you?" I breathe.

"Sure did. It was really fun to plan. We had everything in our heads, everything we wanted to do, everywhere we wanted to go, and it was great to be able to write it down, and actually make it happen."

"I don't want to screw this up for you," I say, turning to look at him. "I mean it. I don't see 'helping a runaway' on this map anywhere." He smiles, and meets my eyes.

When he sees my set face, he laughs.

"Girlie, you are impossible to crack. I know we didn't plan on running into you, but hey, that's the beauty of it. It's spontaneous decisions like this that make life fun, you know? This is going to be an adventure—a true, on the fly, adventure. Grant is going to love it, too." Spontaneous is probably the best word to describe me, so yeah, I get what he's talking about.

"Yes, I know exactly what you mean," I reply.

Jordan sighs loudly. "Finally. This wasn't going to be any fun if you worried about messing it up the whole time. You're one of us now, whether you like it or not." He glances sideways at me to gage my reaction, and I think he's pleased to see the wide grin stretching across my face. I can't help myself. This is probably the first time anyone has ever called me "one of them." And let me tell you—after 17 years of being the odd one out, finally belonging somewhere is really making my day.

I breathe in the smell of Panera and close my eyes for a moment, savoring the delectable aromas of freshly baked bread and hot soup. We've just come from visiting Grant. He was looking slightly better than he had a few hours earlier. He's been moved from the Intensive Care Unit, which is definitely a good sign, and the nurse told us to check back tomorrow for further assessment of his condition. Our visit was cut short by the visiting hours ending, so we had to leave rather abruptly.

"Smells good, huh?" Jordan comments, and I nod enthusiastically.

"My favorite place ever," I answer. "No question." We weave our way through the tables and find a booth in a corner in the back. I settle in on one side of the table and Jordan slides in next to me. His leg brushes mine briefly and he puts more space between us.

"Sorry," he mumbles.

"Only apologize to me if someone died," I say, quoting my soccer coach from awhile back. That makes Jordan smile and it eases the momentary tension. I open Grant's laptop and we both peer at the screen.

"So our plan now really depends on where your parents are. If they don't figure out where we went, then we're free to do what we want. If they somehow figure out where we are, then we'll have to keep moving." I picture this for a moment—me, Ginny Kinsey, loser girl from Bethesda, riding with two of the coolest guys on earth, traveling around the country, kayaking some of the best rivers in the area.

"My poor parents," I say. "They're coming all the way up here only to find that we've moved on. And they're not very determined, so they'll probably end up turning around and going home, and filing a missing child case or something..." A million horrible thoughts suddenly fill my head, and my voice turns more frantic. "...And then I could be on the national news as the missing, rebellious girl who needs to be found immediately, there's a five thousand dollar reward to anyone who can bring her home alive..." Jordan puts a hand over my mouth, stopping my rant midsentence.

"They're not going to do that. Breathe, kid. It's going to be okay. They may involve the police, but you aren't going to make the national news, don't worry. You definitely aren't famous enough for that." I must not look convinced because he takes his hand off my mouth and opens his arms. "Do you want a hug?" I smile and lean into him, and he wraps his arms around me briefly. I press my head into his shoulder.

"Thanks," I say. "I hope you're right."

"So, back to the map." Jordan redirects our attention back to the task at hand. My worries about my parents sending cops after me slowly begin to fade as I immerse myself in Jordan and Grant's detailed plans. Everything sounds perfect, and I feel myself grinning more and laughing more as I imagine myself actually living the dream.

At around nine, Jordan suggests that we find somewhere to sleep. I recommend that we go back to the Ottawa—after all, our sleeping gear is still there. It's late and we're both feeling the fatigue from the long day. Jordan, being the only one of us who wasn't knocked unconscious today, insists that he drive. It's dark out and the air is warm—it's a typical summer night. There are fireflies buzzing about and I hear the insects chirping quietly as well. A breeze ruffles my hair and I turn to face it, breathing in the sweet scent of summer.

The car ride is quiet, and I lean my head against the window, closing my eyes. I think back to our action-packed day, starting with our bacon breakfast and ending with Grant in the hospital and Jordan and me planning our escape. So much had changed. The events from the river are still rolling over me as I drift into a much-needed sleep.

I wake up to Jordan shaking my shoulder. "Ginny," he murmurs. "We're here." I open my eyes, and Jordan's face is close to mine. It looks like he's trying to decide whether or not he should kiss me, but he decides against it, and moves away. I'm too tired to really notice. I stretch groggily and open the door, stepping out into the darkness. Jordan walks around the front of the truck to meet me. I realize we're at his campsite, and I turn around and squint through the darkness, trying to make out my own site. I can't tell if my car is still there, and knowing Jared, it probably isn't. Jordan notices my hesitation.

"Um, if it's not too weird, you can stay with us. Grant's bed is still made from yesterday and you could use that. He has a really nice bag and I'm sure he wouldn't mind if you used it."

I smile at him gratefully. "Thanks," I say. "That sounds wonderful, actually. If you don't mind."

He returns my smile and flicks on a headlamp. "Not at all." He leads the way to a small, two-person tent sent up by the picnic table. He unzips the door and crawls in, and

I follow. It's cozy inside, and seems bigger than it really is. I immediately wiggle into Grant's sleeping bag, and Jordan takes his shirt off before slipping into his own.

"Goodnight, Ginny," Jordan whispers. He props his head on his elbow to turn to look at me. "I had an awesome day, other than the part where Grant and you both almost died."

I prop myself up in a similar fashion and flash a smile at him. "Well, everything worked out, didn't it? I'd say today was extremely successful."

"It was. I enjoyed myself. Did you?"

"Oh yeah. I'm really glad I met you guys, you know." I want to tell him how much it means to me that they took me under their wing, but I don't know how to phrase that without sounding ridiculously corny or romantic. But I try, anyway. "No one's really been this nice to me before. Usually I tag along with someone and never see them again. With you guys it was different."

"Different how?" Jordan asks.

"I actually feel like I've made some friends." I look at him to see if he confirms this.

"Friends? Ginny, I don't think you could make us get rid of you," he replies, and warmth flashes through me. It's such a new feeling. I can't believe some people live with this all the time.

"Thanks, Jordi," I say. I lay my head back on my pillow.

"You're welcome, Ginny," he replies. "Sleep well."

"G'night," I murmur. I fall asleep to the faint sound of the river and the easy breathing of Jordan beside me, reminding me that I am no longer alone.

Part 2
The Road Trip

The light streaming in through a gap in the tent fly wakes me the next morning. Jordan's lying next to me on his side, facing me. It got warmer as the sun came out and his bag is open, revealing his upper body. I can see the definite outline of his IR lifejacket and a long, painful looking scar running across his right pectoral muscle and down his shoulder. His abs are defined, making him appear fit, but not scarily so. His eyelids flutter slightly and he opens an eye to look at me. He smirks when he notices me watching him, and I flush slightly and look away.

"Good morning," he yawns, stretching. "Sleep okay?"

"Fantastically," I reply. "I'd say it's time to hit the road, though. I'm starved."

"Ditto to that," he says, and we both head out of the tent. As I emerge into the morning sunlight and see the soft rays slanting through the trees, I finally get the meaning of the phrase, "Living to see a new day." How close had I been to losing everything yesterday? I glance over at where my old campsite was and notice that both my tent and my car are gone, and I mentally send a thank you to Jared. He's never let me down, in all the years we've been paddling together. I feel Jordan's hand on my shoulder, and I turn to look at him.

"Ready?" he asks, and I nod, ruffling my hair slightly and rubbing some sleep out of my eye.

"As I'll ever be. Let's go." We quickly break camp, throw the gear in the back seat and hop in the car. The ride passes by quietly, both of us absorbed in our own thoughts. I remember the night before, when I thought he was going to kiss me. But the memory is faint and feels almost like a dream. Jordan couldn't like me in that way— could he? I think back to all the time we spent together yesterday, how he hugged me in the restaurant and let me sleep in his tent. They seem like innocent acts but what if they were intended to mean something? I told him that I have a boyfriend, didn't I? I figure that that'll be a good enough cover for me not being into him, if it turns out that he does have feelings for me.

But what about Grant? A voice says in the back of my head. The intense emotions that flowed through me the previous day when I was with him have faded slightly, and I wonder if I dreamed those up, too. Besides, other than Justin, I've never been anyone's crush. I never cared, either. Many people questioned if I even had hormones up until the start of high school, and many people still do a double take when I mention that I have a boyfriend. The chance that Grant likes me back seems very, very slim. But there's something different about hanging with Jordan and Grant, it seems. They don't see me in the same light as the kids at school do. At St. Anthony's, I'm an outcast because I'm different, I'm not cool because I don't spend money on my clothes, and a loser because I don't have many friends. Here, I'm seen as a talented paddler and a hero, even. I definitely earned some respect points (and several insanity points) by throwing myself into that hole to save Grant. What's loser-like at school has suddenly become the ticket aboard the Bolton/Haney express. Who would have thought that I'm not actually the sorry kid the people at school wrote me up to be?

I've honestly never had a serious, head over heels crush on any guy. Justin fell into my life because I wasn't assertive enough to stop it, but I've enjoyed being with him enough that I haven't broken up with him yet. And for some reason, he hasn't broken up with me, either. I was happy with him, but there's something about paddling in general that makes everything else in life seem unimportant and small in comparison. It's the same thing with paddling guys, I've noticed. Since I've met Grant, he's all that I've been able to think about. I remember being happy with Justin but for some reason I can't even picture his face right now. There's something about kayaking that makes me forget my normal life. Being on or near the river puts me in a weird sort of dreamland, one that when I'm in it, I never want to leave.

"Grant," I whisper. He doesn't stir, so I call louder. "Grant!" He jerks awake, and sees me standing above him, and smiles.

"Hey, Ginny," he says. "What's up?" I wish Jordan were here to help break the news to him, but he insisted on going food shopping. We went over the plan on the way here, though. I'm supposed to say hey, how are you, the usual greeting, and make sure that he has called his parents. Then I'm supposed to tell him that *Jordan* had this really good idea to help me run away. He'll ask, why do you want to run away? And I'll tell him about my parents chasing me. Jordan assured me that this would put the whole idea under his name and that I wouldn't sound selfish at all.

"How do you feel?" I ask.

"Better than yesterday. I'm sure they'll let me out soon," he answers, sounding a lot livelier than yesterday.

"Did you call your parents?"

"Yeah, I did."

"Were they worried?"

"Nah, I think they're okay. Where'd you guys stay last night?"

"Back at the site we were two nights ago."

"And how's Jordan? Where is he?"

"He's shopping right now." I hope he takes the bait.

"For what?"

"There's been a slight complication…" I begin. Grant sits up straight, a slightly panicked look in his eyes.

"Wait, what? What's wrong?"

I rush to reassure him. "Nothing, nothing that bad, at least."

He sits back, letting out a sigh. "I thought it was…never mind, it's not important." He's got me interested now.

"What is it, Grant?" I ask.

"Well," he begins, hesitating slightly. "Once we were paddling the Green Narrows in North Carolina, right before the race. We were taking our last runs and I went down Gorilla with a pretty crappy line, flipped, and cut up my face and broke my nose. It sounds bad, but it really wasn't, and when Jordan saw me he just flipped out. He started storming around, yelling that someone should have helped me. I swore he was going to kill someone. He didn't, of course. Obviously, we didn't race the next day. I even talked to one of my teachers about it, and he said it was probably caused by Jordan feeling overly protective of me, or something. I worry now that if I ever get hurt again, which I obviously did yesterday, he'll freak out and actually hurt someone."

"That's weird," I say. It doesn't sound like a big deal to me, but I've never been in a situation like that before so I guess I wouldn't know.

"It is kind of unusual," Grant says, "but it's hard to really picture unless you were actually there. Anyway, what were you saying?"

"Oh," I reply, "my parents found out where I am, and my sister sent word up that they've set off to come get me." I lower my voice to avoid public attention. "Jordan offered to take me with you on your road trip. I told him he didn't have to…"

"Ginny!" Grant's face is lighting up. "Like, we're running across the country? With you?" I catch his enthusiasm and grin too.

"Yeah, that's what he thought would work. Actually, we don't think they'll be able to find us if we leave here. We'll just have to drive around until they give up and go home."

"Ginny! You're gonna love this. We have it all planned out, we're hitting every major river in the US—"

"Yeah, I saw," I interrupt, smiling at him. "You seriously thought of everything. I'm very impressed."

"Have you been out west before?" he asks. I shake my head.

"No. I hope I get to go to Colorado with you guys, I've always wanted to paddle the mountain water up there."

"You will, no worries. And it will be epic," he says, and I hear excitement in his voice. I observe his face, taking in his warm eyes, his defined face, and messy hair, so different from Jordan yet slightly similar, too. Their smiles, for one. They seem more *real* than anything else I've ever seen.

"You think?" I say. Grant meets my eyes and the warmth there floods into me.

"Hell yeah, girl. Just think, we'll be living under the stars, and every day there'll be a new river, a new challenge, and a new adventure. More lines to figure out, waterfalls to boof, holes to surf." I'm grinning now. "When does Jordi want to leave?"

"It all depends on how you feel, and how soon we can get you out of the hospital."

"Don't worry about me. I'll be out as soon as I work some magic on the nurses here." he winks at me, and part of me melts.

"Well you have the morning to work on them. My next two hours are booked. Jordan has our trip preparations all planned out." I smile as I remember him writing down a list titled, "Ginny's Great Escape" with about twenty things we have to do in under two hours, from gas to red bull to super glue and duct tape for his skirt.

"Ha, yeah, that's Jordan for ya. Lists, lists, lists, that's how he thinks. He won't get anything done otherwise."

"Can I borrow your cell? Do you have it on you? I need to call him so we can figure out where we're gonna meet up." I regret leaving mine at home, but this way, people back home have no way to contact me.

"Sure, kid, no problem." He reaches over to his bedside table and hands me his cell. I flip it open and the first thing I see is a picture Jordan and him, tongues sticking out, a waterfall in the background.

"Speed dial 2," he informs me. I thank him and punch it in. Jordan answers on the first ring, and immediately begins talking about the things he's gotten and what we need to do, and concludes with the instructions of meeting him at the movie theatre a few blocks down in the next 10 minutes.

"Bye, Jordan," I say.

"See you in a few," he replies, and I shut the phone and place it back on the table.

"Thanks, bud," I say. "You need anything else?"

"Nah, go meet Jordan, or else he'll call me thirty-seven times wondering where you are." I chuckle softly as I turn to walk away, raising my hand in farewell as I leave his hospital room.

"Take care of yourself, okay?" I say as I exit. I hear him sigh exasperatedly behind me.

"How's he doing?" a nurse asks as she sees me leave.

"Excellent," I say, flashing her a smile. "I've never seen him better."

I meet Jordan five minutes before the time he had requested, and we set off to accomplish number three on the list—camping supplies at Wal-Mart. He managed to accomplish the first two while I was with Grant.

"What do you think? The death of his grandma or his sister's wedding?" Jordan asks, as we discuss possible ways to get Grant out of the hospital.

"Hmm..." I think for moment, then say, "Wedding. His grandma dying is too cynical. Wait, does he even have a sister?"

"Yes, she's older, and she's a music major at James Madison. She's actually lesbian, but that's beside the point." I laugh.

"Alright. Sounds good." I grab thirteen canisters of camping fuel off the shelf and Jordan checks it off his list. I proceed by grabbing matches (six mega-packs, waterproof), Powerbars (24 Performance Energy Bars, six vanilla crisp, six chocolate, six peanut butter, and six milk chocolate brownie), duct tape (four rolls), and a tarp (red, the biggest size possible). Jordan and I separate so we can work faster. He reminds me that if my parents left at approximately five o'clock yesterday, and drove for six before stopping somewhere to sleep, we have about three more hours, assuming they started driving again at eight this morning.

As I've spent more time with him, I've gotten to know more of the real Jordan. It usually works like this: I meet some guys on the river, say goodbye to them at the takeout, and never see them again. My judge of how their personality is comes from how nice they are when they help me with the lines and the variety of adjectives they use to describe the rapids and playboating tricks they throw. But with Jordan, I'm actually getting the chance to get to know him off the river. His quirks make me laugh, our talk is easy and he's more observant than any other guy I know. For instance, earlier today, he pointed out someone he thought was a paddler, because of the way he walked—he went over, asked him if he had run the Ottawa recently, and they proceeded to talk about Buseater for a full ten minutes before I insisted that we move on.

I move over to the freeze-dried food and pick out "Ten meals of choice, as long that they sound tasty". After, I pick out a few DVDs (from the $5 bin ONLY). For long days on the road I'm sure *Juno* and *Mean Girls* will keep us entertained. I wonder where Jordan has the money to fund this trip, and then I remember the side note on his excel sheet: "50% from Kirstin Haney's book sales account, 20% from Jordan, 30% from Grant." I glance at my watch and notice that we only have five more minutes left in the store before we need to move on, so I grab the last few items on my list and head for the check out. I find Jordan paging through an *Outdoor* magazine.

"Hey, I was about to do one of those PA announcements. Glad you showed up." He winks and sets down the magazine. We quickly check out and move on to the next store after placing our purchases in the car.

After hitting the bank and Mountain Equipment (Canada's REI), Jordan decides that we should head back and try to get Grant out of the hospital. But just as he's informing me of this plan of action, his cell rings.

"Hey, G-ster, what's up?" he says into the phone, and I stifle a laugh at his creative nickname. Grant says something on the other end.

"Really? Great! We're just heading back now, in fact. Yes. Uh huh. Yeah, she's right here. No, we haven't spent all our money, don't worry…yes, we've gotten everything we need. You don't need to worry, no. Yeah. Okay, see you in a few." He hangs up and grins at me.

"He's out! In fact, he told them that his cousin was getting married! Now aren't we psychic!" He holds out his fist and I bump it, but he continues on and does a complicated handshake that I do my best to keep up with.

"What was that?" I ask as he finishes with his tongue out and a wave of his thumb and pinky finger.

"Only the best handshake ever! We'll show it to you while we're driving. We're picking Grant up outside the hospital, and then, girlie, we're hittin' the road!"

I imagine a sign beside us, pointing in the direction we're driving, in one of those corny road trip cartoons, reading "Your Adventure Starts Here!" Excitement's building up in me, and I whoop and flash a grin at Jordan. Jordan cranks up the radio and both of us sing along at the top of our lungs, windows open and everything.

I fall asleep about three and a half hours in to the sound of Grant and Jordan talking in the front seat. I wake after an intense dream that I don't remember, and I'm about to sit up when I hear that they're now talking about me.

"We've only known Ginny for three days, how can you be sure?" I think it's Grant's voice.

"Being with her is...I don't even know how to describe it. It makes me..." I don't hear the end of Jordan's sentence, but I hear Grant's reply.

"She is pretty."

"You think?"

"Hell yeah!" This comes out louder than Grant wanted, and he's quiet for a moment before continuing. "But how do you know if...you know..."

"I don't. You know my relationships all end tragically," Jordan sighs.

"Yours? Tragic? At least girls don't spit in your face for telling them the truth! At least they don't kick you in the balls because you aren't in love with them! It's like they'll only be with you if you tell them that you want to be with them forever," Grant's voice is raising as he says this, and Jordan shushes him.

"My last girlfriend, you saw her! That one I met last summer? The one who dropped me in the middle of that concert, loud enough for everyone to hear?"

"Yeah, but at least a girl who you actually liked didn't dump you because she couldn't stand that you didn't want to marry her." I can't stand to hear them bicker any longer, so I stretch then yawn loudly. They both fall silent.

"Hey, Ginny," Grant says mildly. "We're going to stop for lunch at the next exit...I have to go to the bathroom bad and we're both starved. You hungry?" He's covered for himself so well I almost forget that a second ago he was talking about me.

"You bet! Fast food?"

"Yup, probably a Wendy's," Jordan replies, glancing at me in the rearview mirror.

"Awesome," I respond. My mind's still going over their conversation word for word. I decide to think about it more in depth later, maybe when it's dark and they can't see my facial expressions.

"Have a nice nap?" Grant asks, obviously trying to make conversation.

"Oh yeah. It's pretty comfy back here, with all the extra cushioning…" I'm referring to the tarp that I used as a pillow and the bed I constructed out of jackets and clothing bags. "If you want, we can switch out of this spot for sleeping purposes, and we can rotate drivers."

"See? It's good having a female along with us," Jordan says jokingly. "She comes up with plans that we would never have thought of."

"Including the one where she almost killed herself saving my butt?" Grant asks, teasingly, glancing at me and grinning.

"*Especially* that one. It was so fucking insane, I don't think anyone except you would have thought of it," Jordan says, and I laugh.

"It worked, didn't it?"

"Yeah," Jordan says, "it really did."

"Wendy's, next exit," Grant reads off a highway road sign. "Get off here, Jordi, or I think I may have to piss in a bottle."

"Gotcha, bro," says Jordan, and he hits the accelerator and veers quickly off the highway.

We enter the small town of Claydale going about eighty miles per hour. It turns out to be much smaller than we anticipated, so after the exit Jordan slams on the breaks to be able to maneuver on the narrow roads. There are small houses lining the streets, ramshackle as anything, with peeling paint and rickety porches, screen doors on their hinges. In some of the lawns I see kayaks leaning against a shed or a car with a roof rack. As we go over a small bridge, I look over the edge and see a river.

And it's not just any river, either; it's a river with *rapids*.

And then I see the hole.

"Jordan! Grant!" I point excitedly to the beautiful, glassy hole in the middle of the river. "Do you see what I see?" Both of them follow my finger and grin wildly.

"Jordan!" Grant yells. "Pull over!" We find a small parking area and park quickly. There's even a path to the river that seems well used. We're clearly not the only people to have spotted this beautiful river feature.

Grant sprints into the woods to relieve himself and Jordan and I get the playboats from out of the back of the truck. I'm hoping to be able to throw some big tricks—I've been working on my phonix monkey, a pretty advanced trick, and the hole beside us looks perfect for it. It's a pirouette, or spin your bow, then a loop, done in rapid sequence.

I grab my gear back from back as well, and stepping into it feels like I'm stepping into familiar skin. The smell of neoprene makes me feel incredibly high, and I laugh out loud. Grant, who's back from his bathroom break, gives me a funny look as he pulls his skirt over his head.

Once we're all ready, we seal launch off the shore and land softly into the chilly water. It splashes my face and I whoop.

"Who wants the first surf?" Grant asks, and Jordan immediately turns to me.

"Ladies first?" He gestures with his paddle for me to enter the hole, and I paddle towards it. This hole, unlike the killer one on the Ottawa, has flushy shoulders, indicating that you can get a good surf but will be able to get out when you're finished. I enter it from surfer's left, and slip smoothly into the froth. I move around in it for a bit, trying to find the "sweet spot", and once my boat falls into it, I sit back and surf. It's slightly bouncy and after about fifteen seconds of easy surfing I back up onto the pillow of the hole, dig my bow down, and whip my body forward then throw it back, looping my boat, and I land it upright, still in the hole.

"Damn!" I hear Jordan comment from the eddy beside

me, and I throw my spectators a grin before attempting to cartwheel. I get on my edge and move onto my bow before twisting my torso violently and throwing down my stern. I get another bow/stern sequence before I lean too far and flip. I back deck roll up and spin a few times before exiting the hole for good. I paddle back into the eddy and am greeted with open-mouthed stares.

"Holy shit, Ginny! I had no idea you could playboat!" Jordan says, impressed.

"Yeah, no kidding. That was insane, girl! I don't even know if I can match that!" says Grant, grinning at me.

"You probably shouldn't even be on the water now, not after yesterday," I warn Grant.

"Nah, I'm not getting bested by a girl like that," he jokes. "Alright, let's see what I can do..." He paddles into the hole and slips into the spot I was in, and tries to throw a loop too early and flips, and flushes out of the hole. He makes a face at me as he rolls up. Jordan goes in next and is slightly more successful, and manages to land a loop, but lands outside the hole. I go in again and after a couple spins I twist my body, lean forward, throw in a crossbow draw, and my bow spins below me. Once facing forwards again I throw a loop, landing my first ever phonix monkey. Then I hear a yell from the bridge.

"Shred it up, girl!" It sounds so much like Jared I look up, losing my concentration, and flip and get shot out of the hole. When I roll up I turn my attention back to the man on the bridge. He looks to be twenty-something, and has a backwards baseball cap on his head and ear buds around his neck. He's wearing a dark red shirt that outlines his muscled chest and large shoulders, and I know just from one glance that he's a paddler, too. I raise a hand in greeting as I paddle up the eddy. He runs off the bridge and comes to the river shore.

"Who are you?" he asks, a hint of wonder on his voice. "And where are you from?"

"Who are *you?*" I say back. "A stalker?" This makes him laugh.

"Just a local paddler wondering who just invaded his hole. I'm Colton, and this here's Cole's Hole, named after yours truly."

"Seriously?" I say. "That's cool. Sweet hole you got there, Colton."

"I know, right? Best trick hole within some three hundred miles of here. And you didn't answer my question." Grant paddles up beside me in the eddy and shakes the water out of his face.

"Hey," he greets Colton. "I'm Grant."

"I didn't ask you, I asked the lady," Colton says. He raises his eyebrows at me.

"I'm Ginny," I say.

"And what brings you three to Claydale?"

"Paddling," Jordan answers, as he comes up from behind. "What else?"

"No one comes through here unless they're on their way somewhere else. That's how it always is. People come, stay for a day, maybe two if we're lucky, and then skedaddle. So, where you off to?"

"Wausau, Wisconsin, actually," answers Grant. "We'd stay longer, but we're sort of being chased." I shoot him a warning glance but he doesn't acknowledge it.

"Chased?" Colton asks, surprised. "What do you mean?"

"Long story short, we're trying to save Ginny's freestyle career." I cock an eyebrow at him, and he smiles, and mouths, "It's true."

"Oh my God, someone famous has come through Claydale!" Colton exclaims, putting a hand to his head, pretending to get faint. "History has been made! What, are you up there with Emily Jackson? I've actually had a celebrity crush on her since I was fourteen…"

"Um," I begin, not wanting to brag but not wanting to lie, either. "I've seen her around the Ottawa when I've been up there. It was amazing watching her on Garb, I learned a lot."

"You paddled *with* Emily Jackson?" Now Colton

actually looks like he's going to pass out.

"Yeah, it wasn't a big deal, really. I don't think she remembers me at all." Colton still looks impressed.

"You still count as famous," he replies. He glances at his watch. "Well, it was nice talking with y'all, but I have tea with my grandma in five minutes, so I better go." He stands up and brushes off his jeans. "Thanks for visiting Cole's Hole, and I hope you enjoy your visit." He winks at us, flashes us a final grin and jogs up the riverbank and walks back across the bridge.

"Cool guy," comments Jordan. "Weird, but cool."

"Aren't we all?" I question. "Paddlers, I mean. I could say that about any of us."

"You're right," Grant agrees. "Weird, but cool. Very, very cool." I hear the whitewater in the background, calling to me.

"I'm going to get in another surf. You guys game?" I ask.

"What kind of question is that?" Jordan answers. "We're always game for a surf."

"Is that why you both almost died on the Ottawa yesterday?" I ask jokingly.

"Possibly," Jordan replies, smiling. "Now go get back in that hole before the sun sets." I paddle back up the eddy and Grant and Jordan follow, grins on all our faces.

Back in the car, I get shotgun and Grant gets a turn behind the wheel. We're only about six hours in and it's been almost nine hours since we left. I wonder where my parents are, what they're thinking about, how mad at me they are—

"Ginny, phone," says Jordan, interrupting my thoughts. "It's Casey." I take the phone from him and press it against my ear.

"Hello?"

"Ginny! It's Casey," Casey says loudly into the phone. "I got your note and almost sprinted out the door after you, but then I remembered that it was the middle of the night and you had already been gone for six hours."

"I'm sorry I left, Case," I say.

"No, you're not," she says. That's one thing I love and hate about my sister—she can read me better than anyone else. If I'm lying, she knows. If I'm stretching the truth, she knows. It's best just to be honest.

"Okay, you got me. I'm not sorry I left, but I'm sorry I left you behind."

"That's reasonable," she replies. "Anyway, I think I have a way to get up there. Mom and Dad are still trucking through New York, I'm fairly sure they slept in this morning." That's good news. "Where are you, anyway?"

"We just exited Claydale."

"What?" she exclaims.

"Claydale, it's west of Ottawa. We're heading for Wausau, Case."

"Jared told me you found someone to travel with. That's good, Ginny. I'm glad you're not alone. Jared gave me Jordan's number. Who's the other guy?"

"Grant," I say. "Grant Haney." I tried to keep all emotion out of my voice as I said his name, but I know I failed.

"Oh, Grant," she says, and I know she picked up on it, too. I wish I could tell her, because I know she'd stay quiet and listen, and not judge. But I can't, not here. "He's the one who almost died on the Ottawa, right?"

"Jared told you about that, too?" I ask.

"Yup. He told me you had some crazy rescue, too. Anyway, the reason I called was to tell you I have a way to get up there."

"You do?"

"Yes, but...I can't tell you." She falls silent, and I wish she was next to me, so I could rip out her hair. Immoveable as a ten-ton boulder is Casey Kinsey, and I know there's no way I can make her tell me.

"You can't, huh? Why not?"

"It's going to be a surprise. And it really doesn't matter," she answers. "But I do need to know where we should meet you."

"I'm not telling you where to meet me if you don't tell me who you're with," I insist.

"Well," she says, "I guess we'll just have to figure it out by ourselves." There's a click, and the other end goes silent. I stare at the phone, annoyed, before shutting it.

"What'd she say, Ginny?" asks Grant, turning to look at me.

"Well, she said that she's coming up here. And that my parents are somewhere in New York. But she won't tell me who she's coming up with," I say.

"Why is that a problem?" Grant asks. "At least you know she's on her way."

"The thing with Casey," I begin, "is that she's usually honest. She usually speaks her mind and everything on it. You know there's something wrong when she doesn't say anything, or when she hangs up abruptly. And she did both during that phone conversation."

"Don't take this the wrong way," Jordan says, "but why does she feel like she needs to come up at all? Things we do may be dangerous, risky, or crazy. Is this really something we should drag a youngster into?"

"Casey's only fourteen," I reply, "but I think she feels a weird sort of responsibility for me. We've always looked out for each other, and I can remember countless times when I helped her in a tough spot. It's how our relationship works, us looking out for each other."

"That makes sense," Grant says, glancing at me. "I'd feel the same way if I were her."

"What, that I'm a helpless child who needs constant supervision?" I joke.

"No, that if my sibling is in trouble, I need to be there to help."

"You have a sister, right?"

"And I probably wouldn't be here without her." Grant gives me a look saying, "I get you," and I smile, telling him that I got him, too. Maybe this silent communication thing isn't so hard. Maybe you just need to understand the person you're communicating with.

As the moon comes out and the sun slowly sinks below the horizon, a blanket of stars emerges from the dark. I crane my head out the window, feeling the air rush through my hair, to get a better look.

"It's like there's more white than black," I whisper, amazed. Grant, who's still in the driver seat, nods.

"I know, right? It's like you can't tell if it's black stars on a white sky or white stars on a black sky."

"Like a zebra," I say. Grant laughs softly. Jordan's sound asleep in the back, and his soft snores are audible above the roar of the highway.

"What do you do, Ginny, other than paddle? Like, for fun?" Grant asks, keeping his voice low. He glances at me out of the corner of his eye.

"Well…" I think about my life back home, and realize that other than paddling and school, I really don't have much going or me. "I'm kind of a one trick pony." Grant smiles, and takes a hand off the wheel to run a hand through his hair.

"You're kinda like me, then," he says. "I tried soccer, basketball…I wasn't terrible, necessarily, but that's just not what I wanted to do, you know?" I smile, knowing exactly what he means.

"Exactly," I say.

"Jordan's not the same way, though. He has climbing. Has he ever mentioned that before?" I shake my head, glancing at his sleeping form in the backseat. "Well, the beginning of our first semester at New River Academy was spent actually on the New River. The New River Gorge has some of the best climbing in the area, so we all got to try it out, and Jordi loved it. He climbed wherever he could, and got really good, too."

"Is he climbing in Colorado?"

"Nah, he had a pretty bad fall during our senior year…cut himself up pretty good. I think it shook up his confidence a bit, too, so he's taking a break."

"Does he still have a scar from it?" I ask, remembering the one on his right peck.

"Yeah, on the right side of his chest," Grant answers. He keeps his face smooth but I can tell the scar brings back bad memories, so I drop the subject and gaze out the window again and watch the trees flash by, illuminated by the headlights.

"I love nights like this," Grant says, his voice almost a whisper.

"I know," I reply, smiling. "There's definitely something magical about summer nights."

"You think?" Grant asks, turning to look at me.

"Yeah. Definitely. The insects singing, the fireflies glowing, the stars that seem to light up the sky."

"Yeah, I get you," Grant says, and I see a smile on his face as well. We both fall silent, and I close my eyes, feeling the warm breeze on my face and smelling the fresh, summer air.

"Ginny," someone's calling my name. It sounds like I'm underwater, and someone's trying to talk to me from above. "Ginny, we're stopping for the night." I drag myself out of the depths of sleep and blink my eyes open.

"Uhhh, sorry," I mumble. "Where are we?"

"I believe we're somewhere above Michigan. Dunno exactly," Grant replies. His face looks really close to mine, and his features become clearer as my eyes focus. *He's cute in the dark*, I think.

"Alright, I'll help you set up the tent..." I stretch and Grant moves out of the doorway so I can hop out. Jordan is asleep like a rock in the back, and after much poking and prodding he wakes up, groaning about us interrupting his stellar dream about ice cream sundaes.

"Wake up, sluggy, you're sleeping on the gear," Grant says. "Please?"

"Fine, fine, fine..." he moans, stumbling out of the car. He promptly lies down on the grass and falls asleep again.

"He's real helpful when he's tired," I comment. Grant

laughs.

"Tell me about it. I've had to travel with this lump for the past two months." I dig around in the mounds of junk we have stuffed in the back seat and pull out the four-person tent and the bag with the sleeping gear in it.

"You don't mind me sleeping in your tent, right?" I ask, my voice piercing through the quiet night. It seems too loud in the pitch-blackness.

"Not at all. I'm glad we brought the four-person tent, too. I believe Jordan's reasoning on the sheet was, 'for nights we need extra luxury.'" I smile as I remember Jordan's excel sheet with every moment of this trip planned out. Plan for the worst but hope for the best, right? Makes every trip a happy trip, as Jared would say.

"And I'm what, extra luxury?" I joke, and Grant shoves me in the shoulder.

"Not appropriate," he says sternly. I laugh loudly, and Jordan moans on the grass.

"Please shut up..." he mumbles, and Grant kicks him.

"You're not sleeping in our tent unless you help set it up. Get off your sorry ass," Grant commands. Jordan grabs his leg and pulls him down with him, and they proceed to wrestle until Jordan succeeds in pinning Grant against the damp grass.

"If you have enough energy to pin me, then you have enough energy to put up a tent," Grant says. "Now get off." Jordan obeys and Grant gets up. The back of Grant's gray shirt is covered with grass and leaves, and I brush them off as he passes. His back twitches as my fingers touch it, and a weird jolt shoots up my arm. I drop my hands and open up the tent bag, throwing the poles at Jordan and taking out the ground cloth.

"Ah, don't we all love setting up tents in the dark," Grant says. "Anyone have a light?"

"I'll get it!" Jordan is quick to volunteer. I roll my eyes and take over assembling the poles as he jogs over to the truck. The tent is already up and ready to be staked when he comes back.

"Guess you didn't need me after all," he says as he returns. "I'm going to just sit back and relax..." I aim the stake bag at his head and he catches it, barely. "Hey!"

"Stake the tent, Jordi," I say, slightly exasperated. "Please and thank you." He relents and begins to stick the metal pieces into the ground as Grant and I secure the fly.

"Home sweet home," I pronounce as we finish. "For tonight, at least."

"Can I sleep now?" Jordan whines, and Grant and I both laugh.

"Yes, Jordi, now you may sleep," Grant says, and Jordan is the first to dive in as I unzip the door.

The temperature drops severely during the night. I'm on the outside, closest to the door, Grant is in the middle and Jordan is on his other side. I burrow down into the bottom of my sleeping bag, where it is considerably warmer, but I'm now realizing that I can't breathe. I come up for air, and am immediately cold again. I consider going out to the car to get another jacket, but decide that that would be even colder. I don't feel like moving, anyway. I stare at Grant's back and see the gentle rise and fall of his chest, and know he's sound asleep. I flip over and begin doing pushups, seeing no other way to warm up my blood.

I've done maybe thirty-five when Grant turns over and looks at me.

"Ginny?" he mumbles. "What's up?" I stop and look at him sheepishly.

"I'm, uh, incredibly cold," I reply in a whisper. A violent shiver runs through my body, and my teeth begin to chatter. Grant reaches out a hand and touches my cheek.

"Shit, girl, you're frigid," he says. "You want my jacket?" I'm about to refuse, tell him I'll get through the night, when a wind penetrates through the tent walls, making my teeth chatter harder. He makes the decision for me, unzips his coat, and hands it to me. "Here, I don't need it." I smile gratefully at him.

"Thanks, man," I reply. "You sure you don't need it? You're the one who was in the ICU some thirty six hours ago."

Grant smiles at me reassuringly. "The river's like my drug. I feel fine, honest. And my sleeping bag's warm as hell. Put on the jacket," he tells me. I do as I'm told, and I feel slightly warmer. I don't want to bother him anymore, so I thank him again, and try to go back asleep.

But as the night begins to wear on, cold seeps through the jacket and I feel like an ice cube again. I curl into a ball in the bottom of my sleeping bag and don't even feel warm there. What is wrong with me? I've never been this cold before. I know hypothermia can be caused by being submerged in cold water for long periods of time and by freezing temperatures, but none of those things apply to me right now. I feel myself beginning to shake violently and begin to suffocate at the same time, so I emerge out of my sleeping bag and find Grant staring at me.

"You're not okay," he says, concern in his voice. "Come here." He unzips his sleeping bag. "This is going to be awkward, but it's a million times better than you freezing to death." Understanding floods over me, and my eyes widen in the darkness. I'm about to sleep with Grant Haney, in the literal sense. I hesitate, but soon my body makes the decision for me. Human body heat seems like the greatest thing in the world right now.

So without protesting, I unzip my own sleeping bag and roll slowly towards Grant. For a split second, I'm freezing, then I feel Grant's body against mine and he zips his bag up, and his warmth engulfs me. I press my back into his chest and his arms encircle me. I try to tell myself that he's only doing this because I'm freezing to death, but it feels good, too, too good…and soon all I can think about is Grant, Grant, Grant.

I fall asleep to the soft beat of his heart and the warmth of his body heating my own. But my skin isn't the only thing warming up—as I feel his chin pressing down on the top of my head and feel his hands against my chest, I feel my heart, my frozen, numb heart, begin to slowly thaw as well.

When I wake, I hear Grant and Jordan arguing. They're trying to keep their voices down, but they are both failing miserably, and with every sentence each of their voices gets louder.
"What the hell were you thinking?" Jordan hisses.
"She was freezing to death, Jordan! I didn't want her to die! You would've done the same thing!" Grant retorts.
"It wasn't even cold last night! You just wanted to…I don't know…piss me off or something! What did I ever do to you? Do you think you have dibs on her, because she saved your life?"
"What are you talking about?" Grant says, his voice nearing a yell. "She was cold, okay? I've never seen anyone so cold before. I couldn't just sit there and watch her suffer. I'm sorry if I hurt you, Jordan, I really am." He lowers his voice significantly. "It was a freak moment, and I did what I thought was right. It had nothing to do with my feelings, I promise. I just wanted to keep her safe." Jordan lowers his voice as well.
"Okay. I blew up. I'm sorry, too." I breathe a sigh of relief, thankful that the fight didn't grow into something out of control. I stick my head out of the top of the sleeping bag.
"Morning, both of you," I yawn. They both turn to look at me.
"Hey, Ginny," Jordan says, his voice gentle. "Heard you had a rough night last night."
"Yeah, it was crazy." I shudder, partially at the memory and partially for effect. I see Grant give Jordan a "see? I told you so" look.
"I'm sorry, tomorrow night we can give you extra layers," Jordan says. "I have lots of extra blankets and things we packed in case of emergency." This makes me smile.
"You are probably the world's best packer," I

compliment him. "Seriously."

"I'm glad someone appreciates it," he replies, shooting a look at Grant. "I think I do a pretty good job myself, too."

"It's nice for this trip, yes," Grant says, "but you should see him pack for a simple hike, or a beach trip. You wouldn't believe all the *stuff* he brings." Jordan goes on and argues that it's always best to expect the worst, and they argue playfully back and forth for a few minutes as we get out of our sleeping bags and roll them up. I enjoy listening to their banter. It seems so easy, so relaxed, and shows just how strong their friendship really is—and I know, even if I don't want to admit it, that I don't want to do anything to jeopardize it. I may be stupid sometimes, but I'm not selfish. I tell myself firmly that though I have feelings for Grant, I can't act on them, at least not now. He and Jordan are already doing me the biggest favor in the world and I have no right to screw up their relationship, not after everything they've done for me.

"You know," Jordan says, "a while back I got a hole named after me, too." We're in the car again, I'm driving, and Jordan's sitting beside me.

"Oh really?" I prompt.

"Yeah. It was on the New. Super small, but super sticky, and the first time I ran the rapid, I went right into it, got a nice trashing, and then swam. It was so small that our coach didn't even mention it, and the line we were supposed to be running was about fifteen feet away from it. I still managed to get stuck." He laughs. "We called it Jordi's Hole for the rest of my stay at NRA."

"Hey, he's not telling the full story," interrupts Grant from the back. "Every time he ran that rapid he'd aim to miss the hole but would end up going in. Finally, after what, three swims? He managed to surf out."

"Hey! After those three swims, I was a million times less afraid of throwing myself into holes and could shred *my* hole up like no other." I smile to myself. Every time Jordan and Grant talk, they're either arguing about something or boasting about their achievements. Mom has always said that you know you're close to someone if you aren't afraid to fight with them. I have always thought that was absurd, that there's no way you could stay close to someone if you were constantly bickering. Jordan and Grant are currently proving my mother correct.

"...and remember that loop I threw in Angel's that one time? That was epic!" Jordan is now bragging. "I'm pretty sure it was almost all air."

"I didn't see it, couldn't say I believe you," Grant says.

"You heard me talk about it for days afterwards! You better believe it! You even saw that picture that raft guide took!"

"Yeah, even so...that's why they invented Photoshop," Grant points out. Jordan huffs quietly under his breath. I keep my eyes on the road, watching the occasional car pass by. We're nowhere near anything—the last exit was probably thirty miles ago—and thick forest lines either side of the road. The leaves are a brilliant green, the color of summertime. My window is partially open and I breathe in the fresh air, marveling at how clean it is. You breathe in air on the Beltway in DC and you practically get lung cancer. Here, the roads are clear and there's not a police car in sight, so I'm able to cruise along at around eighty. I doubt I've ever gone this fast before.

"Ginny?" Jordan taps me on the shoulder. I look away from the road and meet his eyes.

"Yes?" He looks guilty as he replies.

"I hate to break it to you..."

"Spit it out, man," I say, exasperated.

"I gotta take a piss." I roll my eyes.

"You're a boy, I forgot. You can pee wherever you want. How bad is it? Should we pull over here?" He nods, his face telling me that if I don't pull over now, I'll end up having to watch him urinate in a bottle. "Okay, okay..." I slowly decelerate the car and pull over into the shoulder of the road. I put the car in park and nod for him to get out.

"Thanks, Gins!" Jordan tells me hurriedly as he jumps out of the car and sprints into the woods. I decide some fresh air would do me some good, too, so I step out of the car as well, and Grant follows suit. He walks around the car to stand by me.

"Hey, Ginny," he says, smiling at me. "How do you like the trip so far? Sick of us yet?"

"No, I don't think I could ever get sick of you two," I reply, keeping my voice light. I think he'd run away if he knew how true that really was.

"Really?" Grant asks. "You aren't bored to death by our conversations? We're not very inclusive." I wave this off too.

"Your conversations are very interesting. It's a nice change from listening to my friends back home talk about clothes and boys all the time." There I go again, making it seem like I have a bunch of friends.

"I doubt that's all they talk about."

"Ah, you'd be surprised." It annoys me to hell. By the end of junior year I swore I was going to shoot myself if someone asked me if it was true that so-and-so liked so-and-so or if Brendan was going out with Brynn or Eleanor was going out with Ethan...

Grant's eyes grow wide and at first I think that my last comment *did* surprise him, when I realize it's much more than that. I hear a car pull in behind us. I casually glance over my shoulder and see the black and white of a police car. I guess I should learn to use my mirrors more. An official looking officer steps out. He has a clipboard in his hand and a pencil behind his ear, and he looks up from the clipboard to look at me, his eyes narrowed. I turn back to Grant, and find his eyes boring into my own. They're intense and seem to be hurriedly trying to send me a message. I don't comprehend, though, and what he does next completely catches me off guard.

As the police officer begins walking over, Grant grabs my shoulders, brings his mouth to mine, and kisses me. It's not one of those innocent first-kiss type things either—

it's hard core, full on, tongue and all. First I'm stunned, my body tenses, my mouth resists. But he's gentle, his arms engulf me, and his mouth moves against mine, and soon I feel myself begin to melt into him. My first thought is that he must have kissed a million girls to get as good as he is now. But even that leaves my mind as I begin to kiss him back. He's so damn good that I don't notice the police officer clear his throat behind us, turn around, go back to his car, close the door, and drive away.

My fingers are beginning to lace their way into his thick hair when I hear someone else clear their throat on the other side of us. Grant jerks away, and stumbles so he's about four feet from me, and I lurch in the opposite direction. My face is flushing a deep magenta, and Grant's head is down, hiding his own bright red face. I don't know what just happened, but I know that it wasn't supposed to. Now Jordan's standing in front of us, a look of utter shock on his face, and I know we just messed up. Big time.

"What. The. Fuck?" he says, not even attempting to filter his language. Grant slowly raises his head, and his eyes are full of regret, pain, and I see something else there too, that I see he's trying to hide—passion. My emotions are rolling around like a stormy sea, and I know exactly what he feels like.

"There was this police officer..." he begins, but I can tell Jordan's in no mood for excuses.

"Oh, and what, he walked over here and *demanded* that you kiss her?" His voice is rising now, and I can tell he's furious. "Don't even try to justify that! You know how I feel! You *know!* What did I ever do to you, Grant? Huh? What did I ever do to you to deserve that?" His eyes are wild now, and with every word Grant seems to sink farther into a slump.

"Can you at least listen to my side of the story?" Grant asks, his eyes pleading. "Please? It's not what you thought, I promise." I don't know what Grant's story is exactly, but I know that whatever it is won't be enough to satisfy Jordan. But I know something I can say to fix things, at least for now. Even if it does make me look like a slut, at least Jordan won't be mad at Grant anymore. He'll be mad at me.

"Actually," I say, my voice wavering. I clear my throat, putting on my best straight face. I'm a very believable liar when I want to be. "It wasn't Grant's fault at all. I don't know what I was thinking. I'm...I'm sorry." Jordan's glaring eyes turn to me, and the flame in them suddenly dies. His head drops, his fight leaves, and he looks utterly defeated. My heart leaps out to him. Grant's eyes meet mine, and I give him a small smile. His eyes flash me a message: *what the hell was that?* I give him a tiny shrug in response. I hope he can see the pain in my eyes, so he knows that this isn't easy for me, either.

"Was there a police car?" Jordan asks softly. His voice is flat.

"Yeah," Grant answers. "It came by."

"What did it want?"

"I dunno, I thought maybe he was after Ginny. But maybe I was overreacting." Silence falls over us, and I wonder if I've made a mistake in lying. Then Grant says, "I mean, I guess she thought that kissing me would make the cop think that we were just a runaway couple and not investigate further." If I actually had been the one to kiss him, I could see how this comment would seriously hurt. But I hadn't kissed him, he had kissed me. And finally it all makes sense.

"What?" Jordan says, looking up. "You think she did what?"

"She kissed me to turn away the cops," Grant repeats.

"How do you know that?" he asks. Grant turns to look at me, a pleading look in his eyes. I decide to go with it.

"Cops don't like seeing people make out any more than the next person," I reply. "And my parents definitely told them that I'd be alone. They know how bad I am at making friends." Jordan squints at me, then seems to decide I'm telling the truth.

"That's one weird way to escape the cops," he says, a hint of his former humor in his voice. I breathe a sigh of relief.

"I mean, it worked," Grant says, a small smile forming on his lips. He meets my eyes. *Let's talk about this later.* I nod. *Okay.*

"You want me to drive?" Jordan asks, and I shrug.

"Whatever you want." He holds out his hand and I toss him the keys. He makes his way back to the car and Grant and I follow more slowly.

"Thanks," he breathes. "Though it was my fault." I reach down and squeeze his hand.

"No problem," I whisper back. We all get in the car, and I lean against the window as we begin driving again. As I glance at the side of Grant's head, I can't help but remember his lips on mine. Now I know why he did it, but something tells me that if you stage a kiss, it's not supposed to feel like that. I've never experienced anything like that in my life—when his lips met mine it was like fireworks exploded inside me. For the first time I felt myself let my guard down and lose myself in the moment. I've never felt that exposed near a guy before.

Grant doesn't find time to talk to me during the day, and that night in the tent we sleep on opposite ends. I face the tent wall and don't fall asleep for a long while, listening to Grant and Jordan's heavy breathing and the crickets chirping outside the tent. Jordan has cooled off and gone back to his normal self since our little incident by the road, but I can tell he was affected, maybe a lot, by watching me kiss Grant. Now I know he likes me, and maybe more than he's letting on—which is both scary and flattering. He's only known me for five days, how can he tell I'm a girl he wants to be with? I still don't know why anybody would want to be with me—in "romantic" situations, I freeze up, push the guy away. Maybe not obviously, but how I act is definitely a turn off. Jordan knows the Ginny on the river, but he doesn't know that the

Ginny in normal, everyday life is boring, uninteresting, and antisocial. Jordan's cute, I'll admit. His eyes are the color of the summer sky and I like his sense of humor, but I can't imagine him as anything more than a friend. But obviously he feels otherwise about me.

Then there's Grant, who's a whole other story. Whether he wants to admit it or not, there was definitely some sort of chemical reaction when we made out, even if it was only for a short period of time. But too bad for me, that kiss wasn't supposed to happen, and though I loved it while I was in it, the consequences, as usual, sucked beyond belief. I remember the pain in Jordan's eyes, the look of betrayal he flashed at Grant, and I can only guess the profanity that was flowing through his mind. Is happiness worth the pain of others? I don't think so, at least not here.

I drift into sleep eventually. I sleep fitfully, and I wake up in the dead of night in the middle of a nightmare I can't remember, my heart pounding in my ears. I notice I'm sweating, and my hair is wild, suggesting that I spent the past hour or so thrashing around. Jordan is still asleep next to me, and I pray that he doesn't wake up. I don't want another nighttime debacle. Unfortunately, I see the reflection of someone else's eyes in the dark, and notice that Grant is awake. Shit.

"You okay?" he asks softly. "You've been yelling in your sleep." Oh no. Now I'm dead. Sometimes, when I was younger, I'd have really intense dreams where I'd scream my head off, waking the whole house up, and not remember it all in the morning. I wonder what I had been screaming about this time.

"Really?" I whisper back.

"Yeah. Jordan sleeps through everything, but I'm fairly sure you woke up the whole campground." He's joking, but I feel myself flush. I drop my eyes. "I'm kidding, you know. It wasn't that loud. Promise." I look up and meet his eyes again.

"Thanks," I reply. "And sorry for waking you." Grant

props himself on his arm, and I do the same. We continue to talk quietly over Jordan's sleeping form.

"Do you have some sort of sleeping problem? Like insomnia or something?" Grant asks.

"Nah, I'm not sure what's up with me. I don't usually wake up in the middle of the night."

"Hey, I never got a chance to talk to you about today..." Grant sounds slightly uncomfortable, nervous, maybe. I can tell he's sensitive about this subject too. "Can we go outside? It'll be quick. I just don't want Jordan to wake up."

"You said he sleeps through everything."

"Yeah, but...just, please? I'm not going to pull anything stupid on you, I promise. We're just going to talk." I agree, realizing that it's probably better to not risk waking him. So I exit my cozy sleeping bag and unzip the tent and we both step out into the crisp night air. Again, I'm amazed at the stars, that shine brighter than the streetlights in Bethesda, and make the night seem eerie and beautiful at the same time. Grant and I sit at the picnic table, across from each other.

"So about today..." he begins, his eyes flickering nervously. I wait for him to continue, twirling my thumbs slowly in my lap. When he speaks, it's soft, like a whisper on a nighttime breeze.

"I saw the police car and just freaked. I didn't want you to be brought in, because you're not running away for a wrong reason, you're running away because of something you believe in. The police can't rip you away from something you're passionate about like this. And...honestly? If you want to know the honest truth..." his voice drops so low that I barely make out what he says next. "I didn't want to lose you either." I raise my eyes to meet his, and see that he's telling the truth. I can't stop my heart doing summersaults and jumping up and down and doing back flips, and my face breaks into a grin that I can't control. Grant Haney has feelings for me. I can't believe it.

But I also know that despite everything, I can't be with him. I already determined that.

"That was a good move, you know," I say. "Smart. Spontaneous. Like something I'd do." This makes him smile.

"Ah, not quite. It wasn't exactly a life or death situation."

"But it was," I argue. "If they had taken me back, do you know what that'd do to me? I'm like addicted to paddling, no joke. If I wasn't allowed to ever paddle again, I'm fairly sure I *would* die. You basically saved my life, Grant Haney. Maybe we're even now."

"Ginny..." he trails off, and gazes into the distance. "I try thinking back to that time in the hole and every time I ask myself how the hell you got me out. I don't even know what made you think to do that, and after you made the plan, why you did it..." I want to tell him the truth so bad that it just kind of spills from my mouth. I try to stop it because I know it's the wrong thing to say, but I can't help myself.

"I did it because I love you, Grant," I breathe, and I get up abruptly and walk back to the tent, without looking back. I can't bear to see his reaction.

Grant acts like he didn't hear my closing remark from the night before when we wake up in the morning, and for that, I am grateful. Life continues on as normal, or as normal as it can be on a road trip. We wake up, pack up, and hit the road, and plan to eat breakfast somewhere along the highway. We're nearing the border with Wisconsin now and we want to get to Wausau today.

At the border, I'm afraid someone will pull me aside and take me to the cops. But no one does. We cruise through without further questioning or being pulled over, which is a relief. I sit in the back and listen to Grant and Jordan talk, letting their conversation wash over me, not really absorbing anything but letting the gentle rise and fall of their voices lull me to sleep. I spend most of the ride snoozing quietly. No one wakes me up to tell me that I've been screaming, so I assume that I remained silent. I still wonder what I said the night before.

I must have slept for a while because next thing I know, Jordan's shaking me awake.

"We're here," he says. I must have heard him wrong.

"What?" I mumble.

"We. Are. Here." he repeats. I blink and look around. Sure enough, I recognize the "Wausau Whitewater" parking lot from my last visit here when I was much younger, and notice the visitor's center and rafts leaning up against the wall. I hear whitewater in the distance and the sound of it wakes me up instantly.

"How long did I sleep for?" I ask as I jump out of the car, bathing suit in hand, making my way toward the bathrooms to change.

"Hours. I swear, did you not sleep last night or something?"

"Guess not," I reply. It's amazing how people who know nothing about the truth can come so close to guessing it.

"Ha. Well, I'll meet you in the visitor's center for passes, okay?" I nod and continue on my way to the bathrooms.

Wausau has a great facility. It's not totally artificial, like most world class courses these days, and it's controlled by a dam. Because of this, the eddy lines and holes are more natural, making it more suitable for a river runner like me.

We buy our passes and hit the water. On the first run we take, Jordan and I find a hole that looked scary when I first came here six years ago, but that looks sweet now. During my first surf it practically loops me on it's own, and with a simple shift of my weight it helps me throw ends, and I even half-land a back loop before it window shades me, and then I start getting worked. I realize that I've gotten myself in a bad spot and look upstream, trying to get my balance, when it window shades me again. And again. Maybe this hole isn't as sweet as I thought. *I'm making a huge fool of myself,* I think. First, I went in the hole, on purpose, and now I'm stuck—bad. It's also loud as hell in here, and I can't hear myself think. After a few more window shades, a couple spins, a cartwheel or two, and something that resembles a McNasty, I take a deep breath and attempt to get in control of my situation.

I grab the foam pile hard with my paddle. Keeping my boat balanced under my torso, I begin to stroke on my downstream side, leaning slightly into the foam pile. I stroke slowly, at first, making sure that I stay upright, then faster and faster. The hole pulls against me, trying to force me back into its meat, but I keep fighting, my eyes focused on the nice, green water beyond the foam pile. Finally, after what feels like forever, I feel it release me. I exit the hole and the adrenaline rush leaves, and I'm suddenly exhausted. I hear people clapping, and I look up to see people lining the shore. As I look up they wave and flash me grins and thumbs ups. Some are in paddling gear and bring fingers to their lips and wolf whistle. I see Jordan in the eddy, grinning, and another guy next to him, who screams, "Sweet ride, girl!"

"How long was I in there?" I shout to Jordan as I paddle up the eddy behind him. He shrugs.

"Seemed like thirty seconds, maybe close to a minute. But shit, Ginny, that was intense. That hole was throwing you around like no other. I'm not sure if I've seen anything like that."

"You going in?" I ask.

"Hell no! Not after watching you." I paddle up beside him.

"Okay, then, move, 'cause I'm going in again." I pass him and throw myself into the hole, this time making sure to avoid the meaty part and stay in the friendlier area. After managing to loop a few times, I get out. More people are gathering on the shore. Apparently not many people have the guts to surf this hole. But since I'm brave enough, or maybe crazy enough, to go in it, I get it all to myself. I surf several more times, each time getting a little more bold until finally I get sucked into the sticky part again. This time I know what to do right away and get out pretty quick. Jordan continues down the rest of the river, and Grant passes me, too. He flashes me a grin and takes his hand off his paddle to give me a thumbs up, but doesn't stop to surf, either. After about an hour, I can actually McNasty and throw ends like crazy. I even land a back loop. I check my watch and note that we have been here for an hour and a half and I still haven't made a full run yet. After a successful surf where I get about eight ends and do two loops, I drag myself out of the hole and run the rest of the course.

At the takeout, a young paddler, maybe in his twenties, starts gushing at me.

"How did you do that? You do realize that no one ever goes near that hole in fear of getting trashed. And you did get trashed. Yet you still went in again! And again! Do you come here often?"

"No, the last time I was here I was eleven," I reply, not trying to be cocky. His eyes widen.

"You must be shitting me," he says in disbelief.

"Uh, no, sir," I reply hesitantly. He gives me another look of disbelief before raising a hand in farewell and carrying his boat away from the takeout. I grab my boat and make my to the put in, where I find Jordan and Grant, and we do a quick run together before taking out. The sun is beginning to set and we decide to call it a day.

"You know, Ginny, everyone's talking about you," Jordan says as we walk our boats back to the car. Grant's ahead of us, heading for the bathroom.

"Really?" I say.

"Yeah. No joke. Every person I've passed has been whispering about that 'sick girl in X-Wave.'" I laugh.

"X-*Wave*? That thing was definitely a hole," I say, remembering its fierce recirculation and how it threw me around like I was a foam dummy. Jordi shrugs.

"Maybe it's an inside joke? Who knows," he answers.

A group of guys walk by, whispering amongst themselves.

"Did you see that girl? She was getting massive air loops on X! I don't think I've ever seen a girl go that big before!" One says to another. I shoot a surprised look at Jordan, and he gives me a look saying, *I told you so.*

"I know! She's sick," says another. They then notice me and one of them points.

"You're that girl!" he says. He holds out his hand, talking excitedly. "Hi! I'm Nick. You're insane, if you didn't know. Can I have your autograph? Are you famous?"

"Nah," I reply, laughing. "I'm just a normal girl, promise." He gives me a skeptical look.

"Whatever." He holds out a pen and turns around. "Sign my shirt?" I glance at Jordan who's next to me and he shrugs. *Go ahead.* I uncap the pen and sign my name with a flourish.

"There you go," I reply. This is the first time I've ever signed anything. I feel like a celebrity.

"What's your name, anyway?" he asks.

"Ginny," I reply. "It was nice meeting you, Nick." His friends are smiling at me too. "And the rest of you, too." Jordan grabs my arm and drags me along after him, away from my crowd of admirers.

"Those people are crazy!" I exclaim as soon as we're out of earshot.

"You are pretty awesome, Ginny," he says, smiling at me. I roll my eyes.

"Thanks, Jordan." I notice that his arm is still on mine and he drops it quickly.

"Sorry," he mumbles. I smile at him, telling him that it's okay. We reach the truck and drop our boats in the back.

"How 'bout dinner? I'll treat," I suggest. "I have a bit of money. Not much, but it'll get us a nice meal."

"You sure?" Jordan asks.

"Yeah, you didn't plan for a third person, anyway. It's fine. I owe you."

"I brought extra money, don't you worry. Remember, I

always do plan for the worst."

"And hope for the best, right?" I finish for him. He looks at me, surprised.

"You know that, too?"

"It's all Jared used to tell me," I reply. He smiles.

"He taught you well, then." It's dusk now, and I hear the water growing quieter as they turn the pumps off. Wausau seems oddly peaceful without the roaring of whitewater in the background.

I spot Grant up ahead, waving at us. I wave back.

"Ready to eat?" I call up to him.

"Am I ever. Kayaking sure does work up an appetite," he replies as we get closer. I link arms with my two paddling buddies and we stroll into the eating area, arm in arm, ready for a hearty meal after a hard day of paddling.

"What did you say?" We're sitting at a McDonalds eating breakfast the next morning. Jordan's reading something off of his phone.

"You made the front page of the paper," Jordan repeats. "Here, look." He holds his phone out and I squint at the small screen, and sure enough, I see a close up picture of my "getting trashed in a hole" face. My tongue's sticking out and everything.

"You've got to be kidding me," I say, taking the phone from him. I take a closer look. It's from the cover story of the *Wausau Sun*, their city's newspaper. My picture takes up most of the screen, so I scroll down to read the text.

"A kayaking superstar arrived at the Whitewater Center in Wausau yesterday afternoon. 'I couldn't really believe my eyes,' a local paddler, Zeke Carter, told our reporters. 'I looked over at the course and there was this girl, [called] Ginny, surfing up the one hole that everyone knows to stay away from. [No one] goes into X-Wave unless they're asking for a beat down. But this girl played in the hole for [an hour], and by the end was actually able to land huge tricks...'" The article rambles on about the technical parts of freestyle, and there's another huge color picture of me doing an air loop.

"This is pretty sick..." I murmur. No one has ever gotten good quality pictures of me before, because usually I'm alone or with people I'll never see again.

"It is. I love that picture of you looping," Grant says, in between bites of his breakfast hash brown.

"Me, too," I agree. "I'm not totally sure if it's legal, though...I'm a minor."

"It's captioned without a last name and you were photographed in a public place. And there's so much water in your face that you can't really tell it's you," Jordan replies. "I think it's legal enough. And no one's going to see it who knows you, right?"

"Yeah, I guess."

"I'd say that's not totally true," Grant argues. "You can tell it's her, if you know her. There's that intense look in her eyes that she always has." I give him a funny look.

"You know what I mean?" he continues. "Well, I guess you wouldn't. You can't see yourself paddle. But when you do anything, you get this focused, intense look in your eyes. It'd look violent if I didn't know you better, kind of like you were trying to kill the water." This makes me smile.

"I don't think I've ever seen footage of myself paddling," I answer. "I could look like a complete idiot for all I know."

Grant smiles. "Well, if you're asking, I actually find you quite intriguing when you kayak," he continues. "You seem completely focused, all the time. You don't make the ridiculous faces most people do, your mouth usually remains slightly parted. You shake your head with you roll up and have this characteristic hair flick you do to keep your ponytail out of your way. I'm really jealous of your stroke, you put your whole torso into it, and have a knack for making things look effortless that are actually nearly impossible." Jordan's looking at him now, a slightly confused expression on his face. The way Grant said all of that wasn't even remotely romantic—it sounded more like someone talking about the weather, or describing a homework assignment.

"Wow," is all I say. "I've never really thought about it."

Grant smiles. "Yeah, not many people do."

Jordan's still gazing at Grant, a contemplative look in his eyes. He probably is wondering what's going on in his mind, too—how he knows all that about me, why he knows that much about me, and probably why he decided to tell me. But he doesn't look jealous. Just curious.

"You're mighty observant, Haney," says Jordan. Their eyes meet briefly and some unsaid message flows between them.

"You know, when we show up there, you're going to be like, a celebrity," Jordan tells me, changing the subject.

"I guess I'll be getting my share of the fifteen minutes of fame, huh?" I joke.

"Nah, girl, you've got a hell of a future ahead of you," Jordan says. I raise my eyebrows at him. "I'm serious. I'd put my money on you at Worlds."

"Aw, thanks. But that article made me seem a lot more famous than I actually am. I'm just a normal girl from Maryland, not some crazy playboater."

"You are pretty awesome, Ginny. You just don't know it yet. But we can keep the paparazzi off you, if you want," Grant says. "We'll fend off your fans until you can get into your boat. Once on the water, you can pretend that you can't hear people if they talk to you. Works every time."

"That'd be great, actually. Thanks, guys." I smile, warmth spreading through me. *Grant thinks you're awesome,* a little voice says in the back of my head. *Shut up,* I tell it sternly. *You can't think like that anymore.*

"Yeah, it's our pleasure, really. Then we'll get our fifteen minutes of fame too," Jordan says. I grin at him.

"Yeah, tell them you two are my training partners. But be careful, no last names. We don't want to be able to be stalked by any creepers, or found by the police, if they're actually after me."

"If we see a cop, no shenanigans, okay?" Jordan says,

giving us stern looks. I flash him a nervous glance, to see if he's bringing this up so he can yell at us for it, but his eyes are light and he's smiling.

Grant grins back at him. "Ha, okay. But our stunt last time worked, didn't it?" His eyes meet mine for a moment, and I smile.

Jordan rolls his eyes. "Sure, sure. Don't try that on me ever, or I'll kill you."

"You don't like the idea of making out with me, Jordi?" Grant replies, laughing. He leans towards him and Jordan shoves him back playfully.

It amazes me that they're joking about this now, so soon after it happened. Maybe they had a nice heart to heart while I was sleeping away the ride yesterday and worked it all out. It sure looks like it, the way they're joking about it now. Relief floods me. It all blew over. Thank God. And maybe Grant also forgot about what I told him the other night at the picnic table, when my self-control was at zero and my heart was controlling my mouth. Part of me hopes that he didn't forget, the same part of me that made the words escape my mouth in the first place. The logical, sensible part of my brain hopes that he thought I was just mumbling good night, and didn't catch me declaring my love for him. But both parts agree that despite how I'd like to think otherwise, the words I spoke were true.

"Ready to go, Ms. Kinsey?" Jordan's voice breaks through my thoughts.

"Huh?"

"You're famous now, right? I should get used to referring you as such." I laugh, and shake my head.

"Nah, you guys are my training partners, remember? We're all going to Worlds together. You're just as famous as me."

"I think she's too humble for her own good," Jordan says to Grant.

"You just noticed?" he replies, and we all laugh. I like the idea of us all training together. Our names would fit together, like the three bears or the three blind mice. Ginny, Grant, and Jordan. We'd be known worldwide for our excellence as playboaters and our unique friendship. My parents would notice how amazing we are, and accept me for who I am. They'd no longer worry about my safety because Grant and Jordan would be with me, and they'd even come watch us compete, and be proud to point at me and say, "That's my daughter!" But I know I'm fantasizing way beyond reality, and as we leave McDonalds, the sight of boats in the back of our truck bring me back to the present. I'm ready to face Wausau again. And a little excited, too.

   I don't get mobbed by people as I step out of the car, to Jordan's disappointment. It's not until we're geared up and our boats are on our shoulders that I begin to hear people whispering about me.
   "That's the girl from the paper," a little boy says, pointing at me for his mom to see.
   "It's rude to point, sweetie," the mom replies as she sees me looking. I smile my best charming smile at them and raise my paddle in greeting. The little boy waves excitedly back.
   "She seems nice," he says to his mom as we get farther away.
   As we near the water, we don't attract any more attention. I'm relieved by this, but Jordan's thoughts are otherwise.
   "Man! The only fan base you have is a scrawny eight year old. Bummer," he says. I stab him in the back with the end of my paddle.
   "We are *running away,* remember? We're trying to stay under the radar." He turns around and smiles guiltily.
   "I guess you're right." We reach the put in shortly, and I splash the cool water on my face after I pull my skirt on. Energy begins pumping through my limbs. I love morning paddles.
   "Ah, it this is the life," I say. Grant gives me a knowing

look.

"Wouldn't rather be anywhere else right now, either." Our eyes hold contact for a moment longer before he lets it drop.

"You guys gonna surf today?" I ask. They both turn around and give me incredulous stares.

"What are you smoking, child?" Jordan snorts. "Last time we went into a hole we were warned about we both ended up almost dying. Remember?" I roll my eyes.

"Yeah, but that was what, five days ago?" I answer. I don't press them any further, though, because Jordan brought up an excellent point. With their history of getting stuck and trashed in holes, I'm not sure if I want to risk it, either.

"Yeah, I'm gonna hold back today," Grant says. "I may boof it on the way down but I don't think I'm gonna go in. I found another hole a little ways down that's friendlier, for sure."

"Oh, that's cool," I say. I'm tempted to tell them how freaking easy it is to throw tricks, but I realize that I don't want them going in there after all. Dragging people out of holes is not on my agenda for the day. We hit the first rapid and I'm able to wave wheel easily. I boof a pour-over into an eddy, and ferry my way across into another. I stern stall as I peel out of this one, and float down a little ways vertical. I gaze at the clear sky and smile to myself. I'm drifting down, daydreaming, when I hear a loud bang, and suddenly I'm upside down. I roll back up quickly, and glare at my attacker.

"Jerk!" I splash Jordan with my paddle blade. "That was going to be my all time record." He splashes me back.

"You were definitely asking for it," he says, splashing me again. I'm about to aim a drencher at his head when I realize where we are on the river.

"Left!" I shout, seeing the drop off into X-Wave mere feet in front of us. "Or hard straight!" I pick up speed in a hurry, and boof the hole cleanly. I go straight for the eddy and pray that Jordan does the same. As I cross the eddy line I crane my head around to keep an eye on Jordan. *Please, please, please don't come in sideways,* I think, but when I get a first glimpse of Jordan's boat, it's not even sideways—it's backwards. What the hell is he doing?

"Jordan!" I scream, but either he can't hear me or ignores me entirely. His face is smooth, he seems relaxed, and as he drops in the hole, he actually grins. Crazy bastard.

I watch him get trashed from the eddy, realizing that he probably has a plan and doesn't want my help. First, I watch him go right into the sticky spot. Then, I watch him get window shaded, oh let's say, eight times. Next, he does some flat spins. Then gets window shaded again. He's endered, flips, gets back up, then is endered again. If I knew nothing about kayaking, I'd think he was some pro at Freestyle Worlds. But I know a lot about kayaking, and I know that he's getting über trashed.

Finally, he comes out. When he rolls up, I expect to see him look frightened, or at least surprised. But I'm wrong again. When he rolls up, he meets my eyes, and grins.

"Ginny, that was sick!" he yells as he paddles up.

"Are you crazy?" I bellow back.

"No worse than you!" he replies. I want to smack him for scaring the shit out of me but decide against it. He paddles up beside me. "How dumb did I look?"

"Pretty good, for someone getting trashed," I reply. I search his eyes for any sign of fear or regret, but only see genuine happiness. "What made you go in there, anyway?"

"I don't know," he answers. It looks like he's keeping something from me so I elbow him, and he relents. "I guess I wanted to try being spontaneous...like you." *What is it with these guys?* I think. First Grant, deciding to kiss me randomly by the side of the road. Now Jordan, throwing himself into a killer hole. I am such a bad influence.

"Notice how being spontaneous almost got me killed on the Ottawa?" I say, looking in his eyes and putting my hand on his skirt to emphasize my point.

"Well…"

"Exactly. Just because I'm reckless and stupid doesn't mean you have to be, too. I'm not going to think any less of you. Actually, I may even admire you. For ,being logical, smart, and most of all, alive."

Jordan puts his hand on my skirt and looks me in the eye. "I don't think you're reckless. I don't think you're stupid, either. I think you are the quintessence of the Latin phrase *Carpe Diem.* You live in the moment. You seize the day. You don't let anything stop you from living your own life." His eyes are intense and I can feel the passion behind his words. I feel myself closing off, shutting down, and my flight instinct is telling me to run. I can't deal with mushy heart to heart sessions. Partly because I have no idea how to deal with compliments or flattery, and partly because I don't want to hurt him by saying the wrong thing.

So I do what my instinct tells me to do, as usual. I make up an excuse and leave.

"I think I'm gonna take a chance on X-Wave," I say, pushing away from him slightly. I see the disappointment in his eyes and I feel a flash of guilt, but then it fades. It's safer this way. If Jordan knew how much of a wimp I am on the inside, I doubt he'd be so impressed.

"Don't show me up too badly," he calls, and I flash him a forced smile before throwing myself into the hole. The intense water grabs my boat and I let it throw me around. It clears my head and flushes out my negative energy.

As I close my eyes and let the hole take hold of me, I feel my problems begin to drain away. My brain empties except for the sound of whitewater screaming around me. The wave finally flushes me out on its own, and when I roll up, no one applauds, and the eddy is empty. There's a price to pay for not opening up to people and for running away from situations that I can't handle. *You're a coward,*

Ginny, I tell myself. *A fucking coward.*

I get an urgent phone call the next day, while I'm sitting in the café at Wausau enjoying a hot lunch.

"Ginny!" I hear Casey yell on the other line. "Can you hear me?" I wonder why she's screaming, because it's not noisy on either end and neither of us have hearing problems.

"Yes!" I yell back, to annoy her. "I can hear you!"

"Good," she answers, lowering her voice. "Just checking. Now listen up, this is important." She pauses for effect, and I wait, tapping my foot on the floor to a song stuck in my head. "Mom and Dad know where you are, Ginny. You left a blazing trail for them, once again." What is she talking about?

"What? How? There's no way..." I rack my brain for ways they could of found me. Then I get it. Somehow, they found the article online.

"How the hell did you get into the newspaper, Grace Kinsey?" Casey's yelling again. And she never curses. This is bad.

"I didn't ask to be put in the paper. They just wrote an article about me, and I saw it the next day. And they didn't even use my last name! How did they find me?"

"Are you numb skulled, Ginny?" Casey says, exasperated. I can tell she's rolling her eyes on the other end of the phone. "All they had to do was Google 'Ginny' and 'kayak' in the search bar and bam, that article came up." Fuck. She's right. Why is she *always* right?

"Well, that is bad news," I say, my heart beginning to thud loudly in my chest. How stupid am I?

"Yes, yes, it is," Casey says. "So you're going to leave, right? Where are you going to go?"

"Remember, I can't tell you unless you tell me who you're traveling with." I hear a muffled voice in the background that sounds vaguely familiar, but I can't put a finger on it. It's male, but that's all I can tell. Casey shushes him loudly and sighs.

"Fine, you're leaving a pretty clear trail though, so I'm sure we'll be able to find you. Dad read the article, you know. He called me on my cell when he found out about it. He still thinks I'm on an overnight trip with my friend. Anyway, he sounded mad, as usual, but he read the article aloud while still on the phone with me, and something changed in his voice. I'm not sure what it was exactly, but as he read the caption under that sick picture of you looping, he actually sounded mildly impressed. Usually he just scoffs and grumbles, but he read the line, 'Ginny can get massive air in a hole many local paddlers call insane,' without his usual negativity." As she says this, I suddenly get a crazy idea.

"Well, keep a lookout for those signs," I tell her. "I gotta go. Talk to you later, sis."

"Bye, Ginny," she answers. "I love you." The other line goes dead.

"What was that about, Gins?" Grant asks from beside me. I grimace slightly as I reply.

"My parents found the article," I say. Grant doesn't seem to be fazed by this in the least.

"Bummer," he says. "Guess we'll have to move on, then. We've got a ton of rivers ahead of us, anyway."

"You're not mad that I'm screwing up your plans again?" I ask.

"Nah, Jordan's the one with the plans, not me," he says, and grins. "Your parents on our trail does make this more exciting." That reminds me of the plan that magically appeared in my mind during my conversation with Casey.

"Grant," I begin. "I have this idea." I pause, and he nods for me to continue. "Casey said that when my parents saw the article of me in the paper, they seemed less angry than usual. That got me thinking—what if the reason they're afraid of me kayaking is because they know nothing about it? Ignorance leads to fear, right? What if...what if we purposefully left a trail behind us? For them to follow? And along the way, maybe they'd learn about the sport and actually begin to appreciate it. And accept that I love it and that it's what I want to do for the rest of my life."

Grant cocks his head to the side slightly and rubs his chin with his hand. "Hmm," he says. "Sounds interesting. What kind of trail do you propose leaving? Breadcrumbs? Clues?" I laugh, but Grant remains serious. "No, I'm not kidding. About the clues, I mean. We don't want them biting at our heels, we want them a safe distance away. So our hints can't be *that* obvious."

"You do have a point," I reply, thinking this over. What if we told one of the regulars here to pass a message on to my parents when they showed up? Gave them a set of instructions that lead to a message to where we were going next? Like what if we told them to go rafting, to experience whitewater first hand, and we left a sign by X-Wave, saying that we had passed through, bound for wherever we're off to next? I grin in spite of myself.

"What?" Grant asks as he sees the smile on my face. I inform him of my idea. When I finish, he holds out his fist, and I bump it. He proceeds to turn his fist sideways, fan out his fingers, dip down and high five me, run his hand through his hair and spin around, bump his forearm against mine three times, then wave his thumb and pinky and stick out his tongue. I identify this as the handshake Jordan tried to teach me when Grant was still in the hospital.

"I'll get it eventually," I say, laughing.

"No, sister, you gotta get it now. Every member of our paddling group *must* be able to reciprocate this handshake. It's probably the only rule we have," Grant says, and proceeds to show me it again, step by step, and slower. I soon catch on and am able to do it full speed. Jordan comes up behind me and claps me on the back as I finish a successful run through.

"Excellent! I see Grant has taught you our ways," he says. "What's the occasion?" Grant and I both fill him in on what Casey said and my plan. Jordan grins when we finish.

"That's brilliant!" he exclaims. "Beautiful. Really."

"You think so?" I ask. "You don't think it's crazy?"

"Crazy? Do you see who you're talking to?"

"We live for this kind of stuff, Ginny," Grant says, smiling.

"Handshake?" Jordan prompts, and we all end with a yell, and many heads in the restaurant turn to look at us.

"Ginny's rubbing off on us," Jordan jokes as we turn to leave. I give him a playful shove and he shoves me back and I slam into an innocent passerby. I give her an apologetic smile and fake glare at Jordan.

"Thanks a lot," I tell him. He flashes me a dazzling smile.

"No problem, girlie," he replies, winking. "You asked for it."

We hit the road later that afternoon after leaving explicit directions for the people running the front desk. They all knew me because of the article and my heroics in X-Wave and they were happy to do whatever I wanted. They even said that they'd give my parents a complimentary raft ride, if necessary. Everyone at Wausau was convinced I was a celebrity, and all wished me good luck in the future. I wanted to tell them that I wouldn't have a future in paddling if my parents caught me, but I thought that would be too personal, so I just smiled and thanked them instead.

Jordan, because he's Jordan, wrote the directions down on a piece of paper and gave them to the front desk people as well, in case they forgot. It read:

Dear front desk employees at Wausau Whitewater,

Ginny Kinsey, the girl you read about in the paper this morning, is leaving today. Her parents are following her because they don't completely trust her, and she would like them to know where she's going in a more indirect method. When Nicole Kinsey and/or Rob Kinsey come asking about Ginny, please do the following:

1. Tell them they have to take a raft trip down

> Wausau. Do WHATEVER it takes to get them to obey. (NOTE: That is VERY important.)
> 2. On the raft, get the guides to talk about whitewater sports and how fun they are. Emphasize things like safety and the precautions taken when running a river. Talk a lot about the wonders of whitewater kayaking.
> 3. Before running X-Wave, mention Ginny, and how she came in and wowed the kayaking community here. Tell them that they are about to pass the hole that she surfed. Catch an eddy below the hole and MAKE SURE THEY READ THE SIGN. (NOTE: The sign will read "**GINNY KINSEY WAS HERE. DESINATION: CAÑON CITY, COLORADO**".)
> 4. Make sure they can read the sign!
>
> Thank you for your cooperation. It means a lot.
>
> Yours Sincerely,
>
> Jordan Bolton
> Grant Haney
> Ginny Kinsey

The people at the front desk were very understanding when we stressed the importance of their jobs. They promised that they'd follow through, no matter what. I don't think they quite understood how hard #1 on the list would be, because they haven't met my parents yet, but who knows. Maybe a free raft trip will seem appealing to them.

No one at Wausau suspected me of anything, either, which makes me think that maybe my parents *didn't* file a police report. The only possible explanation for this is that one of them, probably Dad, wants the satisfaction of finding me himself—and they're going to have to go all the way to Cañon City, the home of the grand canyon of

Colorado, to do so. Through it runs the spectacular Arkansas River, with class IV-V whitewater and a view that's supposed to take your breath away. The put in for the 100-mile paddle is in Granite, a small town about eighty miles southwest of Denver, which is where we are heading now. I don't know if my parents will be impressed, or if they'll even like it at all. But I do know that we have to try.

Part 3
The Arkansas

I just want to let you know that the drive from Wausau, Wisconsin to Granite, Colorado is one of the dullest in the country. I'm willing to put money on it. If I see one more cow field I swear I'm going to kill someone. While we're heading through Wisconsin on some long, straight interstate with about five other cars, I propose a "counting cows" game to see how many we drive by. When we get to 200 we promptly give up.

"This is worse than counting sheep," Grant says, yawning. "I'm about to fall asleep." I'm driving, and I completely agree with this statement—the only thing keeping me awake is the hard rock drumming in my ears. It sounds like Three Days Grace, but I can't tell, I'm not an expert on heavy rock.

"Is this Three Days Grace?" I ask, knowing between the two rock junkies one of them will know.

"Sure is," Jordan replies. "I'm impressed, country girl." I grin.

"My boyfriend calls this my band, because it's slightly emo and has my name in it. He believes that I believe in 'pain without love' more than I should," I say. The moment this leaves my mouth I curse myself silently for bringing up Justin.

"I keep forgetting your name is Grace," Grant says,

sounding completely normal. "That's such a girly name. Ginny is so much more...you." I smile at him beside me.

"Yeah, that's what I think, too," I say. I glance at Jordan in the rearview mirror, but his face is in his iPod touch. He seems to find what he's looking for and taps the screen and looks at me in the mirror, and grins. Out of the crackling speakers I hear the lyrics to the only rock song I know by heart.

"Pain! Without love / Pain! / Can't get enough pain! / I like it rough / Cuz I'd rather feel pain than nothing at all..." I lip synch along, not trusting my voice to carry the tune right. I only feel brave when it comes to country music.

"Why does he think this describes you?" Jordan asks. "You're not this sadistic." *Not here, I'm not,* I think. *With you guys, I don't feel like there's anything I have to hide.*

"I'm not like this at school," I say. Jordan cocks an eyebrow at me.

"What do you mean?"

I don't really want to explain, but my reply kind of slips out. "I'm a lot quieter. I keep to myself since I don't really fit in anywhere. There aren't many kids in Catholic school who kayak, you know? I'm different so people stay away." Both Jordan and Grant are looking at me, eyebrows raised. Neither of them reply.

"What?" I ask.

"Are you serious?" Jordan exclaims. "People *avoid* you at school?" I meet his eyes in the mirror again.

"Yeah. I have like, one friend." So now the truth is revealed. I'm not a cool person with lots of friends. I'm your common, everyday loser.

"Wait, so people don't like you because you kayak? That's so weird," Grant says. "And backwards. Kayaking should make you the coolest person in the school. Easily."

"And Ginny," Jordan adds, "it doesn't matter what they think, anyway. *We* think you're cool. We think you're *really* cool. That's what counts." This makes me laugh. Though I typically don't care what other people think of me, having people not think that I'm complete psycho does make me feel good. It's another new feeling that I'm beginning to like. I guess most people call it the feeling of *belonging.*

"Thanks," I answer, smiling. "You guys are all right too."

More fields. More cows. And then, I see a sign for a city. *Madison 115,* it reads. A hundred and fifteen miles, and we'll see something other than flat monotony.

"Any interest in taking a pit stop in Madison?" I ask. "Maybe we could eat something…"

"…And go clubbin'!" Jordan exclaims. "Yes! Now we will put those fake IDs to work. I didn't bring them for nothing, after all." Grant rolls his eyes. "See, Ginny, I have these blank fake IDs that I can fix up, and we can use them to get us into a nightclub." He pauses and glances at me. "Only if you want to, that is."

I think about the last party I went to underage, and that was at this crap club at the end of this year. The music was horrible and the whole place stunk like smoke, and everyone got drunk but me. It was awful because the whole time I felt out of place, but I stayed because Justin wanted me to, and I felt like I at least owed him an end of the year party. But this time I'll be with Grant and Jordan, and we'll be in a club with a bunch of strangers…I'll be able to be whoever I want because I'll never be seeing any of them again…

"Sounds great," I reply, making up my mind. "We'll roll in there at around nine anyway, right in time. There's only one catch…" I just realize the slight problem now. "What the hell am I going to wear? 'Girl's club clothes' definitely weren't on your list, Jordan." I hear him sigh in the back.

"I should've thought of that!" he says, completely serious, and both Grant and I burst out laughing.

"This may be one of the first times you've been caught unprepared," Grant says, grinning.

"And this will be the last," Jordan vows, totally serious.

That makes me laugh again.

"It's okay, I have some money. I'll let you guys go ahead, and I'll buy myself a new outfit at the closest thrift store," I tell them. Nerves suddenly flash in my chest. This is my first opportunity to actually look sexy, and for the first time in my life, I actually want to take advantage of it. I imagine Sara next to me, patting me on the back. "Ginny! I'm so proud of you!" she'd say. But I don't need her, not here. I'm living my own life now.

I look at myself in the full-length mirror in the check out of *Hip Thrift,* the city's second-hand store, and nod. I'm wearing a low cut royal blue tank that makes my blue eyes stand out, along with a cute black skirt and some black heels. I'm wearing some cheap CVS mascara and lip-gloss, and I bought a brush and smoothed out my hair, too. The tank makes my shoulders look strong but they don't appear grossly ripped, and my legs thankfully don't look too bad, either, thanks to a cheap razor I bought and used in a single stall bathroom.

My shopping spree cost exactly $23 and took 37 minutes. I take a deep breath and head out of the store, pointing myself at the "Dexton Street Nightclub" a few blocks down, where I've planned to meet Jordan and Grant at 9:45. I'm thankful for the night air around me, it makes me feel less exposed. Usually, the only times I dress up like this are for the parties I attend once every three months. I pass a guy smoking a cigarette beside an old building, and he checks me out, and I pick up the pace. It would suck to get jumped in my first forty-five minutes in Madison.

As I near the nightclub, I see a large group of people around the entrance, and scan the crowed for the people I'm looking for. I find Grant first, and my heart stops beating in my chest momentarily when I first lay eyes on him. His hair is slightly gelled in a way that makes him look like a movie star, and he's wearing a black, fitted v-neck that outlines his chest perfectly. He's talking on his phone off to the side, but he looks up as I approach. He moves the phone away from his ear and says, "I'll call you back later," to the person on the other end. He walks forward to meet me and gives me a quick hug.

"You look great," he says, meeting my eyes and smiling.

"As do you," I tell him. My voice sounds strange, and I clear my throat. I feel my heart beating in my chest and take a deep breath. I shouldn't be nervous, I tell myself. It's Grant you're looking at. He's the guy you can't be hitting on, remember? The arrival of Jordan provides a welcome distraction.

"Hey," he says as he approaches. He stops when he sees me, and his reaction is similar to Grant's, if not more extreme.

"Hey," I say back. He looks pretty good himself in a red graphic tee and spiked hair. "You guys ready to rage?" Jordan grins and hands me my ID that he made in our time apart. He used a picture I had in my wallet, and as I look at it, I'm impressed. It looks real as hell.

"You rock, Jordi," I say, meaning it. I reach out and give him a hug, too. We get in line and soon, we're inside.

It's dim and the air smells faintly of smoke and heavily of alcohol and sweat. Bodies are moving in a mass on the dance floor, and loud music is blaring from speakers in the ceiling. Many couples are grinding and immediately I have regrets about coming. I can't even kiss a guy without wanting to bolt. How the hell am I supposed to grind?

We blend into the crowd and begin moving to the music. Bodies are pressing in on all sides and I can barely breathe. Some random guy starts grinding into me and I move away quickly, bumping into a couple dancing inappropriately behind me. The music suddenly seems way too loud, the crowd too thick and the heat overwhelming. I push my way towards the outside of the circle. Finally, I break through, and begin to weave my way towards the exit. I have no idea where Grant or Jordan went—I try not to think about Grant grinding with another girl—but they won't miss me if I disappear for a few seconds, anyway. I'm almost to the door when someone grabs me from behind.

"Hey, girlie, wanna dance?" The stranger's words are slurred and his use of Jared's nickname makes me want to punch him in the face.

"No," I say, pulling away.

"Whatdya say?" he slurs.

"I said, NO!" I shout at him, yanking violently away from him. My sudden burst of strength surprises him, and he lets go. I begin to walk towards the exit once more. The stupid bastard follows.

"What's your problem?" he calls. "Why are you being so mean?" I turn around to face him and finally get a good look at him. He has greasy hair, like he was trying to look cool and went way overboard, and jeans and a tank top that shows off a lot more than I want to see.

"Please go away," I tell him. This makes him come closer.

"What did you say?" he sneers. His breath is gross and reeks of beer.

"I said," I tell him, with as much authority as I can muster. "Get. The. Hell. Away. From. Me." He swings a fist in my direction, but I dodge it easily. The best part about drunks is that they're hopeless when it comes to fights. He swings his arm at me again and I deflect it. He swings his other arm at me, but I aim a kick between his legs and he falls with a yell before he can touch me. He crashes into a couple dancing, who both glare at him and move away. I move to stand over him and look into his eyes, my gaze shooting daggers.

"Will you listen to me now?" I ask. He nods vigorously. I give him another kick in the side. "Get up and get out of my sight." He does, and as he walks away, I can almost see a tail between his legs.

I head once again for the back door, ignoring the stares of the people around me. I open the door and the blast of fresh air that hits me feels like a bucket of cold water on a hot day. I breathe in the cool night air and hear the music fade as I shut the door behind me. It's loud in the city and people still crowd the sidewalks, but I manage to find a bench nearby and sit down. After a while, someone comes and sits beside me. Out of the corner of my eye, I see Jordan's red shirt. I look over, and he smiles at me.

"Hey," he says. My stomach flips over. Whether it's nerves or me being uncomfortable about our proximity, I can't tell. I still don't know what to think of him. "Nice show inside."

"Uh, thanks," I say, not really wanting to talk about it. But he's gazing at me levelly with big, honest blue eyes, and I can't get myself to be mad at him. "Sorry I'm kind of ruining your night." Jordan waves the comment aside.

"Don't worry! I wasn't having much fun either. I like dancing, not what was going on in there, if you know what I mean." I smile wryly, but I keep my eyes on a small crack in the sidewalk with a little green shoot of grass emerging from it. It looks so out of place in the rough, man made concrete, and I wonder how it ended up there.

"Are you okay?" Jordan's voice takes my attention away from the grass. He's bending down so his eyes are level with mine, and I can't ignore the concern coloring them. It makes him look cute as hell.

"I've been better," I reply truthfully.

"It was really loud in there," Jordan agrees, still keeping his eyes on mine.

"And hot, sweaty, and gross," I reply.

"Sorry we came here," he says. He looks like he really means it.

"It's okay, really. This beats sitting in a car watching cow fields pass by." Out of the corner of my eye, I catch a person dressed in black, motionless, standing inside near the exit. It's Grant. Of course it's Grant. I turn my eyes towards him and his eyes meet mine. Our gazes lock, and he nods at me, then he turns away from the window. I watch him walk away and offer his hand to a pretty blonde, who takes his hand, and they disappear into the sea of bodies on the dance floor. Part of me is suddenly relieved, because he obviously doesn't like me, so there'll be nothing to encourage my own feelings for him. But the other part of me, the roaring, kicking part trying to get out, is mad, betrayed, and disappointed that the guy I thought was "the one" actually doesn't like me in that way at all.

"Ginny," Jordan says. I notice that it's gone quiet and that I have been staring at the door where Grant had been standing for awhile. I turn to look at Jordan.

"Yeah?" His eyes are deep as he looks at me. I sense that he's about to confess something and my whole body tenses up. But I tell myself to stay put.

But all he says is, "Maybe we should head back inside."

"Jordan?" I ask. His eyes brighten as I say his name. He looks at me expectantly, waiting for me to continue. I swallow loudly. Suddenly I have no idea what I'm going to say. "I...um..." His eyes continue to pierce into my own, not pressuring, but patient. I swallow again. "Thanks for coming out here with me. It was nice...to have your company."

He smiles, and reaches to tuck a piece of my hair behind my ear. "No problem," he says. "It was my pleasure." He stands up, and holds out his hand to me. "Let's head back in." I hesitate before taking his hand, and he pulls me to my feet. He drops my hand as soon as he's standing, and we walk in side by side. *Would it be possible to have both of them?* I think, wistfully. Breaking Jordan's heart is not on my agenda, and I don't think my own heart can give up Grant. But life is never perfect, fair, or full of unicorns. So that seems about as likely as my parents smiling and giving me a hug after my first decent of Great Falls.

Back inside, the people are no more appealing, the music is no more motivating, and the smell is no better. But I blend into the crowd, close my eyes, and let the sea of bodies move me back and forth. It's almost comforting—there's nowhere I have to go, nothing I have to do, and nothing I have to think about. I let myself float, and am swaying to some B.o.B. song when I feel a hand on my waist. I open my eyes, and see a boy standing in front of me, who looks about my age. He's cute and has a skater boy hair cut and a nice smile. His hair is light brown and his eyes are a deep green, and he holds out his hand to me and yells over the music, "You wanna dance?" The song shifts to a slower one, and I smile at him.

"Sure," I say. Maybe I should do something purely for myself for a moment. He slides his hands around my waist and I wrap mine around his neck, and we begin to move slowly with the music. He leans in closer and I let him, and I close my eyes and put my face lightly against his chest, breathing in the smell of Old Spice. I let the music and the stranger I'm dancing with help me focus on the present and not worry about the past or my uncertain future. I just breathe deep and sway, and let the smell in my nose and the music in my ears drown out everything else.

The following morning, we wake up, check out of our cheap motel room and hit the road pretty quickly. I'm refreshed, rejuvenated, and ready to hit the river. Jordan says it's another two days of cows before we reach Colorado. I can't wait.

"The Arkansas is one of the most pristine, difficult, and rewarding runs in America," Grant reads from a book on the Pine Creek to Royal Gorge run that we were going to do. "There are a variety of rapids on the river, ranging from technical and challenging to straightforward and fun. It's mostly continuous and has big wave trains, friendly holes and beautiful scenery." I close my eyes and picture the mountains of Colorado combined with a crazy ass creek, and like what I see.

"Is this a picture book?" I ask from the back seat.

"Can we see pictures?" Grant laughs.

"Ginny wants story time?" he replies. I nod eagerly. "All right. Once upon a time, there were three paddlers..." Jordan punches him in the shoulder.

"I'm actually interested in this river. I don't plan on almost dying again. Please continue," Jordan tells him. Grant flashes him a smile and does.

"'Pine Creek is a moderate class V run. Experience on difficult water is required. The section is continuous and has some sticky spots where swimming would be best avoided.' Isn't swimming always best avoided? Anyway. 'The put in is in the small town of Granite, Colorado off Highway 24. The entrance rapid is pushy but not overly difficult. Do not take it lightly but do not over exert yourself, because the worst (or best, depending on how you look at it) is still to come. The next rapid is called S-Bend, and the feature to avoid is a huge hole near the center of the rapid. You must move right or left to avoid it, which is challenging because the water is moving very fast in that area. Many people do not realize where they are until they are already in the hole. If after you scout you are unsure about your line, it is best to carry around.'"

"Sounds like something we should look out for," Jordan says.

"No shit," I agree, and Jordan flashes a grin at me in the rearview mirror. "Have you seen the footage of this hole on YouTube? It's beyond sticky. It's like a shark mouth. The right line is narrower than the left line, but both are tricky. It's definitely the make or break move on the river." Grant looks impressed.

"If Ginny thinks this is going to be a hard move, then we should be worried," Grant jokes.

"Yeah, right," I say, smirking. "Even the best in the world get trashed in this hole."

"It even says here that 'people have died in the hole at S-Bend because they decide to stay with their gear. Ditch the gear. Save yourself. Get out ASAP, because the river is continuous and cold, especially right after the snow melt,'" Grant reads.

"Dying isn't on our agenda. Let's try to avoid that hole," says Jordan, and I laugh.

"Yeah, it would defeat the whole purpose of this trip if we don't all get out alive," I say. "My parents would show up under the Royal Gorge Bridge and be like, wow, this is pretty cool. Then they'd see paramedics carrying me out on a stretcher, and they'd either start screaming at my dead body or start laughing, saying, 'I told you so.'"

"Nah, Ginny, you're parents aren't that mean," Jordan says. "Once they see you paddle through that gorge with the walls of the canyon around them, they'll definitely start to appreciate the sport more. They've *got* to. If not, we'll move on." I grin at Jordan in the rearview mirror because I love how he makes our adventure seem endless and full of possibilities. If this doesn't work, no problem, we'll just move on to the next place, and keep going on and on and on until we're successful...which I'm beginning to hope is never, because I'm pretty sure that I never want to leave these guys. They treat me more like family than my own does.

We're somewhere in the boring state of Iowa when Casey calls Jordan's cell. He passes it to me and I answer it, not sure what to expect.

"Hey," I say. "It's Ginny."

"Hi!" Casey shrieks. I move the phone away from my ear slightly. "Ginny. Good news. I think we're near you now, depending on how many times you've stopped. Is it okay if we meet you in Omaha?" I remember seeing a highway sign for Des Moines a little while back, so we must not be far.

"How did you catch up with us so quickly?" I ask. "Does your driver have a rocket powered car?" Casey snorts.

"Nope, he's just determined. Anyway, Omaha sound good? We're about three hours away, and you're probably closer, unless we somehow got ahead of you. In the main part of the city there's a mall, and we'll meet you in the Starbucks. If you want to meet us at all, that is."

"Um, I need to talk to Grant and Jordan. I'll call you back, okay?"

"Sure," she says, and we both hang up.

"Jordan?" I ask. He looks back at me in the mirror.

"Yeah?"

"How far are we from Omaha?"

"Um…" he grabs a map and scans it briefly. "Probably about two hours. Why?"

"Casey wants to meet us there."

"That sounds fine," Jordan replies. "What exactly are we going to do with her once we get there, though? Does she want to come with us?"

"I'm not sure…" I reply, realizing that Casey didn't really specify. "I guess we'll find out when we get there."

We pull into the Starbucks parking lot at around six. I scan the parking lot for a familiar car, and my eyes focus on a dark green Escape, and my heart stops beating. The blood drains from my head, I can't breathe, I can't think, and I'm frozen where I am. Grant and Jordan both get out, and I watch them reach the door before turning around to look at me, concerned. I'm still stuck in my seat, not quite believing my eyes.

"Yo! Ginny! You coming?" Jordan calls. He waves Grant ahead and jogs back to stand next to my window. He opens my door and looks at me with questioning eyes. "You okay?" I force my mouth to move and realize that it's gone bone dry.

"Um, I think I've figured out who my sister got a ride with…" I rasp.

Jordan sounds completely unconcerned as he replies. "Really? Who is it?"

"My boyfriend," I whisper. "Justin. The one who thinks kayaking is sadistic." Though he knows nothing about Justin, from my brief description in the car earlier and the horrified expression on my face, Jordan seems to understand.

"I see," he says, keeping his voice level. He leans over and unbuckles me, and I feel like I'm five years old again. He holds out his hand and I take it. "It'll be okay." His eyes are deep and comforting, and they calm my racing heart. I step out of the car.

"I hope so," I murmur, as we slowly make our way to the door. The whole thing feels unreal, like I'm actually outside of my body, watching myself approach my impending doom. Why did Casey ask him, of all people, to drive her? Didn't she know that I wanted to keep him as far away from kayaking as possible? And now here he is, in the middle of my perfect little adventure, about to screw up everything.

Jordan opens the door for me, and I see them right away. I see his familiar dark hair, his blue eyes, and Casey next to him, speaking urgently. As they hear the door, they both look up. Grant waves from a booth as we enter, and I try to focus on him instead of my boyfriend, whose gaze I feel penetrating my back.

"Hey, guys, what took you so long?" Grant asks, and I'm about to reply when Justin leaps up in front of me, barring my path. I step back in surprise.

"So, first I find out that you've run away without telling me, and *now* I find out that you've run away with a couple of guys? What the hell, Ginny?" Justin's furious, I can tell. His voice is rising with every word, and soon everyone in the coffee shop is staring at us. I swallow before attempting to respond.

"I couldn't tell anyone where I was going," I say, keeping my voice as controlled as I can. "You...you wouldn't have understood."

"I wouldn't have understood?" he sneers. "Ginny, we've been going out for what, three years now? And you don't think I understand you?" He's screaming now, and I take a half step backward, and bump into Jordan. He doesn't move back, and I'm thankful for his touch. It gives me the confidence I need to answer.

"I left to be able to kayak, and you've never really been supportive of that part of my life..." I struggle to keep my voice calm. Justin takes a step towards me, and his eyes are smoldering. I've never seen him this mad before.

"I was worried sick, do you know that? Then your sister came up to me and told me that you wanted me with you, wherever you were. She said that you ran away because your parents were mean to you and that I had to help her find you. I believed her. I fucking believed her." He turns his eyes to glare at Casey, and she flinches. I turn to look at her too, appalled. She lied to him to get him to take her? And there I was, trusting her actions completely. I suddenly want to punch both of them. Justin, for being here. And Casey, for betraying me.

"You shouldn't be here," I say softly, my voice menacing. "Either of you." Justin moves towards me quickly and it looks like he's going to punch me, and I tense up, ready for a fight. Then Jordan's hands find my waist and pull me back violently.

"Don't you touch her!" he yells, spit flying out of his mouth. He balls his hands into fists and his eyes are shooting daggers. "She has done absolutely nothing to you."

"And who the hell are you?" Justin yells back. "Am I going to find out now that my girlfriend has been cheating on me, too?"

"Ginny has done nothing wrong!" Jordan retorts, louder than before. Justin makes the move first, and his fist flies out, but Jordan reacts faster than I thought was humanly possible. His arm strikes out, grabs Justin's mid-swing, and twists so violently that I hear a crack.

"Fuck!" Justin screams. It all happens so quickly that I don't have time to stop him. I leap forward to prevent him from doing more damage, but Grant beats me to it.

"Jordan!" he says fiercely. "Drop it! Leave it be! You're only making things worse!" His arms are wrapped tightly around him, and I can see the veins in his arms popping out as he struggles to hold on.

"He can't do that to her!" Jordan howls, struggling wildly.

"I know," Grant says, lowering his voice. The people in the room are now standing, and some are pressing themselves against the walls. I see someone emerge from behind the counter, hands on his hips. The manager.

"Jordan!" I hiss, putting my hand on his arm. "We're screwed. Someone's here to bust us. We gotta get out." At the sound of my voice, some parts of him begin to slowly loosen. Justin's still standing on the other side of him, cradling his arm and glaring at all of us. I gesture for him and Casey to come, too. "We have to go. Now." I manage to herd them all out the door before the man in charge can call the police.

Once safely outside, Grant lets go of Jordan. He meets my eyes as if to say, *That's what I was talking about.* Now I understand. Jordan looks defeated, and he slumps down onto a bench, his head in his hands. Casey approaches me. She tries to meet my eyes but I avoid them. I don't want to talk to her.

"I'm sorry," she says softly. Her voice is so sad that I have to look up. There are tears in her eyes and guilt seems to flow freely from them. "I was wrong. I was stupid. You don't have to forgive me." I look from her, to Justin, who's glowering silently by a tree, and back to Casey again. In normal circumstances, I'd take Casey in my arms and tell her that everything is going to be all right. But this is different. I can't accept her apology yet, not after everything she did.

"You should probably go make sure Justin's all right," is all I say. At the sound of his name, Justin looks up and meets my eyes. They're filled with pain, betrayal, and anger, and I know that it's all directed at me. Casey walks slowly towards him and he turns away from her.

"I can't bear to look at either of you right now," he says, walking away towards his car. Casey turns helplessly back towards me and I shake my head. She needs to figure out how to make things right again.

"I hate to tell you this, but you got yourself into this mess," I say. I know I'm being harsh but I can't help it. "You have to fix this." I turn my back on her and go sit next to Jordan and Grant on the bench. Grant's whispering something in Jordan's ear. Jordan's shoulders are shaking, and I can tell he's crying. I place my hand on his back and begin to rub in small, controlled circles.

"Let it go, Jordan," Grant's saying. "It's okay now. Breathe. Breathe. Life is going to move on." Jordan shudders and both Grant and I reach forward to embrace him. I meet Grant's eyes over Jordan's hunched form, and his concern mirrors my own.

"I couldn't stop myself," Jordan says softly. "I didn't mean to, honest..."

"I know," I whisper. "I'm not mad, Jordan. I'm not mad at you at all." I glance over at Justin, and see Casey next to him, tears still streaming down her face, trying to explain. He's looking at her with a look of pure disgust. I know I should be doing something to help her, because I've always been there for her. But that was back when we always told each other everything, when we never lied or told partial truths. So I turn my gaze back to Jordan and Grant next to me, and I press my face into Jordan's shoulder. Overwhelmed with everything that just happened, I feel tears begin to seep out of my eyes, for the first time in years. Soon I'm sobbing too, and I feel Jordan bring out an arm and wrap it around my waist.

"Oh, Ginny..." Grant murmurs. I feel his hand stroking my hair. The genuine empathy in his voice makes me cry even harder.

Once our tears clear up a little bit, Jordan goes back inside to wash up. Grant and I sit in silence, and I rest my head on his shoulder, thankful for the company.

When Jordan returns, he offers me a steaming cup of hot chocolate, and I accept it gratefully.

"Here," he says. "Thought you might need this." Jordan and Grant share a glance, and it's intense and full of something that I can't quite put a finger on.

"Thanks," I say gratefully. "This is perfect." I wrap both my hands around it, and breathe in the warm steam. Jordan sits down on my other side, and I set my cup down on the ground between my feet. Starbucks serves everything way too hot to drink right away. I reach my arms up and put one around Grant's shoulders and one around Jordan's.

"You guys are the best," I say, meaning it with all my heart. They both laugh softly.

"Sorry this all just blew up in your face," Grant says. "You didn't deserve any of it."

"Often what you get isn't what you deserve," I say. "Unfortunately. Or we'd all lead much easier lives." Jordan chuckles.

"You have a piece of wisdom for everything, don't you?" he says.

I shake my head. "Not even close." I squeeze both their shoulders and drop my arms so I can start on my hot cocoa. The warmth seeps into my insides and I smile. Oh, the wonders of heated, sugary beverages.

"What are we going to do with them?" Grant asks, nodding towards Justin's car, where Casey and Justin are still sitting on the hood. They're no longer talking but are staring into space, both pairs of eyes focused on nothing.

"I don't know," I reply. "I wish I could just turn my back on both of them, but I know I can't do that."

"Casey just wanted to help," Grant points out softly. I can tell he's making an effort to not aggravate me, and I appreciate that.

"I know. But she was out of line to do what she did. Way out of line. I'm not exactly sure what encouraged her to bring Justin here," I say. I gaze at the two of them, my sister and my soon to be ex-boyfriend, two of the only people in the world who actually cared for me back home. I owe them more than this.

"They kind of cancel each other out," Jordan says. I look at him quizzically.

"What?" I ask.

"You know, she really wanted to be here for you, and she was so desperate to get out here that she asked the last person you would ever want to be here to take her."

"That's true," I answer. "What do you think I should do?" This is so *not me*, asking other people for suggestions about decisions in my life.

"Casey needs you, I think," Grant says. "And so does your boyfriend, even if he won't admit it. How close are you guys?"

"Um," I begin, not really sure how to say this. "We were never madly in love. Or even close to it. I think it was almost over by the end of last year, anyway."

"Does he know any of this?" Grant asks.

"No," I reply, shaking my head.

"Maybe you should ask them what they're going to do next. Tell them that they need to get him fixed up. Tell them that you started something and that you have to finish it," Grant says. I meet his eyes and he gives me a nod of encouragement.

"We'll be right here," Jordan says, giving me a little shove. I take a deep breath and walk over. Casey looks at me when I approach and Justin pretends like I don't exist.

"Hey," I say.

"Hi, Ginny," Casey says in a tiny voice. "What's up?"

"What are you going to do now, Case?" I ask softly. She shrugs. Her eyes are bloodshot from crying and she seems so small and innocent that I want to reach forward and hug her. But I wait for her to continue.

"I'm trying to convince Justin that he needs to see a doctor because his arm is broken. But he won't listen. But I think that's what we are going to do next."

"I'm not going anywhere with her," Justin says through gritted teeth. "I can't."

"Well, she's not paddling the Arkansas River with us, either. And our parents are probably freaking out right now. How did you manage to leave, anyway? This is so *not* an 'overnight with a friend.' I thought the neighbors were watching you."

"I...lied to you on the phone. I told them I was going on a trip with Justin. You know how Mom and Dad think that it's important that we bond. They both thought it was a great idea."

More lies. I suck in my anger, and continue, my voice level. "Well, when you don't come back after a day, they're going to be quite worried, aren't they? You really need to go home, Casey. Both of you do."

"Ginny," Justin says in a low voice. "I said, I'm not going anywhere with her."

"You brought her out here, you're bringing her back," I say.

His eyes flash. "She made me! She told me that you wanted me to be with you. So I listened to her. I don't owe her anything."

"You could have used your brain and said no, Casey, I will not help you run away from home to follow your crazy sister. You made the decision to come, not her. She's fourteen, Justin! And you're a legal adult. I'd say that this is just as much your fault as it is hers."

"You are impossible," Justin says, sighing loudly.

"Will you go to the hospital to get that looked at? For me? Casey will take care of you." I lean over and give Casey a quick hug. "I accept your apology," I whisper in her ear. She meets my eyes.

"Thanks," she says. "But will you answer one more question before you leave?" I smile at her.

"Sure."

"What's in Cañon City?" So she ended up reading the sign, too.

"Epic whitewater," I tell her. "Epic, beautiful, whitewater." Casey smiles back.

"I figured," she replies. "Come on, Justin. Whether you like it or not, your arm is broken, and you need to get it looked at..." Her voice has turned back to its normal volume, which is a relief. She tries to pull him towards the car, but he resists.

"Ginny, are you sure you should be hanging out with someone like him?" Justin asks, gesturing at Jordan.

"I know what I'm doing, Justin," I say, annoyed. "He was *protecting* me when he hit you, remember?"

"We're over," Justin says, shaking his head. "We are so over." His eyes meet mine, gauging my reaction.

"I figured that much," I reply. "And do go to the hospital, okay? Casey's right that you need to get that looked at." I wink at Casey, who's standing by him impatiently, and she smiles in return. "I'll see you both at home, okay? And take care. Please." Justin gives me one last, long look, before I turn around and walk back towards where Jordan and Grant are waiting.

Arkansas River, here we come.

The land stretches out forever. The sky outlines the peaks of the majestic mountains and stretches from horizon to horizon. We're standing on the top of Pike's Peak, the tallest mountain in the western US, and let me tell you, the view is incredible. We had some extra time so Grant suggested a ride to the top. Jordan's bad with winding roads, so he stayed behind. We dropped him off at an Arkansas River rafting company to talk about the lines and maybe arrange to tag along with a raft trip. I'm surprised that he allowed Grant five hours alone with me, but maybe they've reached some kind of understanding—that I am a friend, not someone who they need to fight over. I'm just Ginny.

Grant is leaning over the overlook, and a breeze comes and blows his hair out of his face. He has a faraway look in his eyes as he gazes into the setting sun. The long rays of sunlight reflecting off his skin make his face glow with extra warmth. There's a slight grin on his face and as he runs his hand through his hair, there's no doubt in my mind that he's the most attractive guy that I have ever seen. I walk over and stand next to him, but I'm really not looking at the view, though it is fantastic. I'm looking at the man beside me. He looks almost godly standing on the edge of the world, miles of mountains on every side of him, the sun casting soft shadows on his face. He slowly turns and looks at me, and it's so perfect, it's almost movie worthy.

"Ginny?" he says softly.

"Yeah?" I reply.

"So you're with Jordan now?" My heart drops into my stomach.

"Um, what gave you that idea?"

"You know, you guys were hanging at the party, and I know you got close while I was at the hospital. I'm actually really cool with it—" I can't help myself. I use every single ounce of self-control I possess, but it's just not enough. The words coming out of Grant's mouth are so false, though, that I can't hold back.

I kiss him.

I feel his surprise—his lips stiffen against my own, and I feel him shove me back, and I let him. I know what I'm doing is absolutely wrong.

"I'm sorry," I whisper. I search his eyes for some sign of anger or resentment, but find none. "I shouldn't have done that—"

This time he cuts me off. His lips are soft on mine, unlike when he kissed me by the road. They're gentle, but as I begin to kiss him back, it begins to grow. I part my lips and lose myself in the moment, knowing that I'll regret it later but knowing that for once, I think it's worth it.

There's a click behind us, and we break apart in surprise. I see a woman, maybe fifty, smiling sheepishly beside us. She's holding an old Polaroid camera, and her finger is still hovering over the shutter.

"Sorry," she says, looking guilty. "It was too sweet. I couldn't resist. Here." She rips off the print and hands it to me, and I take it. As it slowly develops, I see us, mouths pressed together, eyes closed. It looks like we've been together forever, when in reality, we're not even supposed to be touching.

I smile at the woman who gave us the picture. "Thanks," I tell her. She smiles back.

"You guys seem really good for each other. Keep it that way, we need more love in this world." She winks at us, then turns and walks back to the parking area. I turn my gaze to Grant, already feeling stupid for what I did. Couldn't I have stopped myself? I've screwed everything up. But Grant doesn't speak immediately. He holds my gaze, and his intense eyes make it seem like he's staring directly into my soul. I know he can see everything—from my guilt for kissing him to my actual, true feelings that I've been doing everything in my power to hide.

"I'm not going to lie, that was pretty sweet," he murmurs, slipping his arm around my shoulders and turning me back towards the edge of the mountain. I place mine gently around his waist and lean into him, breathing in his now familiar smell.

"It was," I agree softly, staring off into the picturesque landscape and at the orange sun slipping behind the faraway cliffs. Neither of us mention how much we just messed up, or ask how we're going to deal with Jordan. I pocket the picture and close my eyes, wrapping my other arm around Grant's slim waist and wishing the moment would last forever.

"Are we going to tell Jordan?" I ask on the ride back down the mountain. I know it's the question we've been avoiding the whole drive, but I need an answer.

"I'll tell him," Grant says. "Eventually. Probably not right away. If it doesn't come up, things will fall back into how they were before we left. You know you can't be with me and I know I can't be with you, so unless something changes, this isn't something we should be broadcasting."

"So if he asks, 'How was the trip?' What do we say then?" Grant turns and looks at me.

"You're a smart girl, Ginny. Do whatever you think is right." I'm getting the sense that he's annoyed with me, so I shut up. I take the picture out of my pocket and glance at it briefly, remembering that moment, and I close my eyes and try to imprint it into my memory. No matter what happens, I'll always have those fifteen minutes with Grant Haney. That's really all I can ask for.

We reach the bottom of the mountain and it's like nothing ever happened. It's like it was all too good to be true. We drive to the rafting place, the sun finally gone behind the mountains, as dusk rolls in. We both get out of the car and walk with a good three feet between us to the building. The river is prattling along beside us as we open the door and politely hold it open for each other.

The inside of the building screams "river rat." There are paddles hung up on the navy blue walls surrounding pictures of rafters and kayakers, some flipped over, some on the edge of drops, and some swimming. There are autographed pictures of Eric Jackson, Steve Fisher, and Sam Drevo, and I'm immediately reminded of my room. I get brief flash of homesickness as I remember my own kayaking idols hung up on my pale walls…

A man behind the counter is talking amiably with Jordan, and they both look up as we come in. Behind them is a huge full color map of the river, and I see Pine Creek listed as one of the first rapids, and at the conclusion, in a fancy script, the marking for Royal Gorge. My homesickness vanishes in a flash. Who needs home when you have the river?

"Pikes Peak live up to your expectations?" Jordan asks. Oh hell yes, it did, I want to say. In more ways than you should ever know.

"Yeah," Grant replies. "Great view. We could see for miles. You missed out, bro. It was awesome." Nothing in his face betrays what happened between us. Maybe he forgot. Maybe that's what I should be doing, too.

"You know I get deathly ill on winding roads. I'd like to be healthy and sane for the trip down this river. Marty here has been telling me the horrors of that S-Bend hole, but that it's the greatest thing ever if you're looking for an epic trashing."

"Uh," I break in. "We are *not* looking for epic trashings. I'm not saving your butts again." Marty, the guy behind the desk, cocks an eyebrow at me.

"I sense a good story," he says. His face is lumpy and beat up, probably from epic trashings of his own, and his eyes remind me of the color of the ocean. I can't tell if he's half Indian, half black, or just tan, because his face reminds me of the color of leather. He has a nice smile, and it makes his eyes crinkle, and I can tell he spent a lot of his life laughing.

"Oh yeah," I say. "Great story. For me. For them, not so much…" I trail off as I gesture to Jordan and Grant. They both crack smiles.

"Girl saved your butt, huh?" Marty asks them. They both shrug and pretend to glare at me.

"Oh yeah. They would both be *dead* if it weren't for me," I brag. "No question."

"Well, I will be guiding you through a good part of this river, so I guess we'll have plenty time for story time over cold sandwiches. But first, let me tell you noobs a little about the lines, eh?" I give him a weird look at his use of the word "noob." The only place I've ever heard that is back in third grade when I used to play computer games. He smiles at me and begins to explain. "Noob. You know, like newbie? You've never run the Arkansas before. Therefore, you are a noob."

"Hey! We've run around forty rivers and creeks in the US and have run over twenty in the past three months. We are *not* noobs," Jordan protests.

"Oh, I'm sure you've run some great stuff. But not Arkansas worthy. You are about to experience a real American adventure," Marty replies.

"A real American adventure?" I ask. "That's setting our expectations pretty high."

"You will be surprised, still. I'm doing you a favor so you don't fall over in shock in the middle of your run," Marty says, winking at me. "Now come closer, young Skywalkers. I will now enlighten you about the river you are about to fall in love with." I know he's joking, but there's a passion in his eyes as he brags about the river, and I can tell he's in love with it himself. The way his eyes light up as he says the word *Arkansas* and the way his voice becomes animated and alive make me confident that this will be a run that I am going to love, too. A surge of glee shoots through me as I imagine the river ahead of us. I don't know if I've ever felt more excited in my life.

My leg starts tapping at about quarter note = 500, and as I listen to Marty, my head is filled with beautiful visions of the next day. I can't wait, I can't wait, I can't wait...even as he talks about the treacherous features and the holes that will eat you alive, my mood stays sky high. I remember every detail of what he says, my mind visualizing the lines in my head, my arms tensing as I feel the churning whitewater around me, pulling at my imaginary paddle blades. I shut my eyes as Marty gushes about a rapid called Triple Drop, and I swear water actually splashes me in the face as I imagine perfectly boofing over the third. Then I realize that I'm actually wet.

"Hey!" I say, opening my eyes and seeing Jordan grinning with a cup of water in his hand. All three of them crack up, and I'm stuck standing like an idiot, water dripping off my face. "What was that for?"

"You looked so serious with your eyes shut there, I couldn't resist..." Jordan says, sounding slightly guiltier now. I walk over and cuff him on the side of his face, then lean over and grab his shirt, attempting to wipe the water back on him. He backs up and tries to fight it, but I smear the water all over his shirt and shove him playfully for extra measure.

"That's what you get!" I say. He's about to come at me fists flying when Marty interrupts our skirmish.

"Now onto the Numbers, eh?" he says. We all laugh lightly and huddle around the map once again, and continue on with the lesson. I definitely wish all school was like this.

The night before the big paddle we spend in luxury, or at least the best luxury available in Granite. We drive from the rafting headquarters to a little inn beside a restaurant. We have the best meal of the trip at the Granite Diner, where my meal of chicken and dumplings really hits the spot. After stuffing ourselves we walk next door to the inn. Everything's been packed, Jordan made sure to do that during our Pike's Peak drive (that's part of the why he sent us, so he could get things prepared without us getting in his way), and we're basically set for our trip the next day. We have a tarp to make a shelter with, some slim sacks to sleep in, and food all ready to go in dry bags that we can shove in the back of our boats. I'm a little worried about all our essentials being with us, because that means if we swim, we're toast, but we don't have any other options. I'm even more concerned because the guys dubbed me the most stable, so I ended up with the food, matches, first aid kit, and UV water purifier. No pressure, right? Fortunately I'm paddling a Hero, a boat made for river running that has enough volume to help me stay upright throughout the river.

Grant gets the tarp and Jordan gets the sleepwear. Jordan's paddling a red Liquidlogic Remix, and Grant's in a green Pyranha Burn, boats even harder to flip than mine. We all need the higher volume boats so we can fit gear in them without sinking ourselves. Fortunately, we packed so little that it could probably all fit easily in my school backpack. We're going to have to live off old beef jerky and numerous Powerbars for the next few days. Yum. Food is definitely not what makes overnight paddling trips so great. I'm more looking forward to songs by campfires, stories under the stars, and falling asleep to the sound of the river.

The DVDs we bought a while ago come in handy tonight, and we decide to watch *Mean Girls*. I don't think I've ever seen Grant or Jordan laugh harder. I start the movie off in my own double bed, but the spaces on either side of me begin to seem huge, so I move over to the guys' king sized one. They let me sit between them, both of them moving over to make a Ginny sized space for me. This simple gesture makes me feel like I actually belong with them, and I smile at both of them as I lay down.

So with a huge meal in our stomachs and our spirits high with thoughts about the next day, we fall asleep to Lindsay Lohan and the sound of our laughter ringing in our ears. I don't realize that I fell asleep in between two guys until I wake up the next morning to the blaring of the alarm clock. Jordan moans and stretches, in the process smacking me in the face. I grunt and he rolls over to see who he hit, and he grins as he sees my messy hair lying on the pillow beside him.

"Mornin', Ginny," he says groggily.

"Hey, Jordan," I answer. "Hey, Grant. You guys ready?" I yawn wide, and sit up in bed, running a hand through my untamed hair.

"Ready? I've been waiting for this my whole life…" Grant murmurs, and I smile lopsidedly at him.

"This is going to be an epic trip."

The road is bumpy and uneven, like most roads to remote put-ins in the middle of nowhere. There's a van in front of us with a raft on the top, and inside is Marty and some other ambitious rafters ready to take on the class V. I lean my head out the window and stick my tongue out, enjoying the wind in my hair and face. Grant laughs at me from the front.

"You're reminding me of my dog, Ginny," he says, grinning. There's affection in his voice that I hope Jordan can't pick up. Jordan's listening to his "pre-river soundtrack" on his iPod. I glanced at the playlist once and saw that it was filled with emo rock stuff, which seems like an odd mix of songs to listen to before running a difficult river. I hear the faint pulse of the music radiating from his ear buds and he's bobbing his head to the beat, mouthing the words like he's the rock star in the song. Grant sees me watching him and begins to mock him, mouthing the words to a random song and whipping his mop of hair around. He really does have boy band hair—it's thick, long, and messy, everything that's supposed to turn a girl on. And unfortunately, he's succeeding.

Soon I hear the faint roar of whitewater in the distance, and it gradually gets louder and louder, and my excitement begins to grow. Soon my chest feels like it's exploding, and as we reach the parking area, I literally leap out of the car. I know I'm beginning to grin like an idiot, and when Grant gets out of the car, I can't help myself, and I throw my arms around him. He laughs and hugs me back. We walk around to where Jordan is taking the boats out of the truck, and I engulf him in a bear hug as well before helping him unload.

I slip on my skirt and let the smell of neoprene fill my nose, and I close my eyes and breathe in deep. I pull my dry top over my head, followed by my lifejacket and my bright blue Shred Ready helmet. I glance at my reflection in the truck's windows and smile. Some people may think they look hot in a certain dress, or in low cut shirts. My look is different, unique, and awesome—I definitely feel most confident in kayak gear. I wink at my reflection before grabbing the dry bags from the car. I see Grant gesturing at me from the gathering of rafters, and I walk over, paddle in hand.

"Marty's going through our plan for today. We should probably listen up," Grant says. I briefly scan the group of rafters. Three of them look to be middle-aged men, and there's one woman and an older man. There are five in total, six including the guide. Marty says that we're going to scout first before getting in our boats and running the first section. There's an eddy before S-Bend and we'll get out to scout there, too. If anyone needs a break, he says, we should tell him and he'll try to eddy up. The rafters all nod solemnly, and I can tell that they're nervous. I, on the other hand, have so much penned up energy that I think I'm going to explode. Grant lays a hand on my shoulder as I begin to hop up and down.

"Marty's gonna think you're on something," he whispers.

"I can't really stand still..." I murmur back, and Grant laughs quietly.

"I can tell."

Marty wraps up his speech with some inspirational words ("don't worry that it's a class V—'cause we're all gonna get out alive!") and then we're ready. I place my purple Hero on my shoulder and use my foot to flick my paddle up into my hand. Jordan tosses me my assigned dry bag and I catch it awkwardly, and he smirks as I trip on a root while trying to reposition the bag in my arms.

"You can head down, you three," Marty says, while pulling paddles out of the back of his van. "We'll meet you there." The other rafters are still putting on dry gear (the water is supposed to be very cold) and securing their lifejackets.

"Okay," I reply. "See ya down there." I turn and practically skip down the trail, following the call of whitewater ahead. It's so loud now, I feel it screaming my name, telling me to come, come closer. I feel the longing in my stomach now, the pull of the river tugging at my gut, and soon I'm blazing down the trail.

After what feels like a mile, I see it—the trees end, and I emerge from the woods into a bright patch of sunlight. I step out onto the soft sand of a little beach beside the gentle, swirling waters of an eddy. The water's calm here, but I can hear it roaring up beyond a cluster of boulders. As soon as I set my boat down, I climb them, and the sight on the other side takes my breath away.

There's so much whitewater. It shoots over rocks and dives into eddies, forming high-speed rapids and roaring hydraulics. I breathe in deeply, inhaling the mist created by the froth, and grin, the sweet taste of river in my mouth. I open my arms wide like a bird, and take in the nature around me—the blue sky, the rocks lining the water, the hawk soaring overhead. It's so beautiful that it almost seems unreal.

"Don't jump, Rose!" a voice says from behind me, and I turn around and see Jordan grinning at me.

"You're very noble, Jack," I reply, loving his *Titanic* reference. "Very noble indeed." He reaches up and holds out his hand, and I use it for support as I jump down.

"It's quite a view," I tell him, still in awe. "The rapids are sick. No, beyond sick. Like, comatose, or something." Grant emerges from the woods next, and I wave.

"Hey, slowpoke!" I call.

"Hey, rabbit," he replies. "The rafters are quite a ways back, so we have a little time to chill. We can warm up on the river, above the hairy stuff."

"How far are we going with the rafters?" I ask.

"Pine Creek and Numbers. We'll be on our own for the rest," Grant replies. "Those two are the trickiest sections, though. We'll be able to scout and run the rest of it." I sit down in the sand with my back against a smooth boulder, and Grant and Jordan do the same. We continue to talk about the run ahead of us as we wait for our guide, but finally my excitement gets the better of me.

"I have to get in a boat," I say. "I'm going to have to do jumping jacks if I sit any longer." Despite the amused look I get from Jordan, I jump up, do a couple jumping jacks anyway, and drag my boat into the water. I slip in easily, my butt muscles relaxing easily into my much-used Happy Seat. I grab my sleek carbon paddle and take a few strokes, loving the feeling of water on my blades. I paddle up stream a bit and float back down, in time to see the rafters roll in.

The adventure starts *now*.

My first thought as we hit the first rapid—this is amazing. My second thought—this is more than amazing—this is like, sweet-kick-ass-epic-awesome-tastic. My third thought—I don't think I ever want to leave.

This water is unlike anything I've seen before. I'm used to the warm, pee-filled Potomac River that remains 90 degrees throughout the summer. But this? This water feels like the stuff they give out in bottles. The water is refreshing as it splashes off my face, and as I land a boof with a satisfying skid and am shot through the next section like a kid going down a waterslide, I don't see how anything could go wrong.

The easy section flashes by. I get a good surf on a little wave that has the perfect trough for looping, but sadly, looping a long boat is a little out of my skill range. I spin a few times and twirl my paddle like a baton when I get the attention of one of the rafters. He flashes me a thumbs up and I throw my paddle up and catch it in response.

It's soon after that that I hear it. An increase in volume, an increase in speed, and really, an increase in everything. I find the eddy Marty pointed out last night in the rafting office and dive into it and hop out of my boat. I'm the first one down and I'm already on top of the rocks, scouting the rapid below, when Grant and Jordan join me.

S-Bend is beyond scary. At first glance, all I see is white. The water is moving so fast that I can't even distinguish the holes from the waves. But then I see it. A huge, massive, lion-mouth of a hole in the middle of the main flow. To the left, I see the line we're supposed to take. To the right, I see the other line. If you don't make either...

CHOMP.

I imagine a boat going in, getting snapped in half, and remaining stuck in the recirculation, forever. Ha, we thought that hole on the Ottawa was bad? Well, this puts *bad* in a whole new light. I send a quick prayer to the river god that I nail this line. I'd really like to get out of this rapid alive...

But thankfully for me, the adrenaline in my veins doesn't abandon me. In fact, it increases to such a high level that I honestly feel invincible. My senses are sharp, my mind is focused, and as I set my boat back in the water and hop in, I feel my muscles flex under my dry top, and I know that I am going to nail this line.

I paddle hard out into the main current and fight as hard as I can to stay as far left as possible. The water is moving so fast that I don't realize where I am until I'm right next to the hole. I see it just to my right, a roaring monster with fierce recirculation, and turn my boat left and accelerate as fast as I can. I clip the very edge of the feature, get splashed hard in the face, but pull hard with a good stroke on my right, and slip by unharmed. I crane my head back to see if Grant and Jordan make it down okay, but have to look forward to avoid hitting a boulder. The river is too continuous to stop and wait for my group, so I'm forced to keep going. After maybe a hundred feet of nonstop twists, turns, dives, and waves, I spot an eddy on river left. I slip into it and grab a hold of a rock, and peer upstream, waiting for familiar green and red boats. I see the raft first, and my heart starts to pound faster—we were way ahead of the raft—but then following, I see Jordan, and then finally, Grant. Both of them look wet and slightly fazed, and I can tell just by looking at them that they didn't hit the line right. Well, at least they got out, and their bodies and boats are still intact. So it definitely could have been worse.

I raise a hand at them in greeting, and a couple rafters wave back, telling me to keep going. Apparently I just got nominated leader. I peel out and am taken again by the surging whitewater. I continue to slip through boulders, avoid pour-overs and nail lines for the remainder of Pine Creek. My boat responds to the directions my paddle gives it, and I maneuver the section like I've been running class Vs all my life. It's truly amazing what adrenaline can do to you.

Before I know it we're at Triple Drop. As I boof over the first ledge, I let out a whoop, a huge grin on my face. The water is so strong here that there is little time to think, so I let my instincts take over. Some weird, sixth sense tells me where on the drop to aim my boat, when I should initiate my boof stroke, and where I should place my weight when I land. After a satisfying splash at the bottom of the final drop, I pump my paddle in the air, feeling like an Olympic kayaker who just had a gold-medal-winning run.

I paddle into the next big eddy where Marty instructed us to wait. This is the snack spot, where we'll rest before finishing Pine Creek. I must have gotten down the section a lot faster than anyone else, because it's a good five minutes before I see the next boat. I feel guilty as Grant enters the eddy with an exhausted expression on his face—maybe I should have waited, made sure they were okay instead of just powering down on my own. But when he sees me, he smiles. One of those light-up-the-world smiles that people wear when they've just won the lottery or something. I grin back widely, mirroring his expression. Pine Creek is better than the lottery, or at least it feels like that right now.

"Good run?" I shout over the whitewater. He flashes me a thumbs up as he gets out of his boat.

"Screwed up the line at S-Bend, as you probably noticed. But the rest went smoothly, got pinned on a couple of rocks is all. How about you? You really flew down that section."

"Yeah...I'm feeling really good today," I say, not really wanting to draw attention to myself. Grant joins me on the rock.

"Where's Jordan at?" I ask.

"He got held up by the rafters. I think he's sticking closer to them because he had a problem on one of the lines," he replies. "They were pretty far back, though, because they got held up somewhere above Triple Drop."

I nod response. Grant's close to me now but we're not touching, and I look at him out of the corner of my eye. I love the way his hair sticks out from under his helmet and how natural he looks in his gear. I feel like I should say something, to attempt to convey how I feel about him, but I know that would just make things worse.

"It's a great day to be on the water," I say instead.

"Sure is," he answers. "Best day I've had in a long

while."

"I've only been with you guys for like, two weeks," I continue. "But it sort of feels like a lifetime. It's crazy how paddling will do that to you." I feel him watching me and look over and meet his eyes, and I feel a weird, electric current shoot through my body as our eyes lock. I wonder if he feels it too. Suddenly I want to touch him, to kiss him again, to feel his arms around me...but I know better now.

"You're right," he replies. "I actually don't remember when it was just me and Jordan very well. We had fun together, yeah, but having you along has added extra spice to everything." *Why, because Jordan's in love with me? And I'm in love with you?* I ask silently. "I'm not sure what we'd do without you, Ginny. For one, I might not even be alive. And secondly, I think we'd both really miss having you around."

"I don't know what I'd do without you guys, either," I say, quieter. "Before this, I was alone. And it was my choice, too. When people would try to get closer to me, I'd just shove them away. Not totally intentionally. None of it was my fault..." My voice has dropped to a whisper, and Grant leans closer so he can hear. I don't know why I'm telling him this now. I've waited four years, why not just let the memory die without anyone else getting involved? That was my goal, and so far, it's worked—the only person the incident ended up affecting was me. I'm sure Jackson forgot about me the day after it happened.

"Ginny?" Grant prompts gently. "Do you want to talk about it?" I'm about to say no, I don't, it's my problem not yours, but something in my brain clicks. Maybe it has something to do with running a class V river perfectly and feeling like I can do anything. Or maybe I just trust Grant more than I have ever trusted anyone before. Whatever the reason, I let my protective wall fall.

"It was in eighth grade," I say. I'm speaking so softly that I can barely hear myself. "There was this boy, Jackson. He was the hottest guy in the grade by a mile and when we hooked up at a party one night and he asked me out, I swore that we'd be together forever..." I take a breath. I feel the wall collapse completely, leaving me uncovered, unprotected. Leaving the real Ginny exposed. "But then I caught him making out with this other girl in the hallway, and I was really mad. So I stormed off, and he saw me. He found me after school and offered to walk me home. He told me that he didn't mean anything by kissing the other girl, and that he actually loved me, and then he started kissing me, and then..." I shut my eyes tight, not wanting to remember the rest. But it comes flooding back anyway. The way he grabbed me, the way he pinned me against the wall and the way he touched me...the feeling of panic that built up in me, and the surge of adrenaline that helped me shove him off and run the rest of the way home.

"Oh, Ginny..." Grant murmurs. He wraps an arm gently around me. "What a jackass."

"I've never told anyone that before," I breathe. I expect him to jump up, yell at me for being such an idiot, and ask me why I'd ever keep something like that secret. But he doesn't. He just tightens his arm around me and I lean into him. We stay like that until we both see a flash of red and yellow, and we separate again. I feel oddly at ease, like something huge inside me just got dumped onto the street for everyone to see.

As Jordan paddles up, I jump off the rock to ask about his run, and talk to Marty about the rapids ahead. Then I excuse myself, saying I have to go to the bathroom and don't feel like getting cold in the water, and go into the woods to be alone for a few moments. I lean against a tree, pressing my face into the rough bark, and wonder why exactly I dug up that old memory, reopened that old wound, and destroyed my good mood and my perfect day.

I hear footsteps behind me and feel someone's hand on my shoulder. "Ginny," Grant murmurs. "I'm sorry. For everything that happened to you." I turn to look at him, an almost pleading expression on my face, and he opens his arms and I fall into them.

"Hey, I don't want to make any assumptions here..." Grant begins, "but if you kept that to yourself because you were trying to be selfless and not get anyone else involved, I'm not going to criticize you for that. But I think you need to face this head on and accept that it happened and that it sucked and just move on."

"Grant, when are you going to realize that every assumption you make of me is almost a hundred percent true?" I ask, incredulous that he just figured everything about me out in about half a second, when it took me four whole years to do the same. He laughs quietly.

"I wish I knew more about what was going on in your head, Ginny. A lot of this is lucky guessing. I'm not really a psychic. Or a mind reader. I promise," he says.

I smile up at him. "I know," I whisper. "Thanks, Grant. I mean it." He smiles back, and claps me on the shoulder.

"I think we have a river to run now. You ready?" The previous events of the day come back in a rush, and suddenly it dawns on me that we are on the Arkansas River, and that we have miles to go before we sleep.

"Am I ever," I reply, and we walk back to the group, with me feeling a million times better and Grant humming a tune that sounds vaguely like *Eye of the Tiger*. With Jackson out of my head and the Numbers ahead of me, I hop back into my boat, eager to conquer the rapids ahead and leave the ugly parts of my past behind me for good.

The Numbers on the Arkansas have really great rapid names—Number 1, Number 2, Number 3, Number 4, Number 5, Number 6, and Number 7. After running the first three, we take a lunch break on a large, sunny flat rock. I look up the gorge at the rapids we've come down, and sort of can't believe that I haven't killed myself so far.

Marty packed us food, and we get to feast on turkey and cheese sandwiches, fruit, and bottled water. Grant informs me that this is the last time we'll be eating this well and that I should be savoring it. Personally, I don't mind beef jerky and Powerbars because everything tastes better when you're in the woods, anyway.

Marty tells us that we will be resting here on "Flat Rock" for about half an hour so we can prepare for the steep run ahead, so I strip down to my bathing suit and bask in the warm sunlight. As soon as I lay down on my stomach, a shadow passes over me. "Get outta my sunlight!" I demand, and Jordan laughs.

"Chill, girlie, I just want to save your back from skin cancer." Without my permission, he begins to lather the skin around my sports bra with sunscreen. When I'm sufficiently covered, he lays down beside me. He leaves about a foot of space between us, and for that I am grateful. I don't want anything to be complicated right now. I close my eyes and soak up my vitamin D, feeling like I'm still on the water. I love falling asleep to the gentle rapids rocking me back and forth, back and forth, and feeling like I never really left the river behind.

Soon Jordan's shaking me, though, saying, "Ginny! Paddling time!" At the sound of my name I jump up, and after my head stops spinning, I grab my gear and begin to pull it over my warm limbs.

"Ugh," I complain. Jordan smirks.

"Ew, wet gear," he mocks, and I punch him lightly in the shoulder. We hike up the rocks so we can check out the next rapid, Number 4 (the creativity of these names is still amazing me). It's class IV-V, and immediately I see why— there's a "go left or die" type move where if you go right, you drop off a pour over into the nasty hole at the bottom. The water before is fast moving and doesn't give you much time to plan beforehand. I note a few landmarks and go over my line one more time in my head, and then I'm ready.

I've run so many different lines on so many different rivers that I almost don't remember how to be nervous about it anymore. Either you make it or you don't, it's that simple. But if you don't, it's not the end of the world—I find it quite the opposite. I love the challenge of getting myself out of trouble, and learning to get out of sticky situations is one of the most important skills to have on a river. Jared used to say that the best paddlers don't just hit the right lines; they make lines of their own.

I take a deep breath before the peel out, and focus, visualizing my line one last time. Then I place my paddle in the water, and go. I see the first landmark, a little rock to my left, and cut sharply over above the boulder forming the deadly pour over, and drop through the channel to the left. I feel the jolt of satisfaction of knowing that I hit a line correctly, and rocket through the rest of the rapid, finishing the run with a sweet boof into an eddy on river left. Jordan and Grant flash by and I peel out once again, following their Christmas colored boats down the raging creek.

Numbers 5-6 go smoothly, but it's on the seventh that I really hit the jackpot. Playboaters are always seeking the perfect holes, and there are several world famous ones that everyone knows about. But now and again, you'll run across that perfect, hidden wave, a surf-on-the-fly only wave, that only the special few have been on. I'm shooting down the ultimate Number, trying a sneak line that hugs the right bank, when I fall into it. It's small, but just sticky enough for an easy surf, and I spin around so I'm facing upstream. It's glassy yet bouncy, and I lean back, feeling the hole rock me gently. I see the water rushing into the hole and all the water pouring around me, and I find it miraculous that in all this crazy, hectic whitewater, I'm standing still. It's like I'm frozen in time, not moving forwards or backwards but stuck in the moment. I get a particularly good bounce and throw my torso around and land an epic blunt, and back surf before spinning around to face the front again.

I hear a whistle blow (the signal for "go") from downstream and know my time is up. Reluctantly, I place my paddle on the pillow and pull myself out of my little haven and am once again thrown into the whirling current. It immediately takes my boat and demands my full attention.

At the conclusion of the run, I spot the raft in a little

cove on river left, and I see Grant and Jordan's boats pulled up on the shore as well. The two of them are sitting on a boulder. Grant's talking and Jordan's listening while he scans the river, and I get a glimpse of what it must have been like before I showed up. Grant and Jordan, taking on the world together, without some stupid girl to mess everything up. But soon Jordan spots me and a grin spreads across his face, and Grant murmurs something to him with a smug expression. He raises his hand in greeting and I raise my paddle blade in return.

"Get stuck somewhere?" Marty calls. The rafters are all eating something on the beach as well, sitting in a little circle, laughing and chatting.

"Found a nice little surf hole is all," I reply. It felt like I had only surfed it for a moment, but maybe it was like being in some alternative universe, where one second there is actually an hour in real life. "How long have you been waiting?"

"Only about five minutes," he says. "Don't worry about it." By now, the sun is beginning to set behind the mountains, and the sky is turning a brilliant shade of pink, the clouds looking like fluffs of cotton candy. I paddle into the cove and Jordan and Grant jump off their rock and meet me as I beach myself on the sand.

"We're going to stop here today," Jordan informs me. "It's getting late, and we're pretty beat. That okay with you?" Believe it or not, I'm feeling so high on endorphins that I feel like I could go on forever, but I know it's never smart to keep going after dark. I nod as I pop my skirt and step out of my boat, dragging it onto the shore.

"Sounds great," I say. Marty walks over and offers us some more food, and I realize that I'm ravenous. I smile at him gratefully as I accept the ham sandwich and chips in his outstretched hand and immediately begin to wolf them down.

"Nothing can compare to a river's end meal," Grant says between bites of his own food. The three of us find a log and sit down, but even on land I feel waves beneath me. I close my eyes and imagine that I'm still on my perfect little wave in the middle of Number 7. It was like the eye of the hurricane, a moment of calm in the middle of a wild run.

"Marty," I call, and he looks up from where he's sitting by the other rafters.

"Yeah?" he replies.

"Thanks for taking us down that stretch," I say. "Honestly, if it hadn't been for you, I'd be somewhere at the bottom of the river right now." He laughs and waves my comment off with a flick of his hand.

"Nah, girl, you made that river look easy. It was a pleasure paddling with you three today. Really."

"It was an awesome run," Jordan says. "One of the best I've done, I'd say."

"No question," agrees Grant, flashing a quick smile at me.

"I'm glad you guys enjoyed yourselves, and I hope you like the rest of the river, too. We gotta head outta here now; our shuttle's waiting by the road. Stay safe, ya hear? Watch the skies. If it looks like it's gonna pour, get off. The river gets real nasty at flood stage." I walk over and shake his hand, and Jordan and Grant do the same.

"We will," Jordan says. "And thanks again." Marty winks at us and a few of the rafters raise their hands in farewell.

"See you on the river," Marty says.

"See you," we chorus. Marty and his group pick up their raft and head into the woods. Soon the trees swallow them up, and we're left alone.

I strike a match and light the thin tinder at the base of a log cabin fire, and am rewarded with a burst of flame. It crackles satisfyingly and soon I have a blazing fire. Jordan and Grant both come into the clearing bearing armfuls of firewood, and as they set it down I begin to break the limbs into smaller pieces. Jordan and Grant both sit down on their lifejackets around my fire and put their hands up to warm them. It gets chilly at night in the mountains. Once I'm satisfied with my pile of fuel, I join them around the fire. Jordan and Grant exchange a glance and spontaneously break into song.

"Land of the silver birch,
Home of the beaver,
There still the mighty moose wanders at will.

"Blue lake and rocky shore,
I will return once more
Boom-di-di-a-da, boom, boom
Boom-di-di-a-da, boom, boom.

"Swift as a silver fish
My craft of birch bark
Thy mighty waterways carry me forth.

"Blue lake and rocky shore,
I will return once more
Boom-di-di-a-da, boom, boom
Boom-di-di-a-da, boom, boom."

I close my eyes midway through the song, letting the guys' rough, out of key voices wash over me.

"My heart grows sick for you
Here in the lowlands
I will return to you hills of the north.

"Blue lake and rocky shore,
I will return once more
Boom-di-di-a-da, boom, boom
Boom-di-di-a-da, boom, boom."

When the song concludes, I open my eyes. I stare into the fire, watching the sparks fly up and vanish and the flames dancing and flickering along the logs. I feel the warmth from the flames spread through my limbs and I move my face closer to the fire to get the maximum heat possible.

"Great song," I tell them, smiling in the firelight. "Really." Jordan meets my eyes.

"We hold weekly practices, you know. That's why we're so good." Grant and I both burst out laughing. When our laughter dies down we sit in silence for a bit, mesmerized by the flames.

I remember back to the night that now feels like a lifetime ago, when I was by myself by the Ottawa and Grant found me, sitting by my own fire. That was the last night I was alone.

"I think I'm going to go look at the stars," I tell them, interrupting the silence. "It seems like a clear night." I stand up and brush off my legs, and they do the same.

"We'll come, too," Jordan says, and we walk together back towards the river's edge. We sit on the boulder where they had sat earlier today, and we tip our heads back to gaze at the night sky.

The sky is covered in tiny white lights. I see a bright streak flash across the middle, and follow it with my finger. "A shooting star," I breathe. I close my eyes and wish for a safe trip, because I know that's what I'm supposed to wish for. But as another one flies by, I wish for Grant, even though I know it's wrong. And as I see a third, I wish for Jordan to understand. They're only wishes, right? They're harmless. And never actually come true.

I used to wish for things all the time. I wished for a brother, I wished for a dog, and later, I wished for my parents' support in kayaking. The boy my mom was pregnant with died at birth. The dog we had for two days bit Casey, so we had to get rid of it. And my parents banned me from kayaking forever. So naturally, I don't really believe in the power of wishes, because for me, they don't tend to turn into reality.

"Looks like a storm's rolling in from the west," Grant says, pointing to the western part of the sky. Sure enough, I see a strip of sky where the stars are hidden by a large cumulonimbus cloud.

"Good thing we got through Pine Creek and Numbers, then," Jordan says. "We wouldn't want to be caught in a storm on those."

"Today was an amazing day," I breathe, still staring at the sky. "I don't think I've ever seen a more beautiful river."

"And I've never seen a more beautiful night," Grant says, meeting my eyes and smiling.

It drops into the fifties overnight and our skimpy sleepwear does little to keep us warm, so we set up our tarp with the open end facing the fire. I'm a little worried about leaving a lit fire overnight, but Jordan points out that the ring we built is huge and that we'll feel the flames if they begin to spread, so I give in. I'm not a fan of freezing, either.

We wake up with a layer of dew covering our bodies and to the birds chirping in the trees. I can smell rain on the air as we walk over to check our boats and gear, which we hung in the open by the river, hoping that it would dry. I finger my dry top and am satisfied to find only a trace of water left. An eagle cries overhead and I look up the sky and watch it soar by, and that's when I see the clouds. They're closer now and are a somewhat menacing shade of dark gray, but the majority of the sky remains a bright shade of blue, so I'm not worried. We have hours of sunshine ahead of us.

We meet back by the fire ring to make a plan for the day.

"The next section of the river is called Browns Canyon. It's a moderate run that's ideal for family daylong raft trips. It's about fifteen miles and should take us about a day, maybe a little less. We have a stretch of flat water beforehand so we won't be on whitewater for awhile," Jordan says, squinting at a river map he got from Marty.

"Sounds good," Grant says, and I nod in agreement.

"But we should watch out for a storm. It could be nothing, but Marty did warn us."

"Yeah, that's a good idea," I say. "Better safe than sorry, right?"

I dig through my dry bag and pull out the UV water purifier and three Powerbars secured with a rubber band, labeled "Breakfast, Day 1". I toss them out and grab my water bottle, and head for the river.

"Water, anyone?" I ask. Grant tells me that his bottle is in his boat and Jordan says his is by his gear, and I grab them both and use our UV water treatment kit to purify water in all three bottles.

Soon, we're back in our boats, paddling down the river once more. The river's moving slowly with little riffles here and there, and all three of us look at the swirling eddy lines and wish we had boats we could squirt in. I don't mind being flat in my boat, though. Unlike most whitewater kayakers, I find flatwater very enjoyable. I love the natural beauty of rivers, and the slower moving water allows me to take in my surroundings.

The sheer cliffs on either side of us are majestic and the red rock adds to the serenity of it all. Evergreens grow above the rocks, silhouetted against the sky, towering majestically above us. The sky ahead is clear and cloudless, and there's a moist, cool breeze in the air that's refreshing on my face. We talk easily amongst ourselves. I tell them a little about my life back home and they talk about NRA and how they got into paddling.

"New River Academy was the best place on earth," Jordan is saying. "Before that, I went to a public school, but I didn't really fit in there. Paddling really turned my life around. I first started after I ran into this paddling school by the New River. Grant was one of the kids with them, and he said hi and started gushing about kayaking, and from his description I knew I had to try it." Grant's grinning at the memory.

"Oh yeah. I was with Brett then, right?" Grant asks. Jordan nods, and Grant turns back to me. "Brett Greene is this ancient paddler who starts young kids on the easier parts of the New. I started paddling with him when I was seven, and then we picked up Grant when I was eight."

"Grant was the one who first told me about NRA," Jordan continues. "The moment I heard about it, I knew that I *had* to get in. As soon as I could, I filled out an application and sent it in. I don't know how long I spent editing my essay for that scholarship…" Jordan shakes his head, smiling at the memory.

"Wait, did you get it?" I ask.

"I got a partial scholarship, yeah. The amount we had to pay was still pretty big, though, and my parents and I both worked hard to scrape up enough to pay the difference." I meet his eyes, and I see a flicker of pride there. New River Academy must have been worth it.

"What about you, Grant?" I inquire, curious about the lives these guys led before I met them.

"My parents are more…ah…privileged than Jordan's. I lived in a better part of town and attended a better school and they had good jobs, so when I applied and was accepted, they let me go." He shrugs like he feels guilty about his life being so easy.

"Tell me about NRA," I prompt, switching the subject. "Was it as great as you guys expected it would be?" They both exchange grins and launch into a detailed description of how the school wove together kayak training with education and adventure, and how they travelled all around the world, paddling rivers and learning. Hearing about Jordan's rough childhood also gets me thinking— Grant hasn't really had to work for much in his life, but Jordan's had to work for everything. Jordan's even worked to get me to like him, yet I'm still falling for Grant. Did I not give Jordan a fair chance? After everything he's been through, don't I owe him that much?

We're just getting into some faster moving water when I feel the first raindrops. I look up in surprise, and see that the dark clouds have spread. The only blue sky is the bit in front of us, the only part of the sky that we have been able to see. Maybe we should have looked back, but we were too focused on the water ahead.

"What the hell?" I exclaim a raindrop hits me in the eye.

"Ah, it's no big deal," Jordan says, waving it off. "It's just a drizzle. We'll pull up if things get too much worse." I shrug and agree with him. It's only a little rain, anyway. A few drops couldn't change the water level that much. Marty warned us about downpours, not sun showers. This is nothing.

Soon we're in some easy class IIIs again, and the wave trains make us forget all about the rain. I hit some boofs perfectly and even manage to get vertical on an eddy line. I'm back in my element and loving it. We're entering some slightly bigger water when the sky really opens up. One moment, it's drizzling, and the next, it's like the floodgates have opened on the Mississippi. I don't think I've ever seen rain this heavy. The drops are so big and it's raining so much that it's hard to see the water in front of me.

Marty's warning comes back to me, about how it's dangerous to paddle this river in the rain because of the rapidly rising water. We had shrugged it off earlier, but now I'm not so sure. But this "easy" part of the river is starting to look quite different, because the river *is* rising. The water's turning a hideous shade of pinkish brown, hiding strainers, changing the lines, and altering the river entirely. Rain is now pouring down on us, and I yell ahead at Grant and Jordan, "Eddy up!" Which I soon realize is pointless, because they can't hear me, and there aren't any eddies in sight.

"Ginny! Hole!" I hear Jordan shout, craning his head back to see if I understand. He gestures wildly to the left with his paddle, and I see it. It's massive, and resembles the mouth of a gigantic beast. The recirculation is fiercer than anything I've ever seen—of a boat went in there, it would not come out in one piece. It's almost bigger than S-Bend, and I'm sure that Marty didn't warn us about this when he talked about this section of the river. He said that the stretch after Numbers was a fun, easy recovery spot with lots of *play* holes. This is not a play hole. Not at all.

So I go right, hard. I clip the edge of it, barely, and a surge of fear-induced adrenaline helps me clear it.

But that's not the end of the terrors, no way. The waves are surging now, some nearly four feet tall. Some break on my boat, drenching me in the filthy water, threatening to swallow me before I emerge on the other side. I keep the green and red of Grant and Jordan's boats in sight, making sure they are all right, making sure we are still together. Now the river isn't looking much like a river—it's now resembling more of a bay, or ocean—unpredictable, with uncharted waves and no end in sight. Nothing even remotely resembles the videos on Youtube or the articles in our whitewater books. This isn't the friendly, easy recovery section I expected. For the first time in my life, I feel afraid of the water ahead of me. I'm afraid that we won't be able to make it. I'm afraid of one of us flipping and swimming, and no one being around to help.

That's when I see the strainer. Water is pushing up against it, forming a huge pillow, and at a distance it looks like an innocent boulder. But up close, I can tell that that's not the case—there's a log hiding beneath the water. I no longer see my companions, and I pray that they're not under the log, because I don't see a way around it. I picture myself getting shoved against it, flipping, getting snagged on a branch, pinned under water—I picture it drowning me, sucking the life from my body…

But then a flash of green catches my eye to my right, a bright spot of unnatural color in a sea of dirty pink. Grant. He's found a side channel. Jared's words flash through my head: *Never paddle a river blind.* But paddling this channel blind seems a lot better than facing the alternative. So I lean into the pillow and use my right blade to drag myself towards the opening. The water is screaming at me, threatening to suck me under and eat me alive. But fear of death and the determination to stay upright gives me the strength I need.

I make it past the strainer. I no longer see Grant's boat, but I know he's somewhere ahead. This channel is narrow, rocky, and unpredictable as hell. I'm thrown roughly into a rock and a surge of water hits me, flipping me faster than I have time to react. It's shallow, too, and I feel sharp rocks digging into my face. When I roll up, I feel the warmth of blood running down my cheeks. I taste it on my tongue, and its metallic tang makes me realize the seriousness of the situation.

The creek is so narrow that there isn't much room for paddling. The wild water takes me, shoves me into boulders, rockets me over pour overs, surfs me in holes. There is nothing I can do but brace off what I can, keep control of my edges, and pray that I get down in one piece.

I flip a few more times, and soon the pain in my face and head become a dull throb. I am barely aware of the blood that's gushing out of my facial wounds, trickling into my eyes and occasionally blinding me. When this happens, I shake my head violently to clear the blood, not trusting myself to let go of my paddle. I'm like a ball in a pinball machine, at complete mercy of the shooter. I smash into one rock, shove off of it, and get thrown into a hole. I surf, flip, and get flushed out, the water stinging the cuts on my face and washing the blood out of my eyes. I shoot over a boulder and drop about four feet, and I do my best to initiate a boof stroke so I land flat. I bump over a rock upon landing, sending a jarring pain up my back. I wince, needing a break, before I'm shoved roughly into a slot between two rocks. I'm momentarily stuck, which would have been a relief, if not for the water pushing against me and the treacherous water ahead. I remain stuck until a sharp, piercing whistle breaks into my thoughts. My head whips around toward the sound of it, and that violent motion dislodges my boat. Grant's bright green boat, about six feet from my own, is the last thing I see before I face plant into the rock beside me.

I feel my nose break upon impact and the pain is so great that it clouds my judgment. I can think of nothing but the pain ripping through my head as I bump along the shallow bottom, my face pressed against my skirt. With each rock I hit, it feels like a bullet is ripping through my skull. My paddle is jammed against the bottom, and my knuckles are being rubbed raw as well. I attempt to roll by just hip snapping, but that proves utterly useless—I get up about three inches before being slammed into the rocks again. When I finally manage to roll up, the world is spinning and my vision is blurry. I feel sick and dizzy, and before I know it, I'm upside down again. I try to fight the weakness creeping into my limbs, but I feel myself slipping, slipping into darkness…

And then there is nothing.

Part 4
The River's End

Pain. That's all I feel when I'm conscious again. My head and face feel like they are being constantly run over by a tractor-trailer, and the rest of my body feels like it was put though a blender, a paper shredder, then thrown off the Eiffel Tower. There's this constant throb in my temple that makes me want to get up and barf my guts out, but I'm too weak to do anything but let out a slight moan, and immediately begin coughing up water. The coughs rip through my chest, and I sit up, water pouring out of my mouth. Jolts of pain shoot through me each with each cough, and that on top of the rest of the pain I'm in is too much to bear. I feel strong hands supporting my torso as I cry out, my voice sounding ragged and hoarse.

"Ginny!" a voice calls my name, and I moan again. I feel a hand on my forehead brushing my hair back, and pry open my eyes.

It's dark. A fire's glowing off to my left which lights up the face of the man leaning over me. Grant. His face is bruised, bloody, and marred, and there's a huge scratch down his right cheek that's oozing blood. His hair is matted and sticking out in every direction on his head, his eyes are bloodshot and his right one is slightly bruised. I briefly analyze my pain situation—the worst is definitely coming from my nose, from when I broke it slamming into that rock. There's a cut on my forehead that's throbbing painfully along with a gash down my right jaw line, and the whole left side of my face feels like one huge bruise. I remember being jammed in the rocks and I remember being upside down, but I don't remember anything beyond that.

"What happened?" I rasp. Grant's kneeling and leaning over me, and begins to swab my forehead with a gauze pad. It stings so bad that I have to shut my eyes tight and grit my teeth to prevent myself from screaming.

"You flipped in the best place possible," Grant replies gently. "You were under for a bit but then I was able to reach you, flip you up, and get us safely ashore. You were unconscious but breathing..." He seems to be leaving out a lot of the truth because he thinks I can't take it. But I can. And I want to know all of it.

"Grant," I insist, feeling water in my throat. I begin to cough again, and when I finish I continue, clearer this time. "I need you to tell me the truth." Grant meets my eyes and gives me a small smile.

"Okay," he says. "I saw you pinned between those rocks and wasn't sure what to do. I blew my whistle because I thought you needed to know I was there, but then you flipped, and I knew I had made a serious mistake. I paddled over as quickly as I could, and chucked my paddle downstream in order to give you the hand of god. Once you were upright, the creek had become shallow enough that our boats were no longer moving very quickly, and I was able to get out, stand up, and get you on shore." So basically, I almost died, he somehow managed to save me, and if it weren't for him, I'd still be stuck at the bottom of that God damned creek.

Grant continues to swab my forehead, and I get a glimpse of the gauze pad, and it's covered in blood. He gets a clean one as he begins to tackle my right cheek.

"That sounds pretty crazy," I murmur with my eyes closed, trying to focus on anything but pain on my face.

"Yeah. It was." The sound of his voice makes the pain

ebb, and the sight of concern on his face makes me feel marginally better.

"How bad am I?" I ask, not exactly sure if I want the answer but wanting him to keep talking.

"Beautiful, as always," he replies, winking at me. "And I'm serious," he continues, as he sees my dubious expression. "You look badass as hell right now." I give him a small smile, which probably comes out looking more like a grimace.

"You look pretty hot yourself," I tell him, actually meaning it. His injuries make him look like a fighting hero, and his spiked hair makes him look like he was taken directly out of an action movie. And that's when the world comes crashing down on me, because I realize that with all the pain in my head and everything happening, I totally forgot about Grant's other half, the boy who I know would never, ever forget about either of us…guilt floods me, as his name washes over my mind, over and over again.

Jordan. Jordan. Jordan. Jordan. Jordan…

I imagine him pinned under that gigantic strainer, unable to roll, unable to swim out, praying for a savior that will never come. Jordan, floating to the bottom of the river. Me, not ever being able to see his smile again, hear his laugh, or listen to him tease me. Him, never knowing that I was going to consider giving him a shot. Him, never knowing how much he means to me…

"Ginny? What's wrong?" Grant asks, leaning over me and speaking gently. He brushes a hand across my cheek and I meet his eyes, and I see pain there, too. He knows, but he's been hiding it to pay attention to me. That makes my heart hurt even more. Grant must be dying inside, not knowing where Jordan is. And yet here he is, caring for me.

"Jordan…" I mumble. "Oh shit, Jordan…he's not here, is he?" Grant's eyes fill with pain and determination.

"No. But as soon as we can move, we're going to find him," Grant says, and the certainty in his voice makes me admire him even more.

"I'm ready now," I say, trying to mirror that confidence.

"No, you're not," he insists, but I try to stand up anyway. Immediately, my head starts spinning, and I'm about to fall when Grant wraps his arms around me, supporting me with his chest.

"Guess you're right..." I mumble, mad at myself for being useless at a time when we really need to be moving.

"It's okay, Ginny," Grant says, his voice turning gentle again. "You're more important right now." *Why?* I want to ask. *Because you know for sure that I'm alive?* But I shove that out of my head because I know that I have to be positive if we're going to get through this. Jordan is intelligent, quick-witted, and resourceful. There's no way he got himself stuck in a strainer. We'll find him. We will. Or we'll die trying...

"If he were here, we'd have a plan," Grant's murmuring to himself as he allows me to clean his face. "Jordi always knows what to do..." The pain in his voice is palpable, and I press my lips into his forehead, not knowing how else to comfort him.

"We'll walk up the creek," I say. "We'll go back to the main part of the river. And we'll search. We'll search and search and search and we won't stop until we find him." My voice sounds clear and certain, even if inside, I want to break down and cry. I know I need to keep it together or we'll both fall apart. I imagine a literal explosion, with my brains and guts flying in every direction, and take a deep breath. No one's going to blow up today. I gently move away from Grant and begin wiping his face with the wet gauze, carefully going over his black eye and other bruises. His eyes are closed and he's keeping his face neutral, but I see his hands balled into tight fists and I know he's keeping a lot from me.

"I can't lose him," Grant whispers. "I *can't* lose him." He opens his eyes, and his face contorts into one of pure agony. "Ginny, that guy means everything to me. If we don't find him..."

"Grant," I say firmly. "Look at me." He obliges and his tortured eyes meet my own. The look there hurts more than any of my injuries. "We can't start moving until we're physically able to, right? Heal first. Help second. Okay?" I know I don't sound convincing because I barely believe myself. My brain is telling me to get up and go, go, go, but my body is also telling me that if I stand up, I will just fall back down. Grant can't be in much better shape. We can't leave yet, no matter how much we want to.

"I know," Grant whispers, dropping his eyes. "God, I just fucking wish we could at least find out if he's okay. We could be sitting here, warming by a fire, and he could be somewhere suffering, or...or..." His imagination is going wild and I violently shut out the bloody images that flood my own mind. I can't help but ask myself, *would this all be happening if I hadn't come along?* If they had stayed longer in Ottawa and at Wausau and had gotten to the Arkansas days later, would they have run into the rain? Would they have had a successful run?

What ifs are pointless, because you can't change the past. That's what everyone tells me when I'm overrun with guilt over something I could have done better. But if Jordan doesn't come out alive all because of me, I don't know if I'll ever be able to live with myself.

Jordan's not dead. Normal people don't die kayaking. He's fine. Everything's fine.

This is killing me.

I focus on the gash in Grant's cheek, concentrating on cleaning out every bit of blood, every bit of dirt, and only when he winces and moves away do I realize that I'm probably hurting him. "Sorry," I mumble, deciding to tackle another gash above his left eye. He sits stoically, eyes shut, like he's enjoying the pain.

"Grant?" I whisper, suddenly hating the silence.

"Yes?" he replies, eyes closed.

"I think your face is done." I put a few globs of Neosporin on his cuts before closing up the first aid kit and leaning back so I'm lying facing the sky that has miraculously cleared since the flash flood. The sky is lit up with stars and insects are chirping softly in the trees, sounding sickly optimistic. I want to shoot them. How can they sound so happy when our lives are so screwed up?

As my life falls slowly to pieces
The insects continue singing
Like nothing is wrong
They know nothing about the hole in my chest
Or the pain ripping through my soul
They just keep serenading the night.
It's like they're trying to tell me
That maybe
Just maybe
Everything will be all right
When the sun rises.
When did I become a poet?

Waiting for daylight is like walking through a dark tunnel, waiting for the light at the other end. We both try to sleep but are too wound up with restless energy and soon realize that it's pointless. We sit back to back, by the light of the dying flames, pressing against each other for extra warmth and comfort, reminding each other that we're not alone. We don't talk much aside from a few whispered words about the weather here and there, so I'm left alone with my thoughts.

For some reason my mind drifts back to when I was ten years old, paddling O-Deck for the first time with Jared. Because O-Deck is the rapid right below Great Falls, it was very significant to me and I wanted it to be perfect. But when we got to the sandy beach, the put in, and I learned I had to do a scary ferry, portage over rocks, paddle some more, than portage *again,* I wanted to stop then and there. For one, I hated portages more than anything. And secondly, I didn't want to humiliate myself by not being able to make it.

But Jared insisted that I go. He told me that he knew I could do anything that I put my mind to. He also told me that the words "I can't" should not be in my vocabulary, and made me do pushups on the sand when I told him that I couldn't portage over steep rocks. After throwing down thirty, he let me stop, and dunked me in the pee smelling water for extra measure. Then he started paddling away and told me to follow.

The river was high and even though I'd seen the rapid Fish Ladder millions of times before, it was especially big that day. I didn't think there was any way that I'd get across it without flipping, and I told Jared that, and he shrugged, saying that I could roll, so I shouldn't be worried. I was still nervous as heck as I set my angle and paddled into the froth.

Sure enough, after about two seconds, I flipped. I rolled up quickly, and made almost no headway before flipping again. Rolling was harder the second time, but I finally got up, and paddled into the eddy on the other side, coughing up water. Jared followed me and made the move in two strokes, and as he came closer, he was grinning broadly. And let me tell you—Jared has this killer, movie star smile that I basically lived for, and seeing it then made me think that I could accomplish anything. I was expecting some praise, or at least a good job, but all he said was, "See? I told you so." He flashed me another grin before paddling up the eddy, and called over his shoulder, "You coming?"

That's what I remember most about my time with Jared. Him, looking over his shoulder, asking me if I wanted to continue on with him. And me, being little and not wanting to be left behind or look like a chicken in front of my biggest idol, always following. He had this contagious, confident attitude that made me trust him with my life. So I followed him up the eddy and over the rocks to O-Deck, and had a spectacular day on the river. That's how it was in the old days—just me and Jared, taking on the world. I don't really know how he put up with me. I must have been annoying as hell. But he never, ever left me behind.

Now I've become a Jared of my own. I'm a leader now. And no one in my group is going to be left behind.

So finally, as the sky begins to lighten, and as the first signs of dawn become visible above the horizon, I'm filled with renewed determination. Jared never believed in failure—not in himself, and not in his friends, either. And neither do I. I shake Grant's shoulder gently, whispering that it's morning, finally. I stand up without a hint of dizziness and dig through our packs for breakfast. We're going to need fuel for the long day ahead of us.

"We really did get washed into the middle of nowhere," I comment as I gaze at the creek we are camped next to. It's the same dangerous, horrific monster that almost took both our lives, but today it's been reduced to a little, trickling, harmless stream. Row, row, row your boats, gently down the stream, merrily, merrily, merrily, merrily, God I wish this were a dream...

"Yeah, we really did," Grant agrees. "I can't believe this tiny thing is the killer creek we saw yesterday." His voice sounds lighter, which helps brighten my mood as well.

"No shit," I agree. "It's crazy how flash floods work." He's observing my face, and I remember the pain I was in last night and realize I must look like crap.

"What?" I ask.

"You look even more badass in the daylight," he says, and I suppress a grin. His face turns more serious as he looks upstream. "You ready?"

"Yeah," I answer. "Let's roll." We start up the rocky creek bed. We're carrying all the gear that we had in our boats—the tent, the first aid kit, the UV water purifier, and what's left of the food—in dry bags, and we're wearing our gear in case we get stuck somewhere and have to make it through another cold night. Grant also noted that a helmet will keep us safe if we fall into the river, and I try not to think about that. Grant sets a fast pace and I struggle to keep up, feeling the wear and tear of yesterday's river beating catching up with me. But I suck it up and plow through, knowing that Jordan is more important.

I get a stitch in my side early on that soon turns into a pounding ache. My head follows suit and begins to throb as well, but I plow through and put all my effort into keeping up with Grant. I'm sweating and panting when he finally stops.

"That looks like the log," he says, gesturing to a gigantic, fallen evergreen tree that spreads across the entire river. Branches covered in needles are sticking out everywhere. Now, the riffles beneath it are small and friendly. The strainer forms a bridge, but many of the branches are in the water and the thick needles block the view of what lies below. My eyes begin searching for a familiar red boat, or a blue helmet, or a gray lifejacket—but all I see are the log's tangled branches. I see Grant set his dry bag down and drop mine next to his. The water looks cold and uninviting and the thought of finding Jordan frozen and lifeless even less so.

We stand on a rock by the river's edge and look at each other, and Grant counts to three. We hit the water at the same time. It's ice cold and shocking at first, and the air in my chest is knocked out of me. For a moment, I can't think, I can't breathe, and I sure can't swim. But I force my limbs to move and dive anyway, opening my eyes and searching for signs of our lost companion. It's tough diving with a lifejacket and briefly I consider taking it off, but then realize how unfortunate it would be if I drowned looking for Jordan's drowned body.

I don't want to find anything—I'd rather live in happy ignorance and believe that Jordan is somewhere, *anywhere* else, but I force myself to search meticulously and slowly. But after my legs and arms go numb and I can no longer move my hands, we've still found nothing. I've felt along the bottom of the log and got stabbed with branches multiple times and finally accept that Jordan isn't down here. As I drag myself out of the frigid water, I'm weak with relief. There's still hope yet.

"N-n-no sign?" I chatter to Grant, who's getting out beside me. I'm shivering uncontrollably and begin doing jumping jacks furiously to try to get warm.

"None," he replies, looking cold as well, even though I can tell he's trying to hide it. "If he's not here, then he must have gotten around it somehow..." Or floated under the log. But I don't want to think about that right now.

"When's the last time you saw him?" I ask.

"Um, before the strainer. I saw the red of his boat briefly to my left and then this surge of water carried me violently right, and I ended up in that side channel."

"Yeah, that's when I saw you. Maybe he went left?" I mull this over in my mind as I look at the log again. It spans the width of the river, and it doesn't look like there's any way to get around it.

"The water line is so high, maybe he did," Grant muses. I look over to the left of the log, but the water line is blurry and looks too low, so we both quickly rule out that option. So either he somehow managed to go over the strainer, which isn't really possible, or his body managed to go under it. We both agree that he either went below it, or somehow got out of his boat and went around it. We're hoping fiercely for the latter, but we both know how incredibly unlikely that is. When it comes down to it, though, it really doesn't matter what happened at the strainer—we just hope that he's somewhere, alive.

We leave the log behind and I realize how cold I am. The sun's warm and so are the rocks, but neither seem to be able to get my body temperature above its current, freezing state. Grant's still practically sprinting over the rocks and I'm in no position to stop him.

We walk swiftly along the bank, keeping our eyes peeled for a flash of red or a sign of human life, but find nothing—just red rocks, fast-moving water, and tall trees. Questions are rolling through my mind. If he did manage to get out of his boat, is he passed out somewhere on shore? Or is he somewhere lost in the woods, trying to find a road? But if that were the case, wouldn't we see some sign of a boat, or gear, or something? The sun rises above the trees as it nears noon, and I feel my stomach growling for food, my body longing for warmth, and my legs wanting rest, but I push all those complaints away, because most of all, out of everything, I just want Jordan. The picture of him lying on the bottom of the river, dreams unaccomplished and life unfinished, makes me want to curl up and die myself. Out of all of us, Jordan deserved this the least. Jordan, the one who *always* planned for the worst. Jordan, the one who pulled me out of the river after I dove in after Grant. I owe Jordan my life. It would be all wrong if *he* ended up dead. Jordan never did anything wrong... *Life isn't fair, Ginny*, I hear my mom whispering in my ear. Life isn't fair. Life is never fucking fair, and that, in itself, is the least fair thing of them all.

   I refuse to get discouraged as the day wears on and we've seen nothing out of the ordinary. Grant throws me a Powerbar from his bag at around noon, and I eat it gratefully. It takes me over three minutes to get the wrapper off because my hands are so cold, but I don't complain and I don't ask for help. Grant glances over his shoulder every now and then, and his eyes are filled with intense determination. He's not the sensitive, caring, funny guy I fell in love with anymore—he's all business. And that makes me like him even more.

   At one point, I look back the way we came, and notice that the sky behind us is no longer clear. The clouds aren't storm clouds, they're different. I'm trying to remember the time I learned about weather in science class when a piece of ice smacks me in the nose, sending an excruciating pain through my face and making me scream out.

   "Ah!" I gasp as more ice begins to fall out of the sky. Back home, hail meant small, millimeter sized ice particles sprinkling out of the sky. But here, it's like some weather god is trying to kill us by pelting cubes of ice down from the heavens.

"Ginny!" Grant yells, running back to me. He grabs my hand and jerks me violently toward the water. At first I resist, thinking he's crazy, when I see where he's taking me—there's a small outcrop of rock by the river's edge, and we dive under it. Grant digs the tarp out of his dry bag and puts it over us, and he wraps his arm around me protectively. He feels like a furnace, and I press against him, burying my face into his shoulder.

"Smart thinking," I murmur as the ice pellets rain down on us. It's loud under the tarp. It sounds sort of like we're being ambushed.

"Ginny," Grant says, surprise coloring his voice. "You're cold. No, I take that back. Girl, you're freezing!" I'm immediately reminded of that night in the tent, one of my first nights on the trip, when he spoke those exact words.

"I'm okay," I reply, trying to keep the shiver out of my voice. "Honestly. Jordan's more important right now."

"No, Ginny, I wasn't kidding," he says again, firmer this time. "You're actually freezing. Take off that dry top. I've got the tarp." He holds the tarp up as I struggle to pull the jacket off, my hands too numb to be of much use. After watching me struggle for a few minutes Grant lets go of the tarp and yanks it over my head for me. We both get hit by a few ice chunks before he resituates the tarp above our heads. He then loosens the waist of his jacket and says, "This is going to be weird. But it'll get you warm, I promise. This thing's huge on me. See if you can slip in…" Carefully, I wiggle my way up into his dry top. I get my head and most of my torso in, and curl up in his lap. He places his arms around me and slowly my body begins to thaw.

"Thanks, Grant," I say. My voice sounds unnaturally loud in my ears.

"No problem, girlie," he replies, sounding just like Jordan, and I feel a sharp pang. "What are you, prone to hypothermia or something?" My laugh is muffled by the dry top.

"Guess so," I chatter. We remain silent for a while as the hail pounds the tarp and Grant's heart beats loudly in my ear, and I snuggle against his chest, thankful for the warmth. His arms tighten around me and I feel his chin resting on my head, and we wait out the hailstorm together. Our position is awkward, for sure, but we're alone in our little world under this red tarp, and there's no one out there who can see or judge us.

Except for the someone, or something, behind us.

It announces its presence with a rustle of underbrush, and at first, we're unconcerned. It's the wind, or something. No big deal. We sit in silence for several moments, and I let out a long breath, thinking that there's nothing there after all.

Then I hear it again. First, I think I'm imagining it, but then I feel Grant stiffen against me, and I know that I'm not. There's the shuffling sound of feet moving through leaves right above our heads. Now I'm certain that there's something up there.

"Ginny," Grant whispers. "I'm going to peek at what's out there. It's probably nothing, but just to be sure..." I hear the rustle of the tarp as he moves it, and time seems to slow down. My heart begins pounding and I curl in a tighter ball.

Then he screams.

"Shit, Ginny, bear!" he yells.

He jerks violently, jumping up and taking me with him. We're attached in the most unbalanced way possible, and as he attempts to stand, we both topple over. Unfortunately for us, the ledge we chose to sit under was quite close to the water, and we hit the water with a loud splash.

"Fuck!" I hear Grant yell as the water surrounds us. Now I'm panicking—I can't breathe and I can barely move. I start struggling violently against his chest and I feel his hands trying to yank me out as well. Neither of us have our life jackets on and my helmet is lying on the shore. I'm practically naked underneath Grant's dry top, and the freezing water that hits my bare skin quickly erases any of the progress my body made when warming up beside Grant. I begin to panic as I feel myself beginning to suffocate. My whole body is screaming for air and I begin to flail wildly, shoving and pushing off Grant's body in every way possible, searching for a way out. Air, air, air, I fucking need air...

Then I feel Grant's arms around my lower torso and he pulls down forcefully as he pushes up against a rock on the bottom, and I feel half my hair get ripped out as I escape the confinements of Grant's dry top. Once freed, I kick fiercely towards the surface of the churning water, ignoring the cold biting at my skin. I break the surface, and the first breath I take actually feels like a gift from some holy being.

Then I remember that I'm in the middle of a river without a lifejacket, helmet, or boat. I lay on my back, put my feet up, and lift my butt, getting into the proper "swimmer's position." We practiced this numerous times in my youth to train for this very situation, except we'd always be wearing lifejackets. I guess the instructors assumed that no one would be dumb enough to enter whitewater without one on. Granted, our situation is extremely unusual, and now we are both being forced to keep ourselves afloat using only the air in our lungs and the muscles in our arms.

I'm sculling ferociously with my hands, because unfortunately, having little body fat is not helpful in any way if you're trying to keep yourself on top of the water. With every wave we hit water shoots into my nose, mouth, and eyes, and I have to struggle to get to the surface again. If we were in kayaks, this section would be easy and fun. It's continuous and fast and I slam into a couple of submerged rocks that would be really fun to boof. But for swimmers, this sucks. There are no eddies to swim into and there doesn't seem to be an end in sight, and the water is freezing and my whole body has gone numb. Honestly, I'm not so sure how much longer I'll be able to last before I literally become a human ice cube.

Grant's ahead of me and I can see his brown head bobbing on the surface of the water about fifteen feet downstream. I'd try to catch up if I were able to use my arms more, but the numbness creeping through them is making moving very difficult. To try to avoid sinking I fill my lungs to capacity and hold it for as long as I can before letting it out quickly and filling up again. This leaves me winded and light headed, but I figure that that's better than being at the bottom of the river.

I'm reminded of an article I once read in *Paddler Magazine* about a camp in Darnestown, MD called Valley Mill. There's this one award you can earn called the Red Shirt, and in order to get it need to be able to survive for five minutes with your hands tied to your feet, floating on the surface of the water. I read it and scoffed, thinking that that was the most pointless thing in the world and that you'd never need a skill like that in real life. Well, here I am, unable to use my arms and legs, stuck in a river without a lifejacket. Those folks over at Valley Mill actually are quite smart after all.

I'm beginning to doubt that this rapid will ever end when I hear a loud, shrieking whistle blow from behind me. At first, I think that I must be dreaming, because Grant is the only other human on this river and he is currently ten feet in front of me. But I look behind me anyway, and sure enough, I see a raft. There's a single person on it who's steering the boat alone. I use all my willpower and manage to wave my hand above my head, and shout, "Help!" I've always thought that rafts were stupid, pointless vessels for losers, but the driver on this raft somehow manages to arrive at my side in less than thirty seconds. The person, who turns out to be a she, drops her paddle and reaches her arms out.

"Come here!" she instructs, and I swim stiffly over, and she grips me under my armpits and hauls me aboard. She grabs her paddle again and goes over by Grant, and lifts him aboard as well. I'm lying on the bottom of the raft, staring up at her in awe.

"Hey," she says, glancing down at us. "I'm Savannah Wilson, but most folks 'round here know me as RS." I'm still in a state of shock and know that I'm staring at her open-mouthed, but I can't seem to stop.

"RS? What's that stand for?" Grant asks, and hearing his voice next to me breaks the spell. I look over him and he grins at me, his eyes sparkling. *We made it,* he seems to be saying. *And we're alive.*

"River Savvy. It's my rafting nickname." She turns to me, and gives me a gentle smile, and I feel like I'm nine years old again, and Jared's helping me out of the water after a swim. "And who are you, miss?"

"I'm Ginny," I say, finding my voice at last. "Ginny Kinsey."

"And I'm Grant," Grant says, sitting up in the bottom of the raft and extending his hand for Savannah to shake. "Thanks, for you know, pulling us out of the water."

"I was instructed to take a run down from Numbers to seek out a lost kayak trip. There were three people I was supposed to be looking for—a Ginny, a Grant, and a Jordan. Would you two be part of that?"

"Yeah," I say, my heart sinking. "We are."

"And what exactly happened that resulted in you floating down the Arkansas River without boats or gear, in the middle of a hail storm?" I realize that the hail has stopped, and that the sun is now out and is shining down on our little boat and lighting up the whole canyon.

"It's a very long story," Grant says, quietly. The life is gone from his eyes. "We were on the river during that flash flood." I hear Savannah inhale sharply, but she doesn't interrupt. "You probably saw a huge strainer on your way down here. During the storm a creek formed to the right of it, and Ginny and I went down it to avoid getting stuck. We thought Jordan was with us but it turned out that he wasn't…" Grant drops his eyes, hiding the grief in them. I feel my throat close up too, knowing that we didn't find him, knowing that we failed.

"Oh yeah, that was some strainer, I had to carry around it on the way down. And that must have been a pretty rough creek," Savvy says, peering at our faces and taking in our cuts, scrapes, gashes, and bruises. I bring a hand tenderly to my broken nose and find it huge with swelling. I must look like an abused Rudolf.

"You have no idea," I mutter. Savvy laughs.

"You guys probably found Green's Creek. It's only in at like, seven feet, which only happens during flash floods. You guys should consider yourselves lucky. That's the only part of this whole river, all creeks included, that I haven't run."

"You sound like you're pretty good," Grant says, a slight smile on his mouth that doesn't reach his eyes. Savvy laughs again. It's loud and full, and despite everything, it brings a smile to my face.

"Ah, sure. I know this river like the back of my hand, but that's about it. What about you two? Where are you from?"

"I'm from Maryland," I say.

"And I'm from West Virginia," Grant adds. "We met at the Ottawa a few weeks ago." A wistful expression passes over Savvy's face.

"Never really been out of the area," she says. She has an accent that I'd classify as "western", though I'm not that worldly so I don't know the proper term. It makes her sound half cowgirl and half badass, a description that seems to fit her pretty well.

"I've never been out here 'till now, either," I reply.

"How old are you, kid?" she asks.

"Uh, seventeen," I say, afraid that she'll scoff at my lack of ability, but she doesn't. She actually looks impressed.

"Well, I'm nineteen," she says. "And you've seen many more rivers than I have, I can tell. You any good?" I'm caught off guard by the question, but Grant replies for me.

"Yeah," he says. "Really good." I look over at him at surprise, and I find him looking at me, and as I meet his rich brown eyes, he shrugs. "It's true," he mouths.

"I'm glad I'm not the only one around here," she says, winking at me. She smiles again. Her face is tan, so tan that I think that maybe she actually isn't completely Caucasian. Her hair is dark and thick, and she has it pulled back beneath her blue Sweet helmet. She holds her head confidently but not cockily, and it makes me immediately trust her. She's the first female kayaker I've seen in a long while, and the only one I've seen around my age.

"How did you know we were lost?" Grant asks, and I realize that I was so relieved when she pulled us out of the water that I never wondered how she found out where we were in the first place.

"Well, Marty, after he left you guys at Numbers, asked the trip going out this morning to look for you guys at the takeout for Browns Canyon. You guys weren't there, so just in case, we decided to run a raft down here, to see what's up. And...from the looks on your faces, I'm guessing that guys are worried about Jordan."

"Yeah," we both say together. We're both looking at her, eyes wide, waiting her for her to save our world again, and she's looking down on us like a teacher about to tell a bunch of kindergarteners that recess is canceled for the day.

"I saw that strainer," she says, drawing her words out slowly. "The river's gone down so much that it left most of the branches exposed. There was no sign of a kayaker in them, and I kept my eyes peeled along the river, too, and found nothing. I did find a red tarp, some lifejackets, and a couple dry bags along the shore, and picked them up. I guessed they belonged to you guys." She gestures to red bundle next to her in the raft.

"Yeah, that'd be ours," Grant says, looking at her sheepishly.

"I knew I had found the owners when I saw you two in the middle of the river, lacking all the items that I found," she replies, a smile in her voice. "And you two must be freezing. What kind of trip leader am I, leaving my charges at the mercy of hypothermia?" She reaches into a dry bag of her own and reveals a blanket, two shirts, and two sandwiches in plastic bags. She throws the five things at us, and we accept them gratefully. I slip the shirt over my wet body. Grant and I lean against the front of the raft and we lay the blanket on top of both of us, snuggling together for warmth. He finds my hand under the blanket and squeezes it gently. I lean my head on his shoulder and he rests his head on top of mine.

"I miss him," Grant whispers into my ear. I squeeze his hand, feeling pain radiating off him in waves.

"I know," I whisper back. "I miss him, too." I close my eyes and lean against him, feeling the absence of Jordan like a vast void in my chest. He should be here, not me. This was his trip. His life. I had no right to mess with either.

"Guys, we're getting out at the Browns Canyon take out. I've radioed ahead that I found you and someone's meeting us there to take you to the CRA office. But if you want to come with me to continue looking, I'm willing to do that, too." What kind of question is that?

"That'd be great," I say. Part of me is feeling hopeful that maybe Jordan is actually just down the river a little ways, waiting for us to find him. But the other, larger part of me, doesn't want to reach the river's end where we'll have to say goodbye to Jordan forever.

"Could you get those people to bring boats?" Grant asks, and I hear something catch in his voice. "Jordan would want us to finish the run."

"Sure," Savvy replies softly. Her eyes are full of sympathy as she picks up a walkie-talkie and says, "Sammy! Come in! We need two additional kayaks, with paddles, if possible, at the Brown takeout."

"Sure thing, boss," comes the crackling response. Grant and I look at each other, and suddenly, neither of us can hold it together any longer. I'm the first to break, and he follows shortly after, and soon we're both bawling our eyes out into each other's shoulders. With every sob that rips through my body I remember something else about Jordan—the way his eyes lit up when he laughed, how cute he was the night we tried to party in Madison, and the easy way he ran his hand through his short hair. And with each memory that flashes by I cry harder and harder, gripping Grant as he grips me.

"Shit, Jordi, shit, shit, shit…" Grant is saying through his tears, and his use of Jordan's nickname and the agony in his voice as he uses it makes me cry even harder. As my sobs begin to subside, I wrap my arms tighter around Grant, who must be hurting way more than I could ever imagine.

I hear Savvy in the background, speaking instructions into her walkie-talkie, telling the person on the other end that there's a boater missing, and that they need to send out search parties. She turns to us and asks about the specifics of Jordan's appearance, and I sniffle out a brief description, crying all the while.

Jordan. Didn't. Deserve. Any. Of. This.

And neither does Grant.

As guilt overwhelms me, I think the truest what if of them all—if they had never met me, none of this would have ever happened.

"There's Sam," Savannah says, breaking into my thoughts. I gently unlock my arms from around Grant's now still form, and shake his shoulder gently.

"Hey," I say, my voice husky. "How 'bout we finish off this river the right way?" Grant lifts his head, and I see a flicker of determination in his red, puffy eyes.

"Yeah," he replies, his voice surprisingly calm. He wipes his eyes on the backs of his hands, runs a hand through his thick hair, and manages a small smile. "Let's do this thing."

Sam brought the boats to the takeout, and gives us both looks filled with empathy as we climb ashore.

"I'm Sam," he says, extending his hand. "We'll keep

our eyes peeled for Jordan at all our stations. We'll find him."

"Thanks," I say, shaking his hand and meeting his eyes.

"You guys have a good run," he says, and salutes. Grant salutes back, giving him a small smile.

"We will," he replies.

"I left you guys lots of food in the bag over there," Sam says, gesturing to a large dry bag lying next to our kayaks and paddles. "Along with a nice tent and lots of supplies. You won't need all of it, but you have a whole raft of room, so what the hell, right?"

"You really thought of everything," Savannah says. *Jordan would have, too,* I think.

"I do what I can," Sam answers. "Should I leave you guys alone with the water now? Or do you need anything else?" I'm really beginning to like this Sam guy. Maybe it's because he lightens the mood, but I'm pretty sure it's because he reminds me of Jordan. I suddenly want him to come with us.

"Could he come with us?" I ask, turning to Savvy. She ponders my request for a moment, then shrugs.

"I don't see why not. You up for a little adventure?" she asks Sam, and Sam grins.

"Overnight on the Arkansas? Dude, I'm in," he says, smiling at me. It's a real smile, with real happiness behind it, and it makes me feel the tiniest bit better.

"Cool," I reply. "Like you said, we got rafts of room." He laughs, and flicks his bleached blond hair out of his eyes.

"I'll need to grab my gear from my car, then. I'll be back in a few." He waves and dashes off into the woods.

When he returns, we put the gear in the raft and get ready to depart. The fifty some miles of river left will probably take us two to three days, depending on how long we stop for. So here I am, off on another adventure, with Grant beside me paddling a blue boat and me in an orange one, on the river for one last run. Sam and

Savannah are guiding the raft along behind us, but even with the two new additions to our group Jordan's absence is definitely the elephant in the room. I keep looking back, expecting to see a red boat, a blue helmet, his smiling face. But all I see is a stupid yellow raft and a whole lot of river. Jordan is still nowhere to be found.

That night we camp in high style. Sam brought a roomy, six-person tent, a camping stove, and those freeze dried camping meals that taste like crap and heaven at the same time. After days of living off Powerbars and beef jerky, it tastes pretty damn good. The stars are bright, reminding me of all the nights I spent camping out with Jordan and Grant, and as Grant and I stand on the shore gazing up at them, I know we're both thinking about the same thing.

Grant puts his arm around me and I wrap mine around his waist, and I pick out the big dipper and the little dipper, high in the sky. In the background, I can hear the laughing voices of Sam and Savannah as they hang around the campfire, and I can faintly smell smoke on the nighttime breeze.

Then I see a bright, electric streak fly across the sky, and both Grant and my eyes follow it as it crosses the black canvas. A lone, shooting star, the only one we've seen tonight. We both shut our eyes tight, and wish for the same thing, hoping with all our hearts that it will come true.

The light fades and with it, the hope the star brought. I'm back to missing Jordan. I lean into Grant, glad that there's someone else who I know feels my pain. I remember back to the waiting room, all that time ago, when Jordan had his head in his hands, waiting for news on Grant in the ICU. And now I look over at Grant, and I see that same despair written all over his face. I remember all their easy banter, their speechless communication, and most of all, how whenever I was around them, I knew that this was how a friendship was supposed to be. They made fun of each other, laughed at each other's stupid mistakes, and fought all the time, but through all of it, I know that they really, truly cared about each other. No matter what. For Grant, losing Jordan must be like losing his left arm.

I pull him close, and he leans into me and buries his face into my hair. We stand like this for a while, listening to the sounds of the insects and the gentle lap of the water.

"Grant! Ginny! You guys want marshmallows?" Savannah calls from the fire. I pull away from Grant and we make eye contact, nod at each other, and begin heading slowly back towards the campsite. We put smiles on our faces, put marshmallows on the ends of the sticks they hand us, and laugh and try to act like there's nothing wrong. I think we're trying to believe that ourselves. But as the fire is put out and we're immersed in the dark once more, it's hard to keep Jordan out of my mind. I toss and turn in the tent for a while before shoving my face in my pillow and forcing myself not to move, and slowly, I drift into a restless sleep.

I wake in the early morning and don't expect to see anyone else awake, but I glance to my left where Grant was sleeping and see that his sleeping bag is open and empty. Slightly concerned, I get up, pull a blanket around my shoulders and head out of the tent, making sure to be quiet so I don't wake Savvy or Sam.

I step out into the dawn and find the ground wet with dew. The air is heavy with moisture and smells strongly of summer, and I breathe it in, liking the feeling of the cool air in my lungs. I see Grant sitting on a rock by the river, staring out over the water. While I'm deciding whether or not he wants company, he notices me, and he gives me a small smile and gestures for me to come closer.

"Ginny," he murmurs as I approach. He stands and holds his arms open, and I fall into them. "I never told you, and with everything that's happened with Jordan, I wasn't sure if it was fair to him. But...I also know that if he were here, he'd want me to continue living my life..." I can see him battling the emotions inside of him, and I touch his cheek gently. "Anyway," he continues. "I just wanted to tell you that I love you." He doesn't give me time to respond, he just leans down and kisses me. For a moment, all our problems fade away, and it's just me, Grant, and the river beside us.

After a beautiful few minutes, there's a rustle in the bushes behind us, and Savvy appears.

"Sorry if I'm interrupting something," she says, winking at me. "But I made some breakfast, if you two are interested." She looks older in the sunlight without her gear on. Her hair has natural highlights and is long, pretty, and thick. She's wearing it down, and she runs a hand through it and yawns.

"Sure," we reply together, and follow her back towards the campsite, feeling better for the first time in a while.

Making out with Grant definitely wasn't a permanent fix, though. It was like any short burst of happiness—it makes you feel good for a while, but then it wears off, leaving you back where you started. Thankfully, being on the river makes me feel slightly better again. Kayaking does that. But the river is also where I knew Jordan the best, and being on it without him nearby makes me miss him more than ever.

We find a play hole and I manage to throw ends. Sam and Savvy whoop, and I look over at the eddy, trying to see if Grant or Jordan saw it, too, and only see Grant, who flashes me a thumbs up. My adrenaline rush from successfully cartwheeling fades much quicker than it should have as my heart sinks again, and I'm so distracted that I lose control of my edges and flip. I let the cold water rush around my face. As I roll up, I shake the water out of my eyes and paddle back up the eddy, ready for another surf.

Grant's in the hole now, and his face looks calm. For

once, there's no pain, guilt, or grief—I actually see a flash of a smile as he spins his boat around three times in smooth succession. He then begins back surfing, and he finds my eyes and meets them, then actually grins.

The river's a drug; I don't think I can say that enough. The pain of Jordan is fresh here, because every rapid, every hole, and every wave makes me think of his brilliant smile and bright red boat. But we also lost Jordan on the river. As I think about it now, that's probably how he'd want to go. He was doing something he loved more than anything, and maybe, just maybe, he died happy. Being here not only makes me sad, but it makes me feel closer to him. It's like he's here in spirit but not in body, and if I close my eyes and picture him next to me, it's like he never actually left us at all.

Seeing Grant smile, a real smile, one that reached his eyes, sends a shoot of warmth through my body. I grin back, and as Grant exits the hole, I splash him playfully with my paddle.

"You were shredding that up," I tell him.

"Thanks," he answers, sliding next to me into the eddy.

"Bet even Jordan would've been proud."

"Nah, he's more impressed with loops and throwing ends," Grant replies, and I search for grief in his voice and find none.

"You think he's here?" I ask quieter, putting a hand on Grant's skirt, keeping his boat close to mine. I start to trace the IR symbol with my pointer finger.

"Feels like it," Grant replies in a hushed voice. "Being out here...where I knew him so well..." I hear his voice begin to break and look up at him, but I find his eyes full of unexpected warmth. "We shared so many good times together out here. At the end of our senior year at NRA I swore that if I died the next day, it would be fine by me, because I would have experienced enough fun to fill a lifetime. Jordan agreed with me, saying that if it hadn't been for me and paddling, he wouldn't be anywhere. You know for us guys, it's really hard to say stuff like that, you know?"

"Yeah," I reply, feeling tears in my eyes, not from grief, but from the tenderness of the story. "Jordan's different, though." Grant's eyes focus on my own, and he gives me an odd look.

"Did you love him?" he asks softly. There's no jealousy in his voice, just honest curiosity. I tell him the truth.

"I don't know," I say. "I liked you from the beginning, Grant, from the moment you set foot in my campground. But then I met Jordan, and I began to like him, too. Not romantically, exactly, but more like the best friend I never had. You and him both. You both mean the world to me..." My voice trails off, and I feel my protective wall begin to crumble. I look up at Grant's deep brown eyes and feel like my entire soul is exposed, but for once, I don't feel afraid.

"I thought..." Grant mumbles, and stops, but I give him a look, asking him to continue. He does. "I thought you did. I was okay with it, too, because it's Jordan and he matters to me more than anyone. But then I actually started to wonder why I felt the way I did around you and why I've never felt like that around anyone, not even my girlfriend, before. Then I realized that I *did* care that Jordan liked you." His eyes find mine and they linger there, an almost shy smile on his lips.

"So I wasn't the only one who thought our first kiss was absolutely amazing?" I ask, smiling at the memory.

"No." Grant laughs quietly. "Jordan was furious, but I'm glad that I kissed you. If I hadn't, that cop might have taken you away, and I wouldn't have been able to ever kiss you again."

He raises his head to look over my own, and nods at someone behind me. "They're ready to go." I turn around and see Savvy and Sam float by, grinning and wet after several attempts at surfing.

"Let's do it," I say, letting go of Grant's boat and peeling out into the whitewater once more. I feel the force of the water behind my blade and I focus my mind once again on the river ahead, my mind slowly clearing. Soon the only things I'm aware of are my paddle, my boat, and the water in front of me. And Jordan. Somehow, he's here too. As I head down, I land every boof perfectly, I skirt the holes effortlessly and near the end of the strip of whitewater, I throw this massive wave wheel that I get air off of. When I land, the crisp water splashes me in the face and I feel myself grinning. I know I should be feeling guilty, that I'm here having an amazing time and Jordan isn't, but as I turn around and see Grant floating down in a bow stall, a smile on his face as well, I know we're both thinking the same thing. Jordan never left at all. He's here, with us, on the river. There's no way I could feel like this otherwise. In some obscure fashion Jordan has found a way to never leave the whitewater he loved so much. And in the process, he never left us, either.

That night we camp out in a little clearing in the middle of the Upper Big Horn Sheep Canyon. It's a nice site with pine trees and red rock walls rising up around us. We set up our tents and as we eat beef stroganoff stew around a campfire, we begin to tell stories. We learn about Sam's near death experience on the Colorado River and Savvy's adventures in British Columbia. Sam, I learn, is an ex-slalom boater who trained regularly at the whitewater center in Colorado. He was the third boat on the junior national team when he was 18 and while training intensely for his first senior national team trials, he injured his shoulder. He recovered and began training again, this time for the '08 Olympics. Unfortunately, at the trials in Charlotte, NC, he hurt his shoulder again, this time worse, and had to give up the sport for good. He shrugs as he tells us this, then smiles, saying that if he hadn't gotten hurt he would have never become a raft guide on one of the best rivers in the world. I look at him with new admiration now—if I had all my hopes and dreams of becoming a world class paddler taken away, I wouldn't be handling it all that well at all. My parents took kayaking away from me and I ran away from home. You can't run away from an injury, though. You're stuck with something like that for the rest of your life.

Savvy doesn't say much about herself but I get the idea that she's been a loner all her life, kind of like me. She's bold, self confident, but I also get the idea that she's loved at home and in turn loves others. She seems like the type of person who smiles a lot and makes people laugh without trying. She tells us a story about her first rafting trip on this very river, when she was five, and how she had fallen in and swam down a large section of Browns Canyon. When she got out, she told her parents that she wanted to be a raft guide when she grew up so no more little kids would end up falling into the water. Her mom, I learn, is a quarter Cherokee Indian and her dad is part Hispanic, which explains her skin tone. While she talks, there's something in her voice that draws me into her story. She's funny in the wittiest ways and smiles so effortlessly that I can't help but smile back.

"What about you two?" she asks, directing the question at Grant and me. "I'm sure you guys have tons of stories." I meet his eyes, and I know what he's thinking—every story he has to tell has Jordan in it. But he opens his mouth and begins talking anyway.

"I was thirteen and my parents took Jordan and me down to the Nantahala Outdoor Center for spring break. We were both fairly experienced by then and were excited to get on some new rivers." He's talking to the whole group of us, but every few words he flicks his eyes in my direction, like he's exclusively telling it to me. I give him a small, encouraging smile. He meets my eyes briefly before continuing. "We were running the Nantahala on the second day out. It was cold—probably below freezing, and our instructors had given us pogies and lots of layers to try to keep us warm. Being young and ambitious, we both tried surfing every hole we came across, and ended up getting quite wet. I remember trying to surf the wave Surfers, and flipping and getting my paddle stuck under my boat and taking a little while to roll up. And when I did, the first thing I saw was a snowflake fall onto my nose. Then I looked around and saw millions of flakes dropping around us. I dropped my paddle and held up my hands and tipped my head back, catching flakes on my tongue as I floated down the river. It was so magical. Jordan and I looked at each other and were both like, holy crap, this is awesome. We ran the rest of the river with the snow falling softly on our boats and our helmets." As he speaks, I feel warmth bubble up in my chest. The story isn't epic like some of the ones I have—it doesn't include running huge waterfalls or big rapids—but it's deeper than that. Being surrounded by the hidden beauties in nature is one of the best parts of paddling. But another, almost more significant aspect, is how being on the river brings people together. Grant and Jordan met on the river and forged a friendship deeper than the Grand Canyon and stronger than Earth's gravitational pull.

"Nice, Grant," Savvy comments, nodding at him. "Sounds sweet."

"Ginny?" Sam asks. "You have any stories?" I look at Grant and smile then shake my head.

"Nothing right now," I say. Even as the fire heats my face, I feel like I'm on the Nantahala, and there are snowflakes falling around me. Grant's there, Jordan's there, and we're both little kids again, learning about the wonders of paddling, not worried about our futures but focused on the awesome, beautiful present.

If only Jordan were here now.

"Hey," Savvy says, her voice soft, and both Grant and I look up. "You know, I'm really sorry about Jordan. We radioed in to all our stations along this river and they're all searching. They have helicopters out, too. If he's out there, they're going to find him."

"Only apologize to me if someone died..." I murmur, realizing for once, the truth in my coach's words.

"Thanks," Grant says. "For everything. For pulling us out of the water, for taking us down this stretch of the river, and for sending people after Jordan..." Savvy smiles at him, then at me.

"You guys are great," she says empathetically. "If I were Jordan, I'd want friends like you."

She's talking like he's not dead. There's hope. There has to be. Because right now, that's all we've got.

Grant sleeps with his arm draped over me, and I can't tell if it's on purpose or not. Maybe he wants to know that I'm here, that I'm not going to randomly disappear, like Jordan did. I think about the next day. We're going to reach the end of the river either at the end of tomorrow or the morning of the day after. Suddenly I remember my parents, and how we left that sign at Wausau, directing them to meet us at the river's end. Will they be there? Will they forgive me? Or will they lock me up in the back of the car and never let me out of their sight again? That's very possible. Looking like this, I doubt I'll ever be able to convince them that kayaking is safe. Right now, I have a broken nose, a black and blue face, and cuts, scrapes, and bruises everywhere else. I look like someone who just went through a blender. If I walk up to them and plead my case, they'll say I'm living proof that rivers are something that shouldn't be messed with. I press my face into Grant's shoulder. I have gained so much this trip, and yet I've lost incredible amounts as well. I left home with no idea what was ahead. I had no plan, no destination, only the need to keep kayaking. My life took a trip down a path this summer that I would have never, in my wildest dreams, ever expected.

This summer started with the end of junior year and high hopes for a summer of paddling. It started with days sleeping in late then hitting the water later, the river choice depending on my mood. Some days I'd stay local and just run the Potomac gorge, and others I'd get more ambitious and head up to the Yough and the Tygart in Deep Creek, MD, or go out to the New and the Gauley, over in Fayetteville. Those were the days when I was alone on the river. Depending on the people there, sometimes I'd get weird looks, raised eyebrows, or questions about my age, but for the most part, I was left alone with my thoughts. Looking back now, I'm not sure how I managed. I must have been ridiculously lonely.

Now as I lie here with Grant's arm draped over me I'm reminded that I'm no longer alone. I used to think true love doesn't exist. Now I'm not so sure. I don't know if what Grant and I have is love, it may not even be close—but at least it's a start. I've felt more alive with him than I have with anyone else. I would say that this has been the best summer ever, if Jordan were here. But he's not. Not right now, at least, and maybe...maybe not ever. If we lose him, neither Grant or I will ever be the same again, that's for sure. Not only was he Grant's best friend, but he meant a lot to me, too. I really don't know what we're going to do if we leave the Arkansas without him.

So as I drift off to sleep, I remember the summer I've had so far. It's definitely been a summer to remember. It's had astonishing highs and incredible lows, moments of terror, extreme adrenaline, excitement, happiness, and even love. This whole adventure has been a whirlwind of events and emotions.

I'm definitely not the Ginny I was at the beginning of the summer. That's for sure. Have I changed for the better? Worse? I guess I'll never know.

Then I remember back to that night at the beginning of our Arkansas trip, when we watched the meteor shower rain down on us. I remember my wishes, too. I wished for a safe trip. I wished for Grant. And I wished for Jordan to understand.

We had the opposite of a safe trip. Grant and I are a lot closer now, but that's partly because Jordan's not here, and because of that, he can't understand. *Don't focus on the bad. Focus on the good. Especially when it's all you've got.* Jared told me that once, a long time ago. I don't remember the context. I picture his face in my mind and feel a sharp pang. If only he had been there. Jordan would have never gotten separated from us if he had been leading the trip.

But I listen to him, because Jared, as I've learned, has a tendency to be right. I focus on the one wish that actually came true—Grant. I don't think about the events leading up to it, I just think about how it felt to have him hold me and mean it when the words "I love you" came out of his mouth.

I open my eyes and squint at Grant's face, so close to mine, in the dark. His hair is messy, his face is marred, but there's a slight smile on his mouth, like he's dreaming about something good. I lean forward and kiss his forehead gently.

"Sweet dreams," I murmur, before I snuggle into his side and close my eyes as well.

"Just got a radio from Royal Gorge and we have to get in by the end of today because they need us for a raft trip tomorrow," is the first thing I hear as I wake in the morning. A soft groan escapes my mouth. I feel Grant stir beside me.

"Okay," Grant mumbles and sits up. I stretch and look up at him, and he grins lopsidedly and runs a hand through his bed head hair. *He's really cute in the mornings*, I think. *Really, really cute.* I get a strong rush of affection for the boy next to me. I give him a small smile and as Sam and Savvy leave the tent to start breakfast, I lean up and kiss him gently. He slips an arm around my waist and kisses me back.

"Ready to put this river behind us?" Grant whispers into my ear. I feel his stubble of a beard brush against my cheek. I meet his eyes and rest my head on his chest for a moment, breathing in his smell.

"Am I ever," I reply, my eyes closed. We separate, Grant leaves, and I get my bathing suit on and follow him out of the tent.

The morning air is crisp and smells heavily of dew. The sunlight is bright but not hot, and bathes the whole canyon in a pale yellow. There's a faraway birdcall from over the water and the sound of squirrels chasing each other in the pines overhead. The beautiful smell of bacon wafts over me as I make my way towards our makeshift table.

"Bacon, Ginny?" Savvy asks, offering me a strip on the end of a fork. I take it gratefully and slip it into my mouth.

"Thanks," I reply with my mouth full. "This is delicious." She hands me a bowl of instant oatmeal as well. Sam is by the water, a Nalgene bottle in his hand and a water filter in the other. Grant is nowhere to be found.

"Where's Grant at?" I ask. Savvy shrugs.

"Said he had to take a dump. I think he's off in the woods somewhere. He's either doing that or he just needs some time alone." I'd say the latter.

"Thanks for the food, Savvy," I say. "And thanks for this trip, too." She meets my eyes and smiles.

"No problem, girlie," she replies, and I feel emotion well up in my chest and have to look away so she doesn't see my eyes fill with tears. Out of the corner of my eye I see her watching me with concern. "You okay? Did I say something?"

"Jordan used to call me that, is all," I say.

"Oh," she replies. "I didn't know." There's a short pause before she continues. "What was he like, Jordan? Did he mean a lot to you?" Her eyes are earnest and I get the feeling that she's actually curious, and that she's not just asking because she feels like she has to.

"He was amazing," I say, and then I tear up again, because I realize that we're talking about him in the past tense—Like he's really, actually, truly gone. "He always knew what to say to lighten the mood. He was funny, smart, a great paddler, and an even better friend. I only knew him for about two weeks, and it still kills me that he's not here anymore. If it hurts this much for me, I can't even imagine how bad it must be for Grant. He's known him forever." A tear falls slowly down my cheek and I taste its saltiness as it trickles into the side of my mouth.

"Loss is tough," Savvy says, "and life is messy. But that's how it's always going to be, you know? You just have to do your best to arrange your life into something you can live through. Something you can enjoy. And something that makes it worthwhile." I think about everything that paddling has given me, and all the problems that it's caused. Without it, I'd be nowhere. Because of it, I'm here—In the middle of the Arkansas River, with a guy that means the world to me and without the one who means the world to him. I don't know if my parents still love me, if my sister still loves me, or even if I have anywhere to go once we reach the end of this godforsaken river. *But at least I've come this far,* I think. There's no incredible joy without incredible loss, and paddling has given me both.

"You're right," I whisper to Savvy. "And I think I've found that thing." She gives me a questioning look.

"Kayaking," I say, and she grins.

"Without a doubt," she replies, and I grin, too.

We pack up camp quickly once we finish breakfast and head out onto the water. Grant is quiet and I don't bother him. Once on the river the mood lightens and I feel my body relax. There are railroad tracks running beside us beside the red rock walls, and Sam explains that the Royal Gorge Express passes through hear every three hours to carry tourists through. I don't see why anyone would want to ride in a train when you could be rafting or paddling, but I guess whitewater doesn't appeal to everyone like it appeals to me. The rapids are small here but continuous, and it's after about six miles that Sam informs us that we will be entering the Royal Gorge shortly.

"How soon is soon?" I ask, and he just smiles.

"You'll know," he replies, winking at me. I don't really understand what he means at first, so I just smile and nod in reply. We continue paddling in silence on relatively flat water for a little longer before I notice the walls beginning to seem a bit taller. Then the river curves slightly and we round a bend, and I see it. It's insanely high, dangerously narrow, and looks crazy thin from where we are now. It's the Royal Gorge Bridge—the highest suspension bridge in America.

"Holy shit," I say before I can stop myself. Sam hears me and flashes me a smile.

"Told ya so," he says, winking at me again.

"So, this is the Royal Gorge," says Grant, gazing at the bridge in awe. I look at him in surprise—those are the first words he's spoken all morning.

"This is the Royal Gorge," Savvy confirms. "Welcome to the Colorado's Grand Canyon."

Sure enough, as we get deeper and deeper into it, the walls of the canyon grow higher and higher and higher. Soon we're at the bottom of a deep, deep trench with red rock walls rising up on either side of us for hundreds of feet. I yell, "Echo!" And my voice bounces around the canyon for a good ten seconds. Grant catches my eyes and smiles a smile that actually reaches his eyes.

I paddle over to him and murmur, "This is epic." He nods wordlessly as he scans the colossal walls around us, a look of pure amazement on his face.

"Jordan would have loved this," he whispers.

"I know," I reply, taking in the canyon around me. "He would have loved this so fucking much."

"When we planned this, we thought this was going to be epic. But I had no idea it was going to be *this* epic."

"I'm so sorry he's not here, Grant. I'm so, so sorry…" I feel my tear ducts begin to open, but Grant catches me off guard before I get the chance to cry. He drops his paddle and slips an arm around my neck and kisses me, just as we hit a couple waves and a train rumbles past on the track next to us. I hear some whoops from the train and someone even shouts, "Get a room!" but I'm so caught up in the moment that I don't care. Grant's mouth is soft yet urgent on my own, and he pulls away before I have a chance to respond.

"I know," he murmurs. "But right now, I'm just happy to be here with you." The train is still chugging past, and I wave at the passengers and many of them wave back, and a few even snap pictures. I look back at Grant and meet his gorgeous brown eyes, and I know that we're both thinking the same thing—this is fucking incredible. I give a peace-out symbol to the remaining car, pick up my paddle, and accelerate through the waves. The sun is bright, the sky is clear, there are no rain clouds anywhere, and I know this is going to be a great day.

It's nearing dusk when I see the takeout in the distance. We've just come out of what's called the "Cañon City Wave," a nice play hole that served as a great way to end our day on the water. The raft is ahead of us, and Sam and Savvy are unloading and trying to negotiate a shuttle. There's a boat ramp and I see a parking lot and people milling around. Apparently the Royal Gorge is a popular tourist spot for more people than just paddlers. I'm laughing at one of Grant's jokes when I see it. Or rather, *him*.

There's a lone figure sitting on a ledge of rock about twenty-five feet before the takeout. He's wearing a baseball cap and a bandana wrapped around the lower half of his face, so he looks like a mix between a ninja and a cowboy. It looks like he had to climb out along the rock wall to get there. I peer at the part of the canyon wall he would have had to climb across, and it looks nearly impossible. I'm still trying to figure out how the hell he managed it when I hear Grant inhale sharply, then mumble, "There's only one guy I know who could boulder that." I look at him.

"What?" I ask. Grant shakes his head, as if he's trying to clear a thought from his mind.

"There's no way," he mumbles. "It's not possible." It doesn't seem like he heard me.

"Grant," I say louder. "What is it?" Finally, he turns and looks at me.

"Remember me telling you that Jordan climbs?" Grant's eyes are closed now, and he shakes his head violently. Then he opens them and fixes me with an intense stare, his eyes wide. "But that has nothing to do with this. Nothing at all. Absolutely nothing at all..."

Then the pieces click together in my head. Grant told me that Jordan was a great climber, meaning that he could have gotten onto that ledge. As I scrutinize the figure on the rock, I notice the person's big shoulders, and the way he takes the cap off his head to run a hand through his hair. It's short, and even from this distance, I can tell that it's brown. Hope begins to build up in me, but I quickly crush it. There are millions of guys out there who have big shoulders, short brown hair, and a knack for rock climbing. This is just an easy coincidence.

But as we come closer, more details seem to match Jordan's description. I see the writing on his shirt and see that it's the quick-dry, navy blue one that he had packed in his dry bag for our trip. He's wearing the kayak booties that I've seen him wear every time we've been on the water. And then his eyes met mine, and I see that they were light blue. Jordan's exact shade of light blue. Grant's silent beside me, but I see his eyes growing wide, a mix of hope and fear in them. Then the person stands, pulls his bandana down below his mouth, and takes the hat off his head. His face is marred, with dried blood surrounding a cut on his right cheek, and there's severe bruising around his left cheekbone. Grant begins to paddle faster.

"Jordan!" he yells, his voice cracking. "What the hell...?" I'm too shocked to move. My brain doesn't seem to be functioning. But even so, there's no doubt that the man standing on that ledge is the same man that we thought we lost on the river only three days before. Somehow, Jordan Bolton is standing, alive, in front of us.

"Jordan!" Grant yells again. "Holy shit, man! You're alive! You're alive! Oh my fucking God you are alive!" Grant reaches Jordan's ledge, gets out of his boat, and throws his arms around Jordan. I see his shoulders shaking as he begins to sob. I begin to paddle faster as excitement begins to flood my brain. Jordan's alive. Jordan's here. Jordan isn't at the bottom of the river. I feel tears begin to flow out of my eyes as well as the magic of this miracle truly hits me. Jordan isn't dead. Jordan isn't dead. A burst of happiness so strong runs through my chest that I'm surprised it doesn't burst open. I'm about to reach the ledge and join in the group hug when Jordan loses it.

"What is your problem?" he screams. "Why are you acting like you actually care? I don't want you anywhere near me!" He shoves Grant away from him violently, and he loses his balance and falls into the river next to me. I reach out an arm and grab onto him. My eyes are wide with shock, and I see surprise, hurt, and anger written all over Grant's face as well.

"What?" Grant and I exclaim.

"Don't act like you don't know what you did!" Jordan accuses, jabbing a finger at us. "You *knew* I wasn't okay and yet you didn't do anything about it! I could have been dead. Hell, I almost *was* dead. And what did you two do? You continued the fucking river without me! And you *knew*! You knew all along that I wasn't okay!" Grant and I are staring at him, completely speechless. First, we find Jordan, who we thought was dead and gone at the bottom of the river. Then, we go up to tell him how happy we are to see him, and what does he do? He starts screaming at us. He starts trying to tell us that we did something wrong. Suddenly I'm mad.

"Of course we knew that you weren't okay!" I scream back. "What did you think we did? Throw a party? You think *Grant,* the person who knows you better than anyone else, did anything *but* worry about you when we found you were gone? We cried for days, Jordan! We thought you were somewhere at the bottom of the river! We looked and looked and looked, and notified search parties, and they looked and looked and looked, and then we decided that maybe you'd *want* us to finish this river, if you were alive. We ran the rest of this river for you, Jordan! I haven't been able to go through a single minute of the past three days without thinking about you! And here you are, accusing *us* of not caring?" I'm vaguely aware of tears streaming down my cheeks but I'm too caught up in my livid rant to care. I feel Grant's hand on my arm and look down at him, but he's focused on Jordan.

"What?" Jordan says, looking at me in the eye. His voice is softer, less accusatory.

"You heard what she said," Grant says, his voice low, menacing, almost. "I almost considered ending it for myself after I thought you lost your life in the river. Looks like I would have been doing it for nothing, then." He lets go of my boat and swims over to his own, and pulls himself into it with ease. I paddle over to where his paddle is floating a little downstream and toss it to him. Then we both turn and look back at Jordan. He's staring at us, mouth slightly open, face colored with rage.

"You have always been an excellent liar," he hisses at Grant. "I know how you feel about her. And you knew how I felt about her, too. Then I go ahead and disappear, and bam, you see the opening you've been waiting for—"

"This is not about me!" I shout, interrupting him loudly. I drop my paddle on my skirt and throw my hands in the air. Anger is pulsing through me, stronger than before.

"Then who is it about? Huh?" Jordan sneers, turning to glare at me. "I wouldn't have let you come if I knew you were going to fuck up my life." My jaw drops and any retort I had stored drains quickly away. Jordan's words feel like a direct blow to my gut.

Without waiting for a reply, Jordan boulders across the stretch of rock separating him from the takeout faster than

I thought was possible, leaving Grant and me alone to digest his actions. I feel Grant's hand on my back and I lean into him, not sure what to think.

"What the hell was that?" I whisper. I feel him shiver and realize that he must be quite cold after being submerged in the alpine water.

"I have no idea," Grant replies. I sense a million different emotions in his voice and know that he's just as confused as I am.

"I was so happy to see him alive," I murmur. "And then..."

"It was wrong of him to say that," Grant says quietly. "Some of the other stuff seems like a possible misunderstanding. But he had no right to tell you that you don't belong here." My heart begins to throb rapidly in my chest and a sense of dread wells up in me. Out of all the things that Jordan said, his parting words are what stuck with me the most. Not because of how much they hurt, but because of how much I fear that they are actually true. I think back to everything they've told me about life without me and then to everything that's happened since I've been here, and can't help but draw the conclusion that everything would have been so much better if I hadn't showed up at all.

First off, they would have scouted that rapid on the Ottawa, and neither of them would have ended up in that hole. Grant would have stayed out of the hospital, and they would have been able to run the St. Lawrence and all the other rivers that they had planned on going to. Secondly, I wouldn't have been there to screw up the chemistry of the trip. Neither of them would have fallen for me because they wouldn't have known that I exist. The list goes on and on and on...

Then Jared's words cut through me, stronger than they ever have before. *You're wallowing in self-pity. Stop it. It's pathetic. You can't change the past. Move on, Ginny. Make sure the next minute is better than the one you're in now.* How is it that Jared always comes and rescues me in the exact moments when I need it most? Is his brain somehow wired to my own? Or is my instinct just a lot smarter than I've given it credit for? My head is still pressed into Grant's chest and I sit back up. A breeze hits my face and its refreshing coolness brings me back to the present.

"You okay?" Grant asks, looking at me with concern in his eyes. I give him a small smile.

"Yeah. I think we owe Jordan an explanation," I reply, my voice stronger than I expected it would be.

"Yeah, I guess so," Grant says, picking up his paddle and placing a blade in the water. "Now that I know he's alive, I'd really like to have my best friend back." His tone is light but I know that he really means what he's saying, probably a lot more than he's letting on. Jordan's alive. Jordan's alive. I don't care if he's mad at me or even if he wishes that I never came into his life. What matters is that he's alive.

As we near the boat ramp, I see Sam and Savvy's raft pulled off to the side on a strip of grass, and I see Savvy on a bench, Jordan next to her. Jordan's ear is by her mouth and she's speaking urgently to him. I see his shoulders moving up and down as he cries, and Savvy's hand massaging his back in soothing circles. Sam jogs down the ramp as we approach.

"Hey, guys, I guess you saw that we found your missing man," he says, grinning at both of us. We both grin, realizing how lucky we are.

"I know! I can't believe he's here!" Grant exclaims. Sam grins wider.

"It's a miracle! He told us what happened, and it's pretty insane. You know that log that you guys were talking about? The huge strainer that you didn't see a way around? Well, it turns out that there *was* a way around it. To the far, far left. And that's where Jordan went." Grant and I exchange a surprised glance. *Talk about a decision that decides your fate,* I think. If I had gone left instead of right, I wouldn't have gone down that death channel. But then again, if I had been with Jordan, the whole situation would have been reversed. "He continued down a long stretch of the river, until the section of intense whitewater ended and the rain let up and he was able to get out of his boat. He climbed through the woods and decided that he should try and get help because he thought you two were in trouble. He found a town and got a ride back to the rafting office at Pine Creek, and asked if they knew anything about the whereabouts of you guys. They told him that you were running the river to Royal Gorge, and ran down here to meet you." Some part of this story isn't matching up. Then it hits me.

"Wait, you said he came by the office—why didn't you notify us? Didn't you send out search parties? Did you notify them that you found him?" I ask.

"We have now," Sam says, grinning wider. "Everyone is so relieved. We asked that same question to the people up at Pine Creek, wondering why they didn't recognize him. They told us that he was wearing a bandana over his mouth and a baseball cap pulled low over his eyes, I guess to hide his torn up face."

"And once he found out that we were running the river together..." Grant breathes beside me, and suddenly, I understand why Jordan's so pissed at us.

He thought that we knew he was dead and went ahead and ran the river anyway. He was infuriated that we seemingly took advantage of his absence and hooked up because he wouldn't be there to stop us. But that's not the truth *at all*. But he had no way of knowing any of that.

"Ginny!" The sound of my name breaks me away from my thoughts. I look around for the source and see my sister standing a little ways away. Next to her, one on each side, are the two people who I never wanted to see again—Mom and Dad. And behind them, a little ways back, is Justin, with a cast on his arm. I get out of my boat slowly and place it beside the raft. Grant comes up and squeezes my shoulder.

"I have to do this alone," I whisper. I meet his eyes, and he gives me a nod of encouragement.

"Go get 'em, girlie," he replies, smiling. I hold his gaze for a moment longer before walking slowly over to my happy little family reunion gathering by the riverside.

"Ginny!" Casey exclaims, and runs forward and throws her arms around me. Her enthusiasm catches me off guard. I distinctly remember telling her to go home at the Starbucks in Omaha, and I wonder what the hell she is doing here now.

"Uh, hey, Casey," I mumble into her hair. I look over her head at my parents standing behind her. They both frown when they see my face.

"Grace! What happened to your face?" Mom asks, looking more concerned than I've seen her in awhile. Dad gives me a once over as well and gives me a disapproving look.

"You should have seen the other guy," I say, giving a weak smile. Casey laughs but my parents continue to stand there, staring at me. Justin walks up and stands beside Mom, his arms crossed, and he fixes his eyes on me as well.

"How was the river?" Mom asks. The excitement in her voice is so fake, I almost want to throw up.

"It was great," I say, keeping my voice level. "Thanks for asking."

"Long time no see, huh, kiddo," Dad says, raising his eyebrows. "Are you going to explain your sudden disappearance?" I take a deep breath and swallow hard. From out of the corner of my eye, I see someone walk up behind me. I turn slightly and see Jordan, and he gives me a small smile. *I'm sorry,* his eyes are saying. *I'm so, so sorry.* To my left, a little ways over, I see Savvy and Grant, standing next to each other. Savvy meets my eyes and mouths, "He knows." I nod at her and smile gratefully, before turning my attention back to my parents.

"I left because I had to," I say, my voice firm and confident, hiding my nerves. "Taking away kayaking was like taking away my right arm. I have to paddle, and you guys didn't understand that...by taking it away you were asking for me to do something rash. I'm not saying that it was the right thing to do, but I am saying that it was what I needed to do." Dad's giving me one of those, "Good try, but I'm still right," looks, and I force myself to swallow the anger building up inside of me so it doesn't come boiling out and exploding all over the place.

"The only things you need in life are air to breathe, shelter, food, and water to drink. *Kayaking* falls under none of those categories," Dad says. There's a smug look on his face that makes me want to punch him in the mouth.

"I guess you've never been passionate about anything, huh, Dad," I say, trying to keep the bile out of my voice. He laughs. My hands tighten into fists, and I feel Jordan's arm on my elbow.

"Do you even know what a passion is, Grace?" he asks. "That's just a petty name kids give things they think they like to do. This is just a phase you're going through. In a few years, kayaking's going to seem like a childhood joke." I feel heat rush to my face, and the next words I say through clenched teeth.

"Right. That's why I've spent the last eight years of my life in the sport. I never got any support from either of you, but I didn't let that stop me. And you know why I've done it all these years? Despite all the shit you give me, and all the work I have to go through to make it work? Because I love it. And if you don't believe me, you should just turn around and go home and *leave me alone.*" I know I've pushed it over the edge with that last sentence when I see the vein bulge in Dad's forehead. I feel Jordan's hand tighten around my arm.

"But I guess you ended up getting something good out of everything, huh, Ginny?" These next words completely throw me off guard as Mom speaks them. Something good? Of course I got something good! I got a million good things out of this experience, but not one of them would qualify as good under my parents' standards. I stand there open mouthed for a moment and she takes this as a cue to continue. "You know, the scholarship offering. At the University of Colorado?" She's raising her eyebrows at me in that "surely you haven't forgotten" way. My eyes bulge out of my head slightly and I turn to look at Casey. She's grinning broadly and nods eagerly at me.

"Yeah, Ginny," she says, her voice coated with fake enthusiasm. "You know that school who had scouts in Wausau looking for kayakers, the one who interviewed you? Then you filled out all that paperwork. I know you did, because you had me proof read your essay. I even have a copy here." She holds out a stapled bunch of papers with the words "Kayaking is my Life" at the top. I snatch it from her and scan it, finding bits and pieces of school essays, college application essays, and even poems that I wrote in it. Casey really went all out.

"I had no idea there were even schools that had ridiculous things like kayaking teams," Mom continues. "But when Casey informed us of your scholarship invitation, we finally understood why you continued with it all these years. You knew it would be your ticket to college!" My mom's face breaks out into a wide grin. Jordan is completely still beside me. I see Grant out of the corner of my eye, a baffled expression on his face. I look down at Casey, who's still smiling her fake smile, but it's starting to look a little bit strained.

I think back to the trip that we just completed. I remember all the good times—Cole's Hole in Claydale, the days in Wausau, how bright the stars shone at night, and the first days on the Arkansas. I remember the bad times, too—almost losing Grant on the Ottawa, the love triangle drama between the three of us, and thinking Jordan was dead for a good three days. I've had enough experiences from both ends of the spectrum to last me a lifetime, and I've learned more from them than I have anywhere else. I look at Grant again, and a rush of affection for him floods me, and I look at Jordan beside me, and he meets my eyes and gives me a small smile. I think of the friendship they had before I came and the twisted one they had after I came into their lives. I think about the misunderstanding between the three of us that almost chased Jordan away forever. I look at my parents who both have hopeful, expectant looks on their faces, and at Casey, who has now given up smiling and is regarding me with an urgent expression. I look at Justin, standing behind them, and think about the lie that brought him here as well, a lie that has most definitely broken us apart for good.

I've had enough hectic living to last me for a while. *I owe my parents at least the truth,* I think. Lies only end in people getting hurt. I've hurt people who really matter to me in these past few weeks, all because I felt like being reckless and running away from home and spontaneously joining trips that I wasn't originally supposed to be a part of. I don't think I can live with hurting anyone else. I meet Grant's eyes and mouth, "Sorry." Understanding of what I'm about to do floods his eyes and I speak before he can try to stop me.

"There's no scholarship," I tell my parents. As I say this, I see the light slowly fade out of their eyes. "Casey made that up to try to get you to not be mad at me. I came out here because I wanted to. There was nothing behind my madness. Just...well, me." I give them both a small smile, wondering what punishment is in store for me.

"Well, then," Dad says, his voice surprisingly level. "Looks like we're going to be having a lovely ride home together, huh, Grace. Some quality time in our house with your books will be good for you."

"And you're going to have to explain that broken nose, too," Mom says, eyeing my face. "But we've got a long drive ahead of us. We have all the time in the world to, uh, *talk* about your little adventure." She gives me a sweet smile and then turns to Jordan beside me.

"You must be one of Grace's friends," she says, holding out her hand. "I'm Nicole, her mother. This is Rob, her father." They shake hands.

"Pleasure to meet you," Jordan says. I tap Mom on the shoulder.

"I need to change and get my boat and gear together. Is that okay? I'll be back in fifteen minutes." Mom and Dad exchange a look, and then nod at me.

"Fine," Dad says. "But fifteen minutes. No more." They both begin to walk away towards a building labeled "Gift Shop" and as they leave, Casey jumps in front of me.

"What the heck, Ginny?" she says, throwing her hands in the air. "I worked hard on that essay! And it was such a good plan! Why did you throw it all away?" I give her a long look.

"It was a great idea," I tell her. "But it wouldn't have worked in the long run. What would they have done when the letter never came? When they called the office for details and found out that kayaking teams don't exist? It would have backfired on us, Case. I'm sorry." Casey mumbles something under her breath. I give her a quick hug before turning to Justin, who's leaning against a tree, texting.

"Justin," I say, and he doesn't look up, so I walk closer and say it louder. "Yo. Justin." He slowly raises his eyes to meet my own.

"Yes?" he asks, his voice low.

"Why on earth did you go along with this?" He shrugs nonchalantly.

"She had already dragged me halfway across the country. I have nothing to do this summer. There was nothing to lose, really. Well, except you." He drops his eyes back to his phone. I walk closer so I'm standing right in front of him.

"I didn't want it to end like that, Justin. I really didn't. I'm really, truly sorry. You have every right to be pissed at me." He doesn't say anything; he keeps his eyes on his glowing phone screen. I try again. "I'm not looking for forgiveness or anything near it. I just want you to know that I did care about you. You made high school bearable and I want to thank you for that. I also think you deserve much, much better than me." He still remains silent, but his thumbs stop moving over the keyboard. "I'll see you at school," I say finally, and begin to walk away. I'm halfway to the bench where Grant and Jordan are sitting when he finally speaks.

"See you, Ginny," he says, and when I glance over my shoulder he raises his good arm in farewell. I raise mine in return, meeting his blue eyes for one last time. Looking back, our time together wasn't all that bad—it's just that compared to being with Grant, my time with Justin looks bland, dull, and horribly uneventful in comparison.

Jordan gets up and jogs over to Justin, a guilty expression on his face. As he approaches the tree he begins talking to him in a low voice and every now and then he reaches out and pats Justin's shoulder awkwardly. Seeing Jordan trying to make up for fracturing Justin's arm makes me smile. We all have a lot of apologizing to do.

I reach the bench and sit down next to Grant. We sit in silence for a moment before Grant speaks.

"Why'd you do it?" he asks. I look up and meet his eyes, seeing a mixture of confusion and hurt in them.

"I have to go home," I say, my voice apologetic. I feel tears stinging at the back of my eyes, but I know I have to do this. "If I don't leave now I'll never leave. As much as I wish it were, this isn't my life. This is yours. I need to go back, finish school, plan my own gap year. This isn't about you, Grant. This isn't about Jordan, either. I've had the best summer ever, though. And I have you to thank for that." I lean over and wrap my arms around his neck and bury my face into his bare shoulder. He doesn't argue with me, he just wraps his arms around me and holds me tight.

"It has been a great summer," he murmurs into my hair. "When we get a chance, would you mind if we visited you in Maryland?"

"I'd love that," I say, tipping my head up to look him in the eye. I lean up and put my mouth on his, and we share one last, passionate kiss as the sun begins to sink behind the mountains.

If I've learned one thing this summer, it's that you can't force love. It either comes or it doesn't. It's kind of like a river—if you end up falling on the right wave, you may end up having the ride of your life.

A raft pulls into the takeout with two kayaks in it, one that's purple and the other that's bright green. I jog over, smiling.

"Hey," I say to the man on board.

"Hey, you must be Ginny," he replies, grinning back. "Once RS found you guys she radioed in for someone to pick up your boats. I can't believe you guys survived Green's, that's one hell of a creek." He beaches the raft and hops out, and I help him drag it to shore. I grab my boat and he grabs Grant's, and we lay them on the grass.

"It wasn't really intentional…" I reply, and he laughs.

"How was it? I've heard it's super sketchy, especially at that level."

"Terrifying is a better word for it. It was a crazy ride," I reply, shuttering as I remember how out of control I felt.

"Sounds pretty epic," the guide replies.

"Eh, I wouldn't exactly recommend it," I say. "But I guess I'm probably the wrong person to ask." I extend my hand to the guide. "Hey, thanks so much for grabbing our boats. It must have absolutely sucked to portage them over those rocks." He shakes my hand, grinning.

"It was no problem, really. I'm glad I could help. I'm David, by the way. It's a pleasure to meet you."

"You guys have an awesome company down here," I say, meaning it. "I owe you guys my life. Really." He takes his helmet off his head and runs a hand through his sandy hair.

"Savvy's sick, there's no question about it," he says, and I can tell from his tone that I'm not the only one who admires her.

"For sure," I reply. "I have to head off, but it was really great to meet you." David raises a hand in farewell.

"Good luck, kiddo. Maybe I'll see you around." I raise my hand in return, then grab my boat and head up to the car. Once there, I search the parking lot for Grant and see him talking to David, a grateful smile on his face and his boat already on his shoulder.

As I lift my boat onto the roof of the car, the truth hits me in the chest. It's over. My epic ride on my perfect little wave is over. Tomorrow I'll wake up and there will be no Grant next to me, no Jordan to make me laugh, no river to run, no adventure to plan. In a mere ten minutes I will be back to being Ginny Kinsey, the rebel girl, the loner, the freak. No one will see me as the cool, strong, talented, funny Ginny, because the only two people who see me in that light aren't going to be with me at the end of today.

But maybe that's just the attitude that I've developed over the past few years. Maybe, if I opened up more, other people will like me for who I am. Maybe Grant and Jordan aren't the only two people in the world who I can befriend. Maybe I just need to try harder.

I change out of my wet gear in the bathrooms and when I emerge, I see Jordan and Savvy next to each other on a bench. Jordan's head is bent towards Savvy's and if I didn't know them, I'd think they were a couple chilling after dinner. I step a bit closer so that I can hear what Jordan's saying.

"...we're headed for Washington. There are great creeks up there and we've picked out some of the best to run. I'm so stoked, I've never been up there before and I can't wait to check it out."

"That's weird, because I think a group of guys and I are heading up there as well. Maybe we'll see you."

Jordan gives her one of those smiles that he usually reserves for me. "That'd be awesome," he replies. "And you're obviously a good girl to have around."

"Nah, I was just doing my job," she says, waving away Jordi's compliment. "You would've done the same thing."

"You wanna meet up somewhere? I'm sure Grant wouldn't mind," Jordan suggests. "We could paddle some stuff together, keep each other company."

"Sounds like a plan," she agrees, flashing him a smile. Their eyes lock and I look away, not wanting to invade on a private moment.

A burst of jealousy shoots through me at the thought of Savvy being there without me. What if she decides to join in their group and ditch her own? She'll fill my place, take over my role as the only girl on the trip, and steal the attention of the two guys who I've become so incredibly close with over the past few weeks. What if she's better than I was? What if they like her so much more that their memories of me end up fading, and I become just another girl, completely insignificant in their lives? I know that it was my decision to leave, not theirs, but it's hard to accept that I won't be with them after today. I shove the negative thoughts away—Savvy saved my life. She deserves to be with them just as much as I did.

I see Grant tying a boat on the back of a trailer with Sam next to him, his head turned towards Savvy and Jordan. He catches my eye, smiles, and begins to walk over. I run over to meet him and sink into his arms.

"You think Jordi's found a girl?" he whispers into my hair. I smile into his shirt.

"Possibly. Sorry I'm leaving you to third-wheel it," I say. I lean my head into his chest and breathe in the familiar scent of river and mountain air. "You know, I'm really going to miss you." He's silent for a moment before replying.

"You have no idea," he finally says, so softly that I can barely hear him. "God, Ginny. Losing you is like losing Jordan all over again."

"I'll call," I reply. "Every night. If you don't get service, I'll leave a message." It's then that I realize that he's crying. He reaches into his pants pocket, pulls out an old receipt and a pen and scribbles a phone number down.

"Here. I don't think you have my number," he says, sniffling slightly. I take the paper from him and tuck it safely away in my own pocket.

"Thank you," I whisper.

"You'd better call. Or else." He pulls away so he can look me in the eye. His eyes are watery and there's a lone tear trickling down his cheek. I reach a finger up and wipe it off gently.

"Do you think your plan will end up working?" he asks. I pause to think about that for a moment. My parents seemed really, really mad when they first saw me—but I guess that wasn't totally unreasonable, I did run away from home, and I did break just about every rule they had set in place for me. Maybe they'll calm down on the ride back, and I'll find out that their attitudes about paddling have changed for the better. Then I realize that it doesn't really matter, because October is right around the corner.

"It was a great idea, and it was executed flawlessly. And even if it doesn't work, I'll find a way to get out there," I reply. "Nobody's gonna be able to keep me away from the river." Grant smiles and my heart warms. I'm going to miss him so much.

"I know," he murmurs. "You never give up. That's one of the things I love about you." I take in his beautiful brown eyes and his mop of hair, sticking up from being on the river. I take in his bruises from the Arkansas and the curve of his mouth, his broad shoulders and tan skin, and the way his eyes glow when they meet mine. I'm about to kiss him one last, final time when I hear a yell from across the parking lot.

"Ginny!" my mom yells. "Fifteen minutes is up in two!" I resist the strong urge to give her the finger.

"Nice mom you got there, Ginny," Jordan says, coming up from behind me. I whirl around and throw my arms around him. As his strong arms wrap around my body I begin to cry, too.

"I'm so glad you're okay," I whisper into his shirt. He laughs quietly.

"I'm sorry I was such a jerk earlier. I really, really am. I hope...I hope that's not how you remember me." The guilt dripping from his mouth is almost tangible. I pull away and look him in the eye.

"Jordi," I say, my voice wavering slightly as I hold back a sob. "Don't worry. You're too amazing for me to remember anything but the good stuff." I wrap one arm around Jordan and my other around Grant, and I spend the last minute of my adventure wrapped in the arms of the two greatest people on the planet.

"That was a hell of a trip," Jordan says as we finally break apart. I take one last look at him, then at Grant, and finally, at the river beside us. The sound of whitewater is in the air along with the smell of the great outdoors. I breathe in deeply, savoring the moment, tucking it away into the corner of mind so I never, ever forget it.

"One of the best," Grant agrees.

"Handshake?" Jordan suggests, and tears begin to fall as we run through the handshake Grant taught me all that time ago in the restaurant at Wausau.

A car horn honks in the parking lot.

"You guys are the best," I tell them. "Shred up Washington for me, okay?"

"No problem, girlie," Jordan says, winking at me. A tear escapes out of his eye as well.

I hear the car horn again. I can't keep my parents waiting any longer.

"Bye, Grant, Jordan," I say as I turn to leave. "And thanks. Thanks for everything." I've just turned towards the car when I feel Grant's hand on my shoulder.

"Ginny!" he says. "Wait. Here." He holds out a little paper bag and curls my fingers around it, then brings my hand to his mouth and kisses it. "Take care," he murmurs. I meet his eyes for one last, fleeting moment, before a yell from my dad pulls me away towards my car, towards the rest of my life.

"Bye!" I yell over my shoulder as I turn to leave.

"Bye, Ginny!" Grant and Jordan chorus, and I turn to look over my shoulder one more time and see their arms raised in farewell. Then I head towards my car, tears running freely down my face, leaving my friends, and the river, behind.

As I slide into the backseat, I notice that Casey isn't beside me and that Justin is nowhere to be found.

"We sent your sister with Justin," Mom informs me. "It's just us for the long ride home!" Dad eyes me in the rearview mirror, and I sigh, wiping the tears away from my eyes. This is one road trip that I'm not looking forward to.

I swivel around in my seat and watch Grant and Jordan get smaller and smaller as we exit the lot. I know they can't see me but I wave frantically anyway. When we turn left out of the parking lot and the two guys disappear from my view, I turn my attention to the bag I'm still clutching in my hand.

I open it slowly, not sure what to expect. It's a bag from the Royal Gorge Gift Shop, and as I reach my hand in, my fingers come in contact with a small, metal, cylindrical object. I wrap my hand around it and pull it out of the bag, and when I uncurl my fingers, I find a flashlight sitting in my palm. Wrapped around it is a piece of paper, and I unroll it. On it I see Grant's handwriting, and it reads:

Ginny—

This is to help avoid raccoon attacks in the future. I love you.

Grant

Epilogue

It's October 16th, 2010, also known as my 18th birthday. I'm excited about this for a number of reasons, the main one being that as of today, or, more precisely, as of 1:21 PM, I am legally an adult in the United States of America. I am no longer bound to my parents and I can, to say this simply, do whatever the hell I want.

It's a Saturday, but even so, I'm awake and it's only 6:11 in the morning. It's still dark outside, but I roll out of bed anyway. I need an early morning paddle before my mall shopping date with my buddies. Tonight's a big night for all my friends—it's homecoming, the biggest party of the year, and though I will not be attending, many of my friends are. Sara's going with Elliot and Sadie's going with Nick, and both of them want to look stunning for their senior dance. Unfortunately, I got dragged into helping them pick out shoes.

But before this happens, I need to get on the water. Because my big day is coming tomorrow—Jared's coming down to do some studying in DC, and in honor of my birthday, he is going to be accompanying me on my first decent of the esteemed Great Falls. We're going to do Center Lines, and maybe Maryland, if we're up for it. The first rapid on Center Lines is called Grace Under Pressure. Perfect, right?

All fall I've been training hard, paddling lots, and have gotten myself into the best shape of my life. I'm ready for anything it throws at me. After all, I survived that crazy creek on the Arkansas. After that, I'm fairly sure even Great Falls will look pretty tame.

I grab my mom's old car, my newly purchased Villain already on the roof and my Star in the back, and aim it in the direction of the Lock 6 put in. A quick run down Little Falls will be a good, easy run to get me in the right mindset for tomorrow. When I arrive, the dew is still fresh on the grass and the parking area is empty. I breathe in the smell of the morning and feel the sunshine warm my face. I'm alone, but it's peaceful. There's not a soul out here to ruin the silence but me.

The leaves are bright shades of red, orange, and yellow and a few leaves flutter down and land on my helmet as I reach the put in. *The Potomac is beautiful in the fall,* I think. The huge oaks and sycamores that line the banks look like sleeping giants, sheltering me and protecting this river from the outside noises of the city. It's a hidden sanctuary, the Potomac is. I secure my skirt and pick up my paddle, and my torso rotates effortlessly as I begin to propel my boat forward, my muscles humming as they begin to warm up. This is how it is every morning—it's just me, the river, and the occasional heron, sharing the river together.

Little Falls is at 3.3 feet today, and the wave train is easy but fun. I throw some wave wheels and bounce along on my bow, and get a good wakeup call as I try to loop and fail. The water is chilly but my dry top is warm, and I see my breath in the air as I exhale. I shake the water out of my eyes and continue down the river.

Soon, I'm at the falls. I run the boof on the Maryland side then cut sharply over to Virginia, a move that I've grown to love. I don't even try to get to the correct side of the rock—I punch the hole strongly and skid easily over it. I remember my first trip with Jared, when I went into that hole and swore that it ate me alive. But I've seen some pretty nasty holes since then. Now, the Virginia hole seems friendly in comparison.

Before I know it, I'm at the takeout, and I lean back on my stern for a bit, staring up at the blue sky and at the morning sun rays beginning to peak out above the tree line. It's only 9:33. My day has just begun.

After a bit of a portage and some flatwater paddling I'm back at the car. I still have two hours until our mall date, so I head out to a Starbucks in Chevy Chase for some quality hot chocolate and a blueberry muffin. When I get my wallet out of my purse to pay, a photograph flutters out. I pick it up off the floor and blow on it gently. It's that picture from the top of Pike's Peak, the one taken by the stranger of Grant and me. Our mouths are pressed together and my hands are in his hair. I keep this in my purse, tucked away in a secret pocket, to help me remember that last summer was real. A strong burst of longing shoots through me as I gaze at the picture in my hand.

I shake my head quickly and put the picture away, bringing my thoughts back to the present. The summer's over, I tell myself. It was awesome, but it's over. I read some *Rapid Magazine* and chill in a lounge chair, and before long it's time to go.

I don't bother changing, since I won't be the one shopping. I head over to the Montgomery Mall and meet up with Sara and Sadie inside.

"Have a good paddle?" Sara asks, noticing my wet hair. I smile.

"Yeah, sure did. Little Falls was perfect." They both nod, not exactly understanding what I mean.

"Happy birthday," Sadie says, grinning at me and giving me a hug. I hug her back. I met Sadie this year when she transferred from Cathedral. She's a small, half black girl with a great sense of humor and love for the outdoors. We hit off right away. Now I have two friends, Sara and Sadie. I'm improving.

"Thanks, hon," I say, and Sara gives me a hug as well.

"Your big 18, huh?" she says.

"Sure is," I reply, grinning. She links her arm with mine and leads me into Nordstrom's, and Sadie follows close behind.

They start talking excitedly about homecoming and about the after parties they hope to go to, and I try to pay attention but really can't because all my thoughts are focused on the next day. Will it be as amazing as I've hoped it will be? Will it be challenging? Will I be pushed? Will I go into Subway? Anticipation is building up in me. I grab a shirt off the rack just so I can keep myself busy. Once in a dressing room, I start doing a little spazzy dance in front of the mirror, holding the shirt hanger like a kayak paddle.

Sadie comes rushing in, a deep purple dress in her hand, and I stop dancing. She acts like she didn't see anything and holds the dress up, grinning broadly.

"I found this. Ginny. You have to try it on. Please." Her eyes are glowing, and I oblige, just because I don't want to crush her excitement. She zips me up and I yank my hair out of my ponytail and ruffle it, then turn around and look at myself in the mirror. Sadie gasps.

I look good. Actually, better than good. I've never looked this good in a dress. Ever.

"I'm buying that for you," Sadie says, without asking for my permission. She ushers Sara over, and they both agree that I look stunning, and that I have to come to homecoming tonight. I inform them that I have a big day tomorrow and need rest, but they don't listen. Sadie ends up buying the dress for me and some shoes for herself, and Sara gets some heels as well. We go our separate ways then, because try as they might, neither of them can convince me that going to a dance is more important than resting for Great Falls.

As I round the corner onto my street, I see a familiar car parked in front of my house. My heart stops beating. My hands freeze on the steering wheel. It can't be. I'm dreaming. This is not possible.

But it is. Because sitting on the tire swing hanging from the tree in my front yard is Grant Haney, a wide grin on his face. I pull up behind his familiar red truck, my heart still pounding way too fast for me to function properly, and I leap out. My legs carry me swiftly into his awaiting arms.

"How did you find me?" I whisper, as I wrap my arms around his neck.

"Casey," he replies. He kisses me, and I kiss him back, hard. I feel like fireworks are exploding in my chest and my heart feels like it's going to burst open. He's here. Grant is here. In my yard. In my arms. For real...

"Happy birthday, Ginny," he says when we finally break apart. All I can do is stand there, mouth slightly parted, eyes wide. "I kind of made a lot of assumptions when deciding to come here. First, that you'd still want me. Second, that you'd actually be here. And third...that you needed a date to homecoming tonight." He gives me this cute, nervous look, like he's afraid that I'm going to turn him down.

"Who the hell do you think would ask *me* to homecoming?" I ask, and he laughs.

"So will you go with me?"

"Yes," I reply, a grin forming on my lips. "Yes, yes, yes, yes!" I throw my arms around him again and he laughs harder.

"Now go get ready," he tells me. "I know how long you girls like to labor over your hair, and I wouldn't want you to have to rush." I give him one last kiss before grabbing my Nordstrom bag and heading into the house, feeling completely on top of the world.

After a shower and some hair styling, I'm about ready. I apply the last dab of mascara and admire myself in the mirror. *Sara is going to be so proud*, I think. My parents even seemed excited when I told them that I had a date to homecoming. I rush down the stairs just as I hear a knock at the door.

I turn the doorknob, and before me stands Grant, who looks…incredible. I'm too busy staring at him that I don't realize that he's staring at me in the same way until I look up to meet his eyes. We both flush.

"Hey, you," he says.

"Hey," I reply. "Ready to go?" He nods and holds out his arm, and I take it, smiling up at him.

"Mom! Dad!" I call. "My date's here! We're late! Gotta run!" I close the door before I can hear their response.

Once outside, Grant leans down and whispers in my ear, "You look amazing tonight." I meet his eyes and grin.

"You polish up nicely, too." This makes him laugh, and before he gets a chance to lean down and kiss me, I know one thing that would absolutely make my life complete.

"You and Jordan want to run Great Falls with me tomorrow?" I ask. Grant's face breaks into a gleaming smile, the kind that made me fall in love with him in the first place.

"What kind of question is that, Ginny?" My face stretches into a grin to match his. *This is definitely going to be the greatest birthday ever,* I think. *No doubt about it. It'll be a great birthday to mark the end of a great year.*

He holds open the door of the passenger side of the car that took me across the country, and I enter, breathing in the familiar smells of last summer. Then he steps on the gas and we accelerate into the night.

Acknowledgments

This book reflects my life and many of the people in it, and I'd like to give a shout out to a few of those people now. First off, to Valley Mill Camp and the Valley Mill Racing Team, where I learned to kayak and met some of the greatest people on the planet. I wouldn't be the same person I am today if it hadn't been for Bruce, Gigantor, Callum, Ashley, and all my paddling buddies. You guys mean the world to me. Ginny's road trip, too, was inspired by our team's numerous trips crammed in our classy white van. I have so many fabulous memories of driving across interstates at 90 mph, setting up camp in the dark, peeing at the side of the road, eating McDonalds at midnight, singing songs at the top of our lungs in Wal-Mart parking lots, getting lectured about brushing our teeth, having intense Slim Jim and sock wars, and so many more. Extra thanks to Bruce and Gigantor, our fearless Adventure Camp counselors, who taught me the CPR Ginny needed to save Grant on the Ottawa and for showing me what a true paddler is supposed to be like. I owe Bruce, especially, a huge thanks for teaching me just about everything I know—about paddling, the river, being a good trip leader, and life in general. You've been the greatest coach anyone could ever ask for. Also special thanks to Callum for leading my first trip to Canada and for helping me *not* almost die on the Ottawa, and to the rest of the Valley Mill lake staff for being the greatest coworkers ever. Thanks to the numerous holes I've gone in that have taught me both courage and caution, especially to Lily's Hole at Dickerson (and thanks to my team for naming the hole after me). Thanks to my moms, Ellen and Denise, for introducing me to the outdoors and for teaching me how to deal with the woods, wilderness survival, bears, raccoons, camping, and hypothermia. Also, special thanks to Ellen, our fearless leader, whose "scrambled egg" kayak started it all, and to Denise, whose tendency to over pack drives me crazy but helps us prepare for the worst. Without their support and love I wouldn't be anywhere. Then to Michelle, who's endless lists and plans inspired Jordan's tendency to do the same, and to June for teaching me about being a good sibling. An important thanks, too, to Adrianne, Maddie, and Natalie, for being the greatest friends ever, on and off the water. Also, to all my other friends and first readers who gave me the support and encouragement that motivated me to actually do something with this story, especially to all of you who gave me feedback and helped me edit. A big thanks, too, to the people at NaNoWriMo who helped me write the first 50K. And finally, to the Potomac River and Valley Mill Camp, for introducing me to the awesome sport of whitewater kayaking and for giving me an amazing childhood.

Glossary of Paddling Terms

(All) Star – a Jackson kayak made for playboating
American Whitewater – an organization promoting US rivers and paddle sports – visit www.americanwhitewater.org for more information
Back deck roll – a type of roll where you slide your body across your stern, and if done correctly, your head remains dry
Back loop – a trick where your boat flips backwards, bow over stern
Black River– A river in upstate New York
Boof – *n.* a pour over or small waterfall that a boater can go over *v.* the act of going over a pour over or small waterfall and landing flat instead of vertically. When done right, the hull hitting the water sounds like "boof"
Bow – the front of the boat
Bow stall – balancing vertical, on the bow of your boat. Likewise, a **stern stall** is balancing vertically on your stern.
Brace – *n.* a paddle movement used to keep your boat upright if you are about to flip *v.* to keep your boat upright using your paddle
Buseater – A large wave on the Ottawa that only appears at very high water
Cartwheel – a freestyle trick where the boater goes from his/her bow to the stern, much like a cartwheel in gymnastics. Also called **"throwing ends"**
Class I-V – international whitewater classification system, with I being easy/beginner and V being extremely difficult. To put this into perspective, class VI is considered not runnable
Cockpit – the part of the boat you sit in
Creeking – extreme whitewater kayaking on high gradient (steep) rivers

Eddy – river feature formed behind a rock or other obstructing object. Water in an eddy actually moves against the main flow of the current. The **eddy line** separates an eddy from the main flow

Eddy turn– going from the current to an eddy

Ender – *n.* any move where your boat is vertical on its stern *v.* to go onto your stern, either on purpose or with the help of a hole or eddy line (in this case, it is also called a "**stern squirt**")

Ferry – going from one side of the current to the other

Flat spin – spinning your boat around while keeping your hull relatively flat in a hole/wave

Foam pile – the part of a hole where water recirculates. It literally looks like a pile of foam

Freestyle/playboating – type of kayaking done in holes and on waves where a boater does tricks. In competition, these tricks are judged and scored

Garburator – a breaking, standing wave on the Ottawa River, known for its fast moving water and easy access

Great Falls – a series of Class V rapids on the Potomac River. There are three different lines you can run— Maryland Lines (on the MD side of the Potomac), Virginia Lines, and Center Lines (in the middle).

Hole – a river feature where water recirculates, creating a hydraulic. This can be formed by a rock or other obstructing object

Hull – the bottom of the boat

Jackson Kayaks – brand of kayaks started by Olympian and world champion Eric Jackson. Jackson makes many different types of boats for many different styles of kayaking, and more information can be found at www.jacksonkayak.com

Lachine – a rapid consisting of large waves on the **St. Lawrence** in Montreal

Level – height of the river, which is measured by a gage at a certain point in the river and posted for people to be able to check. You can find "river stages" in most newspapers

Line – a route down a rapid
Little Falls, Lock 6 – locations on the Potomac. On Little Falls, there are two lines you can run, Virginia and Maryland. A large rock separates the two channels.
Loop – literally looping your boat, stern over bow. It's called an **"air loop"** when your boat stays mostly out of the water during it
McNasty – freestyle trick where you start in the feature backwards, do half a spin and then loop
New River Academy (NRA) – real traveling boarding school named for its home base on the New River. Visit www.newriveracademy.org for more information
New River, Youghiogheny (Yough) – rivers in West Virginia
Paddle roll – a move used to right your boat after you flip, using your paddle and a movement of the hips (called a **"hip snap"**)
Peel out – going from an eddy to the current
Phonix monkey – an advanced playboating trick, where your boat spins around on its bow then loops in rapid sequence
Potomac River – a river separating Maryland and Virginia
Put in – the location where you enter the river to start your trip
Scout – looking at a rapid and picking out your line before going down it in your boat
Shuttle – getting back to your car from the takeout
Skirt – piece of kayak gear that you wear around your waist to keep water out of your boat
Slalom – kayaking through gates set up over a whitewater course. It's a race done in individual runs, and the paddler with the fastest time wins.
Stern – the back of the boat
Subway – a drop on Great Falls that goes into an underwater cave that is impossible to get out of
SUP – an abbreviation for Stand Up Paddleboarding, it's done on a board that resembles a surfboard with an extra long paddle

Surf – staying on a wave/hole using gravity and the feature's recirculation

Swim – when you flip and are unable to roll up, which results in you exiting your boat

Takeout – where you get off of the river

Tellico, Ocoee, Nantahala – rivers in the North Carolina area

Tongue – refers to the channel of green water, usually shaped like a "V", and is usually the safest and smoothest line to take down a rapid

Trash/trashing/trashed – term referring to getting thrown around unwillingly in a hole. Usually occurs when the boater is **"stuck"** in the hole, meaning that the recirculation is keeping their boat in place

USACK – USA Canoe/Kayak, the Olympic committee for paddle sports – visit www.usack.org for more information

Villain – Jackson kayak designed for creeking and extreme whitewater kayaking

Wave wheel – a cartwheel done over waves

Window shade – when a hole flips you over and flips you back up again without you doing anything

About the Author

Lily Durkee was inspired to write *Chasing Grace* by her own love of paddling and the outdoors. Growing up she spent her summers camping, hiking, and backpacking with her family and learning to whitewater kayak with the amazing people at Valley Mill. Since getting in a boat for the first time at age 8 she's paddled rivers, raced slalom, and surfed waves in numerous locations across the country. She also runs track and cross-country for her high school and plays the clarinet. She lives with her two moms, sister, and dog in Takoma Park, MD. She wrote *Chasing Grace* when she was fifteen and hopes that her non-paddling readers get inspired to get out onto the water and experience kayaking for themselves.